ARTEMIS FOWL

aurum potestas est

ARTEMIS FOWL is a child prodigy from Ireland who has dedicated his brilliant mind to criminal activities. When Artemis discovers that there is a fairy civilization below ground, he sees it as a golden opportunity. Now there is a whole new species to exploit with his ingenious schemes. But Artemis doesn't know as much as he thinks about the fairy People. And what he doesn't know could hurt him . . .

For Ciarán, who will hear many rugby stories

PUFFIN BOOKS

UK | USA | Canada | Ireland | Australia
India | New Zealand | South Africa

Puffin Books is part of the Penguin Random House group of companies
whose addresses can be found at global.penguinrandomhouse.com.

www.penguin.co.uk   www.puffin.co.uk   www.ladybird.co.uk

Penguin
Random House
UK

First published by Puffin Books 2010
This edition published 2017
002

Text copyright © Eoin Colfer, 2010
Map illustrations by Kev Walker and Tony Fleetwood
All rights reserved

The moral right of the author has been asserted

Set in Perpetua by Palimpsest Book Production Ltd, Falkirk, Stirlingshire

Printed in Great Britain by Clays Ltd, Elcograf S.p.A.
A CIP catalogue record for this book is available from the British Library

ISBN: 978-0-241-33565-9

All correspondence to:
Puffin Books, Penguin Random House Children's
80 Strand, London WC2R 0RL

www.greenpenguin.co.uk

MIX
Paper from
responsible sources
FSC
www.fsc.org   FSC™ C018179

Penguin Books is committed to a sustainable
future for our business, our readers and our
planet. This book is made from paper certified
by the Forest Stewardship Council.

EOIN COLFER

ARTEMIS FOWL

AND THE ATLANTIS COMPLEX

PUFFIN

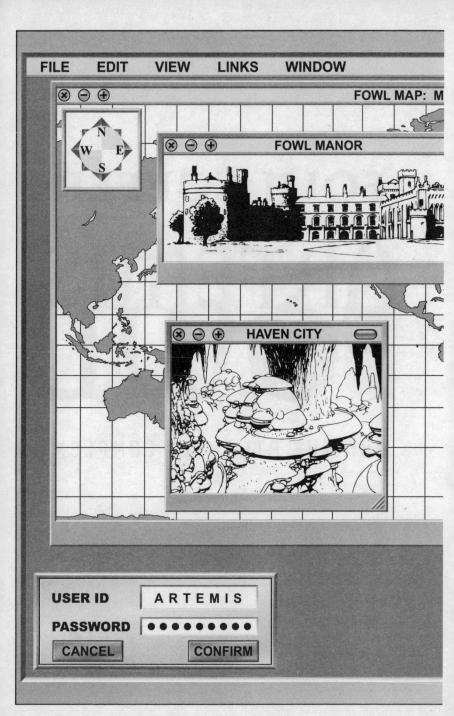

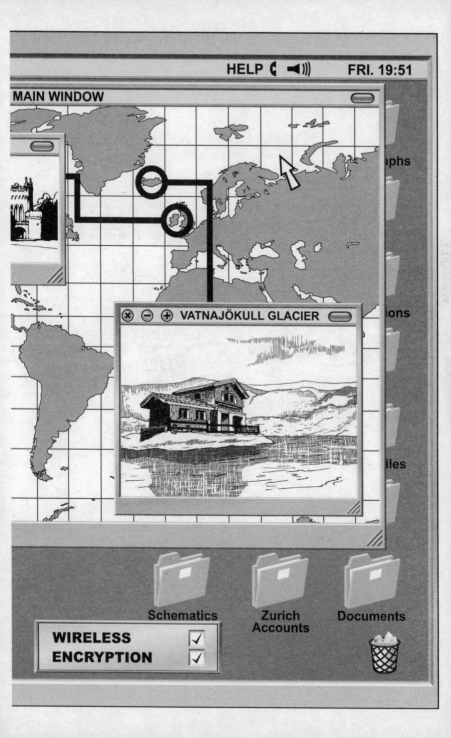

Contents

ARTEMIS FOWL: SO FAR
SO BAD

THERE was once an Irish boy who longed to know everything there was to know, so he read book after book until his brain swelled with astronomy, calculus, quantum physics, romantic poets, forensic science and anthropology among a hundred other subjects. But his favourite book was a slim volume which he'd never once read himself. It was an old hardback that his father often chose as a bedtime tale, entitled *The Crock of Gold*, which told the story of a greedy bucko who captured a leprechaun in a vain effort to steal the creature's gold.

When the father had finished reading the last word on the last page, which was *Fin*, he would close the worn leather-bound cover, smile down at his son and say, 'That boy had the right idea. A little more planning and he would have pulled it off,' which was an unusual opinion for a father to voice. A *responsible* father at any rate. But this was not a typically responsible parent – this was Artemis Fowl Senior, the kingpin of one of the world's largest criminal empires. The son was not so typical either. He was Artemis Fowl II, soon to become a formidable individual in his own right, both in the world of man and in the fairy world beneath it.

A little more planning, Artemis Junior often thought as his father kissed his forehead. *Just a little more planning.*

And he would fall asleep and dream of gold.

As young Artemis grew older, he often thought about *The Crock of Gold*. He even went so far as to do a little research during school time and was surprised to find a lot of credible evidence for the existence of the fairy folk. These hours of study and planning were nothing but light-hearted distractions for the boy until the day his father disappeared in the Arctic following a *misunderstanding* with the Russian Mafiya. The Fowl empire quickly disintegrated, with creditors crawling out of the woodwork and debtors burrowing into it.

It is up to me, Artemis realized. *To rebuild our fortune and find Father.*

So he dusted off the leprechaun folder. He would catch a fairy and ransom it back to its own people for gold.

Only a juvenile genius could make this plan a success, Artemis correctly concluded. *Someone old enough to grasp the principles of commerce, yet young enough to believe in magic.*

With the help of his more than capable bodyguard, Butler, twelve-year-old Artemis actually succeeded in capturing a leprechaun and holding it captive in Fowl Manor's reinforced basement. But this leprechaun was a *she* not an *it*. And remarkably humanoid with it. What Artemis had previously thought of as temporarily detaining a lesser creature now seemed uncomfortably like abducting a girl.

There were other complications too: these leprechauns were not the hokey fairies of storybooks. They were high-tech creatures with attitude, members of an elite fairy police squad: the Lower Elements Police Reconnaissance Unit, or LEPrecon to use their acronym. And Artemis had kidnapped Holly Short, the first female captain in the unit's history. An act that had not endeared him to the well-armed fairy underworld.

But in spite of a niggling conscience and LEP attempts to derail his plan, Artemis managed to take delivery of his ill-gotten gold and in return he released the elfin captain.

So, all's well that ends well?

Not really.

No sooner had the Earth settled from the first fairy–human stand-off in decades, than the LEP uncovered a plot to supply the goblin gangs with power sources for their Softnose lasers. Number one suspect: Artemis Fowl. Holly Short hauled the Irish boy down to Haven City for interrogation only to discover, to her amazement, that Artemis Fowl was actually innocent of something. The two struck an uneasy bargain, where Artemis agreed to track down the goblins' supplier if Holly would help him to rescue his father from the Russian gang that held him prisoner. Both parties upheld their respective ends of the bargain and in the process developed a respect and trust for each other that was underpinned by a shared sharp sense of humour.

Or at least this used to be the case. Recently, things have changed. In some ways he is as sharp as ever, but a shadow has fallen across Artemis's mind.

Once upon a time Artemis saw things that no one else could see, but now he sees things that are not there . . .

CHAPTER I: **COLD VİBES**

 VATNAJÖKULL is the biggest glacier in Europe with an area of more than five thousand stark blue-white miles. It is for the most part uninhabited and desolate, and, for scientific reasons, the perfect place for Artemis Fowl to demonstrate to the fairy People how exactly he planned to save the world. Also, a little dramatic scenery never hurts a presentation.

One part of Vatnajökull that does see human traffic is the Great Skua restaurant on the shores of the glacier lagoon, which caters to groups of ice tourists from May to August. Artemis had arranged to meet the proprietor at this *closed for the season* establishment very early on the morning of September first. His fifteenth birthday.

Artemis steered his rented snowmobile along the lagoon's rippling coastline where the glacier sloped into a black pool dotted with a crazy-paving pattern of broken ice plates. The wind roared around his head like an excited crowd in a stadium, carrying with it arrowheads of sleet that peppered his nose and mouth. The space was vast and unforgiving, and Artemis knew that to be injured alone on this tundra would lead to a quick and painful death – or at the very least abject humiliation before the popping flashes of the tourist season's tail end, which was slightly less painful than painful death but lasted longer.

The Great Skua's owner, a burly Icelander in proud possession of both a walrus moustache with the wingspan of a fair-sized cormorant and the unlikely name of Adam Adamsson, stood in the restaurant's porch, popping his fingers and stamping his feet to the rhythm in his head and also finding the time to chuckle at Artemis's erratic progress along the lagoon's frozen shore.

'That was a mighty display,' said Adamsson when Artemis finally managed to ram the snowmobile into the restaurant's decking. 'Hell, *harður maður*. I haven't laughed that hard since my dog tried to eat his reflection.'

Artemis smiled dourly, aware that the restaurateur was poking fun at his driving skills, or lack thereof. 'Hmmph,' he grunted, dismounting the ski-doo as stiffly as a cowboy after three days on a cattle drive, whose horse had died, forcing him to ride the broadest cow in the herd.

The old man actually cackled. 'Now you even sound like my dog.'

It was not Artemis Fowl's habit to make undignified entrances, but, without his bodyguard Butler on hand, he had been forced to rely on his own motor skills, which were famously unsophisticated. One of the sixth-year wits at St Bartleby's School, the heir to a hotel fortune, had nick-named Artemis *Left Foot Fowl*, as in he had two left feet and couldn't kick a football with either of them. Artemis had tolerated this ribbing for about a week and then bought out the young heir's hotel chain. This choked the teasing off abruptly.

'Everything is ready, I trust?' said Artemis, flexing fingers inside his patented sola-gloves. He noticed that one hand was uncomfortably warm; the thermostat must have taken a knock when he'd clipped an ice obelisk half a mile down the coast. He tugged out the power wire with his teeth; there was not much danger of hypothermia as the autumn temperature hovered just below zero.

'And hello to you,' said Adamsson. 'Nice to finally meet you face to face, if not eye to eye.'

Artemis did not rise to the *forge a relationship* lure that Adamsson had tossed out. He did not have room in his life at the moment for yet another friend that he didn't trust.

'I do not intend to ask you for your daughter's hand in marriage, Mr Adamsson, so I think we can skip over any ice-breakers you may feel obliged to offer. Is everything ready?'

Adam Adamsson's pre-prepared ice-breakers melted in his throat and he nodded half a dozen times.

'All ready. Your crate is round the back. I have supplied a vegetarian buffet and goodie bags from the Blue Lagoon Spa.

A few seats have been laid out too, as bluntly requested in your terse e-mail. None of your party turned up, though – nobody but you – after all my labours.'

Artemis lifted an aluminium briefcase from the ski-doo's luggage box. 'Don't you worry about that, Mr Adamsson. Why don't you head back to Reykjavik and spend some of that extortionate fee you charged me for a couple of hours' usage of your frankly third-rate restaurant and perhaps find a friendless tree stump to listen to your woes?'

A couple of hours. Third-rate. Two plus three equals five. Good.

Now it was Adamsson's turn to grunt and the tips of his walrus moustache quivered slightly.

'No need for the attitude, young Fowl. We are both men, are we not? Men are entitled to a little respect.'

'Oh, really? Perhaps we should ask the whales? Or perhaps the mink?'

Adamsson scowled, his wind-burnt face creasing like a prune. 'OK, OK. I get the message. No need to hold me responsible for the crimes of man. You teenagers are all the same. Let's see if your generation does any better with the planet.'

Artemis clicked the briefcase's lock snap precisely twenty times before striding into the restaurant.

'Believe me, we teenagers are not all the same,' he said as he passed Adamsson. 'And I intend to do quite a bit better.'

There were more than a dozen tables inside the restaurant, all with chairs stacked on top, except for one, which had been dressed with a linen cloth and laden with bottled glacier water and spa bags for each of the five places.

Five, thought Artemis. *A good number. Solid. Predictable. Four fives are twenty.*

Artemis had decided lately that five was his number. Good things happened when five was in the mix. The logician in him knew that this was ridiculous, but he couldn't ignore the fact that the tragedies in his life had occurred in years not divisible by five: his father had disappeared and been mutilated, his old friend Commander Julius Root of the LEP had been murdered by the notorious pixie Opal Koboi, both in years with no five. He was five feet five inches tall and weighed fifty-five kilos. If he touched something five times or a multiple of that, then that thing stayed reliable. A door would remain closed, for example, or a keepsake would protect that doorway, as it was supposed to.

Today the signs were good. He was fifteen years old. Three times five. And his hotel room in Reykjavik had been number forty-five. Even the ski-doo that had got him this far unscathed had a registration which was a multiple of five, and boasted a 50 cc engine to boot. All good. There were only four guests coming to the meeting, but including him that made five. So no need to panic.

A part of Artemis was horrified by his newfound superstition about numbers.

Get a grip on yourself. You are a Fowl. We do not rely on luck — abandon these ridiculous obsessions and compulsions.

⠿ • ⋃ ⌂ ◊ ⫝̸ ⤳ • ⁂ ⩎ ⊗ ⌑ • ⊗ ⌑ • ☽ ⫝̸ ⊛ ⊖ ⤳ ⌂ ⫝̸

Artemis clicked the case's latch to appease the number gods – twenty times, four fives – and felt his heart slow down.

I will break my habits tomorrow, when this job is done.

He loitered at the maître d's podium until Adamsson and his snow tractor had disappeared over a curved ridge of snow that could have been a whale's spine, then waited a further minute until the vehicle's rumbling had faded to an old smoker's cough.

Very well. Time to do some business.

Artemis descended the five wooden steps to the main restaurant floor (*excellent, good omen*), threading a series of columns hung with replicas of the Stora-Borg mask until he arrived at the head of the laid table. The seats were angled to face him and a slight shimmer, like a heat haze, flickered over the table top.

'Good morning, friends,' said Artemis in Gnommish, forcing himself to pronounce the fairy words in confident, almost jovial, tones. 'Today's the day we save the world.'

The heat haze seemed more electrical now with crackles of neon-white interference running through it and faces swimming in its depths like ghosts from a dream. The faces solidified and grew torsos and limbs. Small figures, like children, appeared. Like children, but not the same. These were representatives of the fairy People and among them perhaps the only friends Artemis had.

'Save the world?' said Captain Holly Short of the LEPrecon. 'Same old Artemis Fowl, and I say that sarcastically as *saving the world* is not like you at all.'

Artemis knew he should smile, but he could not, so instead he found fault, something that would not seem out of character.

'You need a new shield amplifier, Foaly,' he said to a centaur who was balanced awkwardly on a chair designed for humans. 'I could see the shimmer from the front porch. Call yourself a technical expert? How old is the one you're using?'

Foaly stamped a hoof, which was an irritated tic of his and the reason he never won at cards. 'Nice to see you too, Mud Boy.'

'How old?'

'I don't know. Maybe four years.'

'Four. There, you see. What sort of number is that?'

Foaly stuck out his bottom lip. 'What *sort* of number? There are *types* now, Artemis? That amplifier is good for another hundred years. Maybe it could do with a little tuning, but that's all.'

Holly stood and walked lightly to the head of the table.

'Do you two have to start with the sparring right away? Isn't that getting a little clichéd after all these years? You're like a couple of mutts marking territory.' She laid two slim fingers on Artemis's forearm. 'Lay off him, Artemis. You know how sensitive centaurs are.'

Artemis could not meet her eyes. Inside his left snow boot, he counted off twenty toe-taps.

'Very well. Let's change the subject.'

'Please do,' said the third fairy in the room. 'We've come

across from Russia for this, Fowl. So if the subject could be changed to what we came here to discuss . . .'

Commander Raine Vinyáya was obviously not happy being so far from her beloved Police Plaza. She had assumed command of LEPgeneral some years previously and prided herself on keeping a finger in every ongoing mission. 'I have operations to get back to, Artemis. The pixies are rioting, calling for Opal Koboi's release from prison, and the swear-toad epidemic has flared up again. Please do us the courtesy of getting on with it.'

Artemis nodded. Vinyáya was being openly antagonistic and that was an emotion that could be trusted, unless of course it was a bluff and the commander was a secret fan of his, unless it was a double bluff and she really did feel antagonistic.

That sounds insane, Artemis realized. *Even to me.*

Though she was barely a metre tall, Commander Vinyáya was a formidable presence and someone that Artemis never intended to underestimate. While the commander was almost four hundred years old in fairy terms, she was barely middle-aged and in any terms she was a striking figure: lean and sallow, with the reactive feline pupils occasionally found in elfin eyes, but even that rarity was not her most distinctive physical characteristic. Raine Vinyáya had a mane of silver hair that seemed to trap any available light and send it rippling along her shoulders.

Artemis cleared his throat and switched his focus from numbers to the project, or, as he liked to think of it, *THE*

PROJECT. In the end, when it came down to it, this was the only plan that mattered.

Holly punched his shoulder gently.

'You look pale. Even paler than usual. You OK, birthday boy?'

Artemis finally succeeded in meeting her eyes – one hazel, one blue – framed by a wide brow and a slash of auburn fringe that Holly had grown out from her usual crew-cut.

'Fifteen years old today,' muttered Artemis. 'Three fives. That's a good thing.'

Holly blinked.

Artemis Fowl muttering? And no mention of her new hairstyle – usually Artemis picked up on physical changes straight away.

'I . . . ah . . . I suppose so. Where's Butler? Scouting the perimeter?'

'No. No, I sent him away. Juliet needed him.'

'Nothing too serious?'

'Not serious but necessary. Family business. He trusts you to look after me.'

Holly's lips tightened as though she had tasted something sour.

'He trusts somebody else to shepherd his principal? Are you sure this is Butler we're talking about?'

'Of course. And, anyway, it's better that he's not here. Whenever my plans go awry, he's close at hand. It's vital, *imperative*, that this meeting goes ahead and that nothing goes wrong.'

Holly's jaw actually dropped in shock. It was almost comical to see. If she understood Artemis correctly, he was *blaming* Butler for the failure of previous schemes. Butler? His staunchest ally.

'Good idea. Let's go ahead, then. The four of us should get this show on the road.'

This from Foaly who had spoken the dreaded number with no thought for the consequences.

Four. Very bad number. The absolute worst. Chinese people hate the number four because it sounds like their word for death.

Almost worse than saying the number four was the fact that there were only four people in the room. Commander Trouble Kelp had apparently not been able to make it. In spite of their historic dislike for each other, Artemis wished the commander were here now.

'Where is Commander Kelp, Holly? I thought he was attending today. We could use the protection.'

Holly stood at the table, ramrod straight in her blue jump-suit, acorn cluster glittering on her chest.

'Trouble . . . Commander Kelp has enough to deal with in Police Plaza, but don't worry. There's an entire squadron of LEPtactical hovering overhead in a shielded shuttle. Not even a snow fox could make it in here without a singed tail.'

Artemis shucked off his snow jacket and gloves. 'Thank you, Captain. I am encouraged by your thoroughness. As a matter of interest, how many fairies are there in an LEP squadron? Exactly?'

'Fourteen,' replied Holly, one jagged eyebrow raised.

'Fourteen. Hmm. That is not so . . .' Then a light-bulb moment. 'And a pilot, I presume?'

'Fourteen *including* the pilot. That's enough to take on any human squadron you care to throw at them.'

For a moment it seemed as though Artemis Fowl would turn round and flee the meeting that he himself had requested. A tendon tugged at his neck and one forefinger tapped the chair's wooden headrest. Then Artemis swallowed and nodded with a nervousness that escaped from him like a canary from a cat's mouth before being swallowed back down.

'Very well. Fourteen will have to do. Please, Holly, sit. Let me tell you about the project.'

Holly backed up slowly, searching Artemis's face for the cockiness that usually dwelled in his smirk lines. It was not there.

Whatever this project is, she thought, *it's big.*

Artemis placed his case on the table, popped it open and spun the lid to reveal a screen inside. For a moment his delight in gadgetry surfaced and he even managed a faint grin in Foaly's direction. The grin stretched his lips no more than a centimetre.

'Look. You'll like this little box.'

Foaly snickered. 'Oh my stars! Is that . . . could that possibly be . . . a laptop? You have shamed us all with your brilliance, Arty.'

The centaur's sarcasm drew groans from everyone.

'What?' he protested. 'It's a laptop. Even humans can't expect anyone to be impressed by a laptop.'

'If I know Artemis,' said Holly, 'something impressive is about to happen. Am I right?'

'You may judge for yourself,' said Artemis, pressing his thumb against a scanner on the case.

The scanner flickered, considering the proffered thumb, then flashed green, deciding to accept it. Nothing happened for a second or two then a motor inside the case buzzed as though there were a small satisfied cat stretching in the case's belly.

'Motor,' said Foaly. 'Big deal.'

The lid's reinforced metal corners suddenly detached, blasting away from the lid with a squirt of propellant, and suckered themselves to the ceiling. Simultaneously the screen unfolded until it was more than a metre square with speaker bars along each edge.

'So it's a big screen,' Foaly said. 'This is just grandstanding. All we needed were a few sets of v-goggles.'

Artemis pressed another button on the case and the metal corners suckered to the ceiling revealed themselves to be projectors, spewing forth streams of digi-data that coalesced in the centre of the room to form a rotating model of the planet Earth. The screen displayed the Fowl Industries company logo surrounded by a number of files.

'It's a holographic case,' said Foaly, delighted to remain unimpressed. 'We've had those for years.'

'It is not a holographic case – the case is completely real,' corrected Artemis. 'But the images you will see are holographic. I have made a few upgrades to the LEP system. The case is synced with several satellites and the onboard computers can construct real-time images of objects not inside the sensors' range.'

'I've got one of those at home,' mumbled the centaur. 'For my kid's game console.'

'And the system has smart interactive intelligence so I can construct or alter models by hand, so long as I'm wearing v-gloves,' Artemis went on.

Foaly scowled. 'OK, Mud Boy. That *is* good,' but he couldn't help adding the PS: 'For a human.'

Vinyáya's pupils contracted in the light from the projectors. 'This is all very pretty, Fowl, but we still don't know the point of this meeting.'

Artemis stepped into the hologram, and inserted his hands into two v-gloves floating over Australia. The gloves were slightly transparent with thick tubular digits and an unsophisticated polystyrene-look render. Once again the briefcase's sensor flickered thoughtfully before deciding to accept Artemis's hands. The gloves beeped softly and shrank to form a second skin around his fingers, each knuckle highlighted by a digi-marker.

'The Earth,' he began, ignoring the impulse to open his notes folder and count the words. He knew this lecture by heart.

'Our home. She feeds us, she shelters us. Her gravity prevents us from flying off into space and freezing, before thawing out again and being crisped by the sun, none of which really matters as we would have long since asphyxiated.' Artemis paused for laughter and was surprised when it did not arrive. 'That was a little joke. I read in a presentation manual that a joke often serves to break the ice. And I actually worked ice-breaking into the joke, so there were layers to my humour.'

'That was a joke?' said Vinyáya. 'I've had officers court-martialled for less.'

'If I had some rotten fruit, I would throw it,' added Foaly. 'Why don't you do the science and leave the jokes to people with experience?'

Artemis frowned, upset that he had ad-libbed and now could not be certain how many words were in his presentation. If he finished on a multiple of four which was not also a multiple of five, that could be very bad. Perhaps he should start again? But that was cheating and the number gods would simply add the two speeches together and he'd be no better off.

Complicated. So hard to keep track, even for me.

But he would continue, because it was imperative that *THE PROJECT* be presented now, today, so that *THE PRODUCT* could go into fabrication immediately. So Artemis contained the uncertainty in his heart and launched into the presentation with gusto, barely stopping to draw breath in case his courage deserted him.

'Man is the biggest threat to the Earth. We gut the planet of its fossil fuels then turn those same fuels against the planet through global warming.' Artemis pointed a v-finger at the enlarged screen, opening one video file after another, each one illustrating a point. 'The world's glaciers are losing as much as two metres of ice cover per annum, that's half a million square miles in the Arctic Ocean alone in the past thirty years.' Behind him the video files displayed some of the consequences of global warming.

'The world needs to be saved,' said Artemis. 'I realize now, finally, that I must be the one to save it. *This* is why I am a genius. My very *raison d'être.*'

Vinyáya tapped the table with her index finger. 'There is a lobby in Haven, which has quite a lot of support, that says roll on global warming. The humans will wipe themselves out and then we can take back the planet.'

Artemis was ready for that one. 'An obvious argument, Commander, but it's not just the humans, is it?' He opened a few more video windows and the fairies watched scenes of scrawny polar bears stranded on ice floes, moose in Michigan being eaten alive by an increased tick population and bleached coral reefs devoid of all life.

'It's every living thing on or underneath this planet.'

Foaly was actually quite annoyed by the presentation. 'Do you think we haven't thought about this, Mud Boy? Do you think that this particular problem has not been on the mind of every scientist in Haven and Atlantis? To be honest I find this lecture patronizing.'

Artemis shrugged. 'How you feel is unimportant. How I feel is unimportant. The Earth needs to be saved.'

Holly sat up straight. 'Don't tell me you've found the answer.'

'I think so.'

Foaly snorted. 'Really? Let me guess: wrap the icebergs maybe? Or shoot refracting lenses into the atmosphere? How about customized cloud cover? Am I getting warm?'

'We are all getting warm,' said Artemis. 'That is the

problem.' He picked up the Earth hologram with one hand and spun it like a basketball. 'All of those solutions could work, with some modifications. But they require too much interstate cooperation and, as we all know, human governments are not good at sharing their toys. Perhaps, in fifty years' time, things might change, but by then it will be too late.'

Commander Vinyáya had always prided herself on an ability to read a situation, and her instincts were loud in her ears like the roar of Pacific surf. This was a historic moment; the very air seemed electric.

'Go on, human,' she said quietly, her words buoyed by authority. 'Tell us.'

Artemis used the v-gloves to highlight the Earth's glaciated areas and rearranged the ice mass into a square. 'Covering glaciers is an excellent idea, but even if the topography were this simple – a flat square – it would take several armies half a century to get the job done.'

'Oh, I don't know,' said Foaly. 'Human loggers seem to be getting through the rainforests a lot quicker than that.'

'Those on the fringes of the law move faster than those bound by it, which is where I come in.'

Foaly crossed his front legs, which is not easy for a centaur in a chair. 'Do tell. I am all ears.'

'I shall,' said Artemis. 'And I would be grateful if you would stifle the usual expressions of horror and disbelief until I conclude. Your cries of astonishment every time I present an idea are most tiresome and they make it difficult to keep track of the word count.'

'Oh my gods!' exclaimed Foaly. 'Unbelievable.'

Raine Vinyáya threw the centaur a warning look. 'Stop acting the bull troll, Foaly. I've come a long way for this and my ears are very cold.'

'Should I pinch one of the centaur's nerve clusters to keep him quiet?' asked Holly with barely a grin. 'I have studied centaur incapacitation, as well as human, if we happen to need it. I could knock out everybody here with one finger or a sturdy pencil.'

Foaly was eighty per cent sure that Holly was bluffing, but all the same he covered the ganglia over his ears with cupped fingers.

'Very well. I'll keep quiet.'

'Good. Proceed, Artemis.'

'Thank you. But keep your sturdy pencil at the ready, Captain Short. I have a feeling that there could be some disbelief on the way.'

Holly patted her pocket and winked.

'2B hard graphite, nothing better for a quick organ rupture.'

Holly was joking but her heart wasn't in it. Artemis felt that her comments were camouflage for whatever anxiety she was feeling. He rubbed his brow with a thumb and forefinger, using the gesture as cover to sneak a peek at his friend. Holly's own brow was drawn in and her eyes narrow with worry.

She knows, realized Artemis, but what Holly knew he could not say exactly. *She knows that something is different, that the even numbers have turned against me.*

Then Artemis reviewed this last sentence and for a second its lunacy was clear to him and he felt a fat coiled snake of panic heavy in his stomach.

Could I have a brain tumour? he wondered. *That would explain the obsessions, the hallucinations and the paranoia. Or is it simply obsessive compulsive disorder? The great Artemis Fowl felled by a common ailment.*

Artemis spared a moment to try an old hypnotherapist's trick.

Picture yourself in a good place. Somewhere you were happy and safe.

Happy and safe? It had been a while.

Artemis allowed his mind to fly and he found himself sitting on a small stool in his grandfather's workshop. His grandfather looked a little sneakier than Artemis remembered and he winked at his five-year-old grandson and said:

Do you know how many legs are on that stool, Arty? Three. Only three and that's not a good number for you. Not at all. Three is nearly as bad as four and we all know what four sounds like in Chinese, don't we?

Artemis shuddered. This sickness was even corrupting his memories. He pressed the forefinger and thumb of his left hand together until the pads turned white. A trigger he'd taught himself to elicit calm when the number panic grew too strong, but the trigger was working less and less recently, or in this case not at all.

I am losing my composure, he thought with quiet desperation. *This disease is winning.*

Foaly cleared his throat, puncturing Artemis's dream bubble. 'Hello? Mud Boy? Important people waiting, get a move on.'

And from Holly. 'Are you OK, Artemis? Do you need to take a break?'

Artemis almost laughed. *Take a break during a presentation? If I did that, I might as well go and stand beside someone wearing an I'M WITH CRAZY T-shirt.*

'No. I'm fine. This is a big project, the biggest. I want to be sure that my presentation is perfect.'

Foaly leaned forward until his already unsteady chair teetered dangerously. 'You don't look fine, Mud Boy. You look . . .' The centaur sucked his bottom lip, searching for the right word. 'Beaten. Artemis, you look beaten.'

Which was the best thing he could have possibly said.

Artemis drew himself up. 'I think, Foaly, that perhaps you do not read human expressions well. Perhaps our faces are too short. I am not beaten by any manner or means. I am considering my every word.'

'Maybe you should consider a little faster,' advised Holly gently. 'We are quite exposed here.'

Artemis closed his eyes, collecting himself.

Vinyáya drummed the table with her fingers. 'No more delays, human. I am beginning to suspect that you have involved us in one of your notorious plans.'

'No. This is a genuine proposal. Please, hear me out.'

'I'm trying to. I want to. I came a long way for that exact purpose, but all you do is show off with your suitcase.'

Artemis raised his hands to shoulder level, the movement activating his v-gloves, and tapped the glacier.

'What we need to do is cover a significant area of the world's glaciers with a reflective coating to slow down the melt. The coating would have to be thicker around the edges where the ice is thawing more rapidly. Also it would be nice if we could plug the larger sink-holes.'

'A lot of things would be *nice* in a perfect world,' said Foaly, once again making smithereens of his promise to keep quiet. 'Don't you think your people would get a tad upset if little creatures pop out of the ground in spaceships and start carpeting Santa's grotto with reflective foil?'

'They . . . we . . . would. And that is why this operation has to be carried out in secret.'

'Secretly coat the world's glaciers? You should have said.'

'I just did say and I thought we agreed that you would hold your peace. This constant haranguing is tiresome.'

Holly winked at Foaly, twirling a pencil between her fingers.

'The problem with coating the icebergs has always been how to deploy the reflective blanket,' continued Artemis. 'It would seem that the only way to do it would be to roll the stuff out like carpet, either manually or from the rear of some kind of customized snow crawlers.'

'Which is hardly a stealth operation,' said Foaly.

'Exactly. But what if there were another way to lay down a reflective covering, a seemingly natural way?'

'Work with nature?'

'Yes, Foaly. Nature is our model; it should always be.'

The room seemed to be heating up as Artemis drew closer to his big reveal.

'Human scientists have been struggling to make their reflective foil thin enough to work with, yet strong enough to withstand the elements.'

'Stupid.'

'Misguided, centaur. Not stupid, surely. Your own files . . .'

'I considered the foil idea briefly. And how did you see my files?'

This was not a real question. Foaly had long since resigned himself to the fact that Artemis Fowl was at least as talented a hacker as he himself was.

'The basic idea is sound. Fabricate a reflective polymer.'

Foaly chewed his knuckles. 'Nature. Use nature.'

'What is the most natural thing up here?' said Artemis, giving a little hint.

'Ice,' said Holly. 'Ice and . . .'

'Snow,' whispered the centaur almost reverentially. 'Of course. D'Arvit, why didn't I . . . Snow, isn't it?'

Artemis raised his v-gloved hands and holographic snow rained upon them.

'Snow,' he said, the blizzard swirling around him. 'No one would be surprised by snow.'

Foaly was on his feet. 'Magnify,' he ordered. 'Magnify and enhance.'

Artemis tapped a holographic flake, freezing it in mid-air.

With a couple of pinches he enlarged the ersatz flake until its irregularity became clear. It was irregularly regular, a perfect circle.

'A nano-wafer,' said Foaly, forgetting for once to hide how impressed he was. 'An honest-to-gods nano-wafer. Smart?'

'Extremely,' confirmed Artemis. 'Smart enough to know which way is up when it hits the surface and configure itself to insulate the ice and reflect the sun.'

'So we impregnate the cloud province?'

'Exactly, to its capacity.'

Foaly clopped into the holographic weather. 'Then when it ruptures we have coverage.'

'Incremental, true, but effective nonetheless.'

'Mud Boy, I salute you.'

Artemis smiled, his old self for a moment. 'Well, it's about time.'

Vinyáya interrupted the science love fest. 'Let me see if I've got this straight. You shoot these wafers into the clouds and then they come down with the snow?'

'Precisely. We could shoot them directly on to the surface in dire cases, but I think for security it would be best to have the seeders hovering shielded above the cloud cover.'

'And you can do this?'

'We can do it. The Council would have to approve an entire fleet of modified shuttles, not to mention a monitoring station.'

Holly thought of something. 'These wafers don't look

much like snowflakes. Sooner or later some human with a microscope is going to notice the difference.'

'Good point, Holly. Perhaps I shouldn't lump you in with the rest of the LEP as regards intellect.'

'Thanks, I think.'

'When the wafers are discovered, as they inevitably will be, I will launch an Internet campaign that explains them away as a by-product from a chemical plant in Russia. I will also point out that for once our waste is actually helping the environment and volunteer to fund a programme that will extend their coverage.'

'Is there a pollution factor?' asked Vinyáya.

'Hardly. The wafers are entirely bio-degradable.'

Foaly was excited. He clip-clopped through the hologram, squinting at the enlarged wafer.

'It *sounds* good. But is it really? You can hardly expect the People to stump up the massive and ongoing budget for such a project without proof, Artemis. For all we know, it's one of your scams.'

Artemis opened a file on the screen. 'Here are my financial records. I know they are accurate, Foaly, because I found them on your server.'

Foaly did not even bother blushing. 'They look about right.'

'I am prepared to invest everything I have in this project. That should keep five shuttles in the air for a couple of years. There will be profit on the back end, naturally, when the wafers go into production. I should recoup my investment then, perhaps even turn a respectable profit.'

Foaly almost gagged. *Artemis Fowl putting his own money into a project. Incredible.*

'Of course I hardly expect the People to take anything I say on face value. After all, I have been –' Artemis cleared his throat – 'somewhat less than forthcoming with information in the past.'

Vinyáya laughed humourlessly. 'Less than forthcoming? I think you're being a little gentle on yourself for a kidnapper and extortionist, Artemis. *Less than forthcoming?* Please. I find myself buying your pitch, but not everybody on the Council is as charitable towards you.'

'I accept your criticism and your scepticism, which is why I have organized a demonstration.'

'Excellent,' said Foaly eagerly. 'Of course there's a demonstration. Why else would you have brought us here?'

'Why else indeed.'

'More extortion and kidnapping?' suggested Vinyáya archly.

'That was a long time ago,' blurted Holly, in a tone she would not usually take with a superior officer. 'I mean . . . that was a long time ago . . . Commander. Artemis has been a good friend to the People.'

Holly Short thought specifically of a close call during the goblin rebellion when Artemis Fowl's actions had saved her life and many more besides.

Vinyáya apparently remembered the goblin rebellion too. 'OK. Benefit-of-the-doubt time, Fowl. You've got twenty minutes to convince us.'

Artemis patted his breast pocket five times to check on his phone.

'It shouldn't take more than ten,' he said.

Holly Short was a trained hostage negotiator and found that in spite of the importance of the topic she was rapidly shifting focus away from nano-wafers and towards Artemis Fowl's mannerisms. Though she commented occasionally as the demonstration progressed, it was all she could do not to cradle Artemis's face in her hands and ask him what was the matter.

I would have to stand on a chair to reach his face, Holly realized. *My friend is almost a grown man now. A fully fledged human. Perhaps he is fighting his natural-born bloodthirsty desires and the conflict is driving him crazy.*

Holly studied Artemis closely. He was pale, more so than usual, like a creature of the night. A snow wolf maybe. The sharp cheekbones and triangular length of his face added to this impression. And perhaps it was frost, but Holly thought she could see a streak of grey at his temples.

He seems old. Foaly was right: Artemis looks beaten.

Then there was the number thing. And the touching. Artemis's fingers were never still. At first it seemed random, but, on a hunch, Holly counted and soon the pattern was clear. Fives or multiples of five.

D'Arvit, she thought. *Atlantis Complex.*

She ran a quick search on Wicca-pedia and came across a brief summary:

Atlantis Complex: (at-lan-tyss kom-pleks) is a psychosis common among guilt-ridden criminals, first diagnosed by Dr E. Dypess of the Atlantis Brainology Clinic. Other symptoms include obsessive behaviour, paranoia, delusions and in extreme cases multiple-personality disorder. Dr E. Dypess is also known for his hit song 'I'm In Two Minds About You'.

Holly thought that this last bit was possibly Wicca-humour.

Foaly had reached the same conclusion about Artemis and said as much in a text message he buzzed over to Holly's helmet, which sat on the table before her.

Holly tapped her visor to reverse the readout then read the words.

Our boy is obsessing. Atlantis?

Holly called up a Gnommish keyboard on the visor and typed, slowly, so as not to attract attention.

Maybe. Fives? She sent the message.

Yes, fives. Classic symptom.

Then seconds later.

A demonstration! Fab. I ♥ demonstrations.

Holly managed to keep a straight face in case Artemis happened to stop counting long enough to glance her way. Foaly could never concentrate on anything for very long, unless it was one of his beloved projects.

Must be a genius thing.

It seemed as though the Icelandic elements held their breath for Artemis's demonstration. The dull air was cut with haze that hung in sheets like rows of laundered gauze.

The fairy folk felt their suit thermocoils vibrate a little as they followed Artemis outside to the rear of the restaurant. The rear of the Adam Adamsson establishment was even less impressive than the front. Whatever lackadaisical effort had been applied to making the Great Skua hospitable obviously did not extend to the back of the building. A whale mural, which looked like Adamsson had painted it himself using a live Arctic fox for a brush, stopped abruptly over the service entrance, decapitating an unfortunate humpback. And in several spots large sections of plaster had split from the wall and been tramped into the mud and snow.

Artemis led the small group to a tarpaulin, which had been pegged over a large cube.

Foaly snorted. 'Let me guess. Looks like a common garden tarpaulin, but is actually cam foil with rear projection set to look like tarp?'

Artemis took two more steps before answering, then nodded towards everyone to fix them in their places. A bead of sweat ran down his back, generated by the stress of losing his battle to obsessive behaviour.

'No, Foaly. It looks like a tarpaulin because it is a tarpaulin,' he said, then added. 'Yes, a tarpaulin.'

Foaly blinked. 'Yes, a tarpaulin? Are we in one of your Gilbert and Sullivan operettas now?' He threw his head back and sang, '*I am a centaur, yes, a centaur is what I am*. It's not like you to wax, Artemis.'

'Foaly is singing,' said Holly. 'Surely that's illegal?'

Vinyáya snapped her fingers. 'Quiet, children. Contain

your natural disruptive urges. I am most eager to see these nano-wafers in action before taking a shuttle closer to the warm core of our planet.'

Artemis bowed slightly. 'Thank you, Commander, most kind.'

Five again, thought Holly. *The evidence mounts.*

Artemis Fowl twirled a hand at Holly Short as though introducing himself to a theatre audience. 'Captain, perhaps you would remove the cloth. You have an aptitude for taking things apart.'

Holly was almost thrilled to have something to do. She would have preferred to have a serious talk with Artemis, but at least tackling a crate did not involve ingesting more scientific facts.

'Happy to,' she said, and attacked the tarp as though it had insulted her grandmother. Suddenly there was a knuckle knife adorning the fingers of her right hand, and three judicious slices later the tarp fluttered to the ground.

'You might as well do the crate while you are about it, Captain Short,' said Artemis, wishing he could sneak in an extra word to bolster the sentence. Immediately, Holly mounted the crate and apparently punched it into sections.

'Wow,' exhaled Foaly. 'That seemed excessively violent, even for you.'

Holly descended to earth barely making a footprint in the snow. 'Nope. It's more of a science. *Cos tapa*. The quick foot. An ancient martial art based on the movements of predatory animals.'

'Look!' said Foaly, pointing with some urgency into the vast steel-grey gloom. 'Someone who cares!'

Artemis was glad of the banter as it distracted from his loosening grasp on the logical world. While the fairies enjoyed their customary back and forth, he allowed his spine to curve for a moment, let his shoulders dip, but someone noticed.

'Artemis?'

Holly, of course.

'Yes, Captain Short.'

'Captain? Are we strangers, Artemis?'

Artemis coughed into his hand. She was probing. He needed to ward off her attentions. Nothing to do but say the number aloud.

'Strangers? No. We've known each other for more than *five* years.'

Holly took a step towards him, her eyes wide with concern behind the orange curve of visor.

'This five thing, Arty. I'm worried about that. You're not yourself.'

Artemis swept past her to the container that rested on the floor of the crate.

'Who else would I be?' he said brusquely, cutting short any possible discussion on the state of his mental health. He waved impatiently at the ice haze as though it were deliberately obstructing him, then pointed his mobile phone at the container, zapping the computerized locks. The container looked and sounded like a regular household refrigerator, squat, pearlescent and humming.

'Just what they need in Iceland,' muttered Foaly. 'More ice-makers.'

'Ah, but a very special ice-maker,' said Artemis, opening the fridge door. 'One that can save the glaciers.'

'Does it make Popsicles too?' asked the centaur innocently, wishing his old buddy Mulch Diggums was there so they could high five, a practice so puerile and outmoded that it would be sure to drive Artemis crazy, if he weren't already crazy.

'You said this was a demonstration,' snapped Vinyáya. 'So demonstrate.'

Artemis shot Foaly a poisonous look. 'With great pleasure, Commander. Observe.'

Inside the container sat a squat chrome contraption, which resembled a cross between a top-loader washing machine and a stubby cannon, apart from the jumble of wires and chips nestled under the bowl.

'The Ice Cube is not pretty, I grant you,' said Artemis, priming the equipment with an infra-red signal shot from the sensor on his phone. 'But I thought better to get production moving along than spend another month tidying the chassis.'

They formed a ragged ring round the device and Artemis could not help thinking that had a satellite been observing the group they would look like children playing a game.

Vinyáya's face was pale and her teeth chattered, though the temperature was barely below freezing. Chilly in human terms, a lot more uncomfortable for a fairy.

'Come on, human. Switch this Ice Cube thing on. Let's get the dwarf on the mudslide.'

A fairy expression which Artemis was not familiar with, but he could guess what it meant. He glanced at his phone.

'Surely, Commander. I will certainly launch the first pouch of nano-wafers just as soon as whatever unidentified craft is passing through the airspace moves on.'

Holly consulted her visor readout communicator. 'Nothing in the airspace, Mud Boy. Nothing but a shielded shuttle full of hurt for you, if you're trying to pull some kind of trick.'

Artemis could not stifle a groan. 'No need for the rhetoric. I assure you, Captain, there is a ship descending through the atmosphere. My sensors are picking it up quite clearly.'

Holly thrust her jaw forward. 'Well, *my* sensors aren't picking up a thing.'

'Funny, because my sensors *are* your sensors,' countered Artemis.

Foaly clopped a hoof, chipping the ice. 'I knew it. Is nothing sacred?'

Artemis squared his shoulders. 'Let's stop pretending that we don't spend half our time spying on each other. I read your files and you read the files I allow you to steal. There is a craft which seems to be heading straight for us and maybe your sensors would spot it if you used some of the same filters I do.'

Holly thought of something. 'Remember Opal Koboi's ship? The one completely built from stealth ore? Our pet geeks couldn't detect that but Artemis did.'

Artemis arched his eyebrows as if to say *even the police officer gets it.* 'I simply looked for what should be there but wasn't. Ambient gases, trace pollution and such. Wherever I found an apparent vacuum I also found Opal. I have since applied the same technique to my general scans. I am surprised you haven't learned that little trick, *Consultant* Foaly.'

'It will take about two seconds to sync with our shuttle and run an ambience test.'

Vinyáya scowled and her annoyance seemed to ripple the air like a heatwave.

'Run it then, centaur.'

Foaly activated the sensors in his gloves and screwed a yellow monocle over one eye. Thus wired he performed a complicated series of blinks, winks and gestures as he interfaced with a v-system invisible to all but him. To the casual observer it would seem as though the centaur had inhaled pepper while conducting an imaginary orchestra. It was not attractive, which was why most people tended to stick with hardwired hardware.

Twenty seconds more than two seconds later, Foaly's exertions ceased suddenly and he rested palms on knees.

'OK,' he panted. 'Firstly, I am nobody's *pet geek*. And, secondly, there may be a large unidentified space vehicle headed our way at high speed.'

Holly instantly drew her weapon, as though she could gun down a spaceship that was already falling on them.

Artemis rushed towards his Ice Cube, arms outstretched

maternally, then literally stopped in his tracks as suspicion filled his heart with heat.

'This is your ship, Foaly. Admit it.'

'It's not my ship,' protested Foaly. 'I don't even have a ship. I come to work on a quadrocycle.'

Artemis fought the paranoia until his hands shook, but there seemed to be no other explanation for the arrival of a strange ship at this precise time.

'You're trying to steal my invention. This is just like the time in London when you interfered in the C-Cube deal.'

Holly kept her eyes on the skies, but spoke to her human friend.

'I *saved* Butler in London.'

Artemis's whole frame was shaking now. 'Did you? Or did you *turn* him against me?' The words he spoke disgusted him, but they seemed to push through his lips like scarab beetles from the mouth of a mummy.

'That's when you made your alliance against me, wasn't it? How much did you offer him?'

For a long foggy breath, Holly was speechless, then: 'Offer him? Butler would never betray you. Never! How can you think that, Artemis?'

Artemis glared at his fingers as if he half hoped they would reach up and strangle him. 'I know you're behind this, Holly Short. You have never forgiven me for the kidnapping.'

'You need help, Artemis,' said Holly, tired of talking around the problem. 'I think you may have a condition. It might be something called the Atlantis Complex.'

Artemis stumbled backwards, knocking against Foaly's hindquarters. 'I know,' he said slowly, watching his breath take form before him. 'Lately, nothing is clear. I see things, suspect everyone. Five. Five is everywhere.'

'As if we would ever do anything to hurt you, Artemis,' said Foaly, patting the hair Artemis had ruffled.

'I don't know. Would you? Why wouldn't you? I have the most important job on Earth, more important than yours.'

Holly was calling in the cavalry.

'There's a UC in the atmo,' she called into her communicator, using that soldier shorthand that seemed more confusing than plain speaking. 'Descend to my seven for evac. Stat.'

A fairy shuttle fizzled into visibility seven metres overhead. It appeared plate by plate from nose to stern, the soldiers inside visible for a brief moment before the hull solidified. The sight seemed to confuse Artemis even further.

'Is that how you're going to take me? Scare me into voluntarily coming aboard, then steal my Ice Cube?'

'It's always cubes with you,' noted Foaly somewhat randomly. 'What's wrong with a nice sphere?'

'And you, centaur!' said Artemis, pointing an accusing finger. 'Always in my system. Are you in my head too?'

Vinyáya had forgotten the cold. She shrugged off her heavy coat to gain some ease of movement.

'Captain Short. The crazed human is your contact – put him on a leash until we get out of here.'

It was an unfortunate phrase to use.

'Put me on a leash? Is that what you've been doing all this time, Captain Short?'

Artemis was shivering now, as though a current passed through his limbs.

'Artemis,' said Holly urgently. 'Wouldn't you like to sleep for a while? Just lay your head down somewhere warm and sleep?'

The notion took hold in some corner of Artemis's brain. 'Yes. Sleep. Can you do that, Holly?'

Holly took a slow step forward. 'Of course I can. Just a little *mesmer* is all it takes. You'll wake up a new man.'

Artemis's eyes seemed to jellify. 'A new man. But what about THE PROJECT?'

Easy now, thought Holly. *Move in gently.* 'We can take care of it when you wake up.' She slipped the thinnest wafer of magic into her upper registers; to Artemis it would sound like the tinkling of crystal bells on every consonant.

'Sleep,' said Artemis, softly in case volume broke the word. 'To sleep, perchance to dream.'

'Quoting theatre now?' said Foaly. 'Do we really have the time?'

Holly hushed him with a glare, then took another step towards Artemis.

'Just a few hours. We can take you away from here, from whatever's coming.'

'Away from here,' echoed the troubled boy.

'Then we can talk about the project.'

The shuttle's pilot fluffed his approach, carving a shallow

trench in the surface with his rear stabilizer. The cacophonous splintering of sugar-glass-thin ice plates was enough to sharpen Artemis's pupils.

'No,' he shouted, his voice shrill for once. 'No magic. One two three four five. Stay where you are.'

A second craft introduced itself to the melodrama, appearing suddenly in the distant skyscape as though crashing through from an alternate dimension. Huge and sleek like a spiralling ice-cream cone, trailing tethered boosters, one errant engine detaching and spinning off into the heavy grey clouds. For such a huge ship, it made very little noise.

Artemis was shocked by the sight.

Aliens? was his first thought, then: *Wait, not aliens. I have seen this before. A schematic at least.*

Foaly was having the same thought. 'You know, that looks familiar.'

Entire sections of the giant ship were flickering out of sight as it cooled down from its steep atmospheric entry, or re-entry as it turned out.

'That's one from your space programme,' said Artemis accusingly.

'It's possible,' Foaly admitted, a guilty tinge blossoming on his rear cheeks, another reason he lost at poker. 'Difficult to tell with all the erratic movements and so forth.'

The LEP shuttle finally touched down, popping a hatch on its port side.

'Everyone in,' ordered Vinyáya. 'We need to put a little distance between us and that ship.'

Foaly was three or four steps ahead. 'No. No, this is one of ours. It shouldn't be here, but we can still control it.'

Holly snorted. 'Sure. You're doing a great job of it so far.'

This comment was one more than the centaur could bear. He finally snapped, rearing majestically on his hind legs, then bringing his front hooves smashing down on the thin ice.

'Enough!' he roared. 'There is a deep-space probe bearing down on us. And even if its nuclear generator does not explode, the impact blast wave alone will be enough to destroy everything in a fifteen-mile radius, so unless that shuttle of yours can travel to another dimension, boarding will be about as much use as *you* would be at a scientific convention.'

Holly shrugged. 'Fair enough. What do you suggest?'

'I suggest you shut up and let me deal with this problem.'

The term *probe* generally brings to mind a small, spare craft, with perhaps a few sample jars in its hold and maybe a rack of super-efficient solar cells clamped to its back, but this machine was the polar opposite of such an image. It was huge and violent in its movement, jarring the air as it bludgeoned through, jumping in lurching leaps, dragging tethered engines behind like captured slaves.

'This thing,' muttered Foaly, blinking to activate his monocle. 'Seemed friendlier when I designed it.'

The soldiers were ordered to hold their positions, and the entire group could only watch as the giant ship bore down on them, screaming ever louder as its soundproofing waffling was scored. Atmospheric friction tore at the probe with jagged fingers, tearing huge octagonal plates from the hull. And all the while Foaly tried to gain control of it.

'What I'm doing is going through the shuttle's antennae to get a good fix on the probe's computer, see if I can find the malfunction and then maybe I can program in a nice friendly hover at thirty metres. A little more shield would be nice too.'

'Less explaining,' said Vinyáya through gritted teeth, 'and more fixing.'

Foaly kept up his line of drivel as he worked. 'Come on, Commander. I know you military types thrive on these tense situations.'

Throughout this exchange, Artemis stood still as a statue, aware that should he release the tremors they would engulf him perhaps forever and he would be lost.

What has happened? he wondered. *Am I not Artemis Fowl?*

Then he noticed something.

That ship has four engines. Four.

Death.

As if to confirm this thought, or indeed prompted by the thought, an orange bolt of energy appeared at the very tip of the descending craft, roiling nastily, looking very much like a bringer of death.

'Orange energy,' noted Holly, shooting it with a finger gun. 'You're the explainer guy, Foaly, explain that.'

'Worry not, lesser intellect,' said Foaly, fingers a blur across his keyboard. 'This ship is unarmed. It's a scientific probe, for gods' sake. That plasma bolt is an ice-cutter, no more than that.'

Artemis could hold in the tremors no longer and they wracked his slim frame.

'Four engines,' he said, teeth chattering. 'F-f-four is death.'

Vinyáya paused on her way to the shuttle gangway. She turned, a sheaf of steel hair escaping her hood. 'Death? What's he talking about?'

Before Holly could answer, the orange plasma beam bubbled merrily for a moment then blasted directly into the shuttle's engine.

'No, no, no,' said Foaly, speaking as one would to an errant student. 'That's not right at all.'

They watched horrified as the shuttle collapsed in a ball of turgid heat, rendering the metal shell transparent for just long enough to reveal the writhing marines inside.

Holly dropped low and dived towards Vinyáya who was searching for a pathway through the flames to her men inside.

'Commander!'

Holly Short was fast, actually getting a grip on Vinyáya's glove before one of the shuttle's engines exploded and sent Holly pin-wheeling through the superheated air on to the roof of the Great Skua restaurant. She flapped on the slate like a butterfly on a pin, staring stupidly at the glove in her hand. Her visor's recognition software had locked on to Commander Vinyáya's face and a warning icon flashed gently.

Fatal injury to central nervous system, read a text on her screen. Holly knew that the computer was saying the same thing in her ear, but she couldn't hear it. *Please seal off the area and call emergency services.*

Fatal injury? This couldn't be happening again. In that nanosecond she flashed back to her former commander Julius Root's death.

Reality returned in a fiery heatwave, turning the ice to steam and popping the heat sensors in her suit.

Holly dug her fingers into the roof slush and hauled her upper body higher. The scene played around her like a silent movie, as her helmet noise filters had expanded and ruptured in the nanosecond between the flash and the bang.

Everyone in the shuttle was gone . . . that much was clear.

Don't say gone, *say* dead *– that's what they are.*

'Focus!' she said aloud, pounding a fist into the roof to emphasize each syllable. There would be time to grieve later; this crisis was not yet past.

Who is not dead?

She was not dead. Bleeding but alive, smoke drifting from the soles of her boots.

Vinyáya. Oh gods.

Forget Vinyáya for now.

And in a snowdrift underneath the eaves she spotted Foaly's legs doing an inverted gallop.

Is that funny now? Should I be laughing?

But where was Artemis? Suddenly Holly's heartbeat was loud in her ears and her blood roared like the surf.

Artemis.

Holly's journey to a crouch was harder than it was supposed to be and no sooner had her knees found purchase

•◌• ✦◌ ◐ ⏃) ⌗⍜ ✦ → •⸜⸝) ✦ •⋃ ⏃) ⏀ ⚡ •◌•

than her elbows gave way and she ended up almost back where she'd started.

Artemis. Where are you?

Then from the corner of her eye Holly saw her friend loping across the ice. Artemis was apparently unharmed, apart from a slight drag in his left leg. He was moving slowly but determinedly away from the burning shuttle. Away from the crank and blackening of contracting metal and the mercury drip of stealth ore finally reaching its melting point.

Where are you going?

Not running away, that was for sure. If anything, Artemis was moving directly into the path of the still-falling space probe.

Holly tried to scream a warning. She opened her mouth but could only cough smoke. She tasted smoke and battle.

'Artemis,' she managed to hack after several attempts.

Artemis glanced up at her. 'I know,' he shouted, a ragged edge to his voice. 'The sky appears to be falling but it isn't. None of this is real, the ship, those soldiers, none of it. I realize that now. I've been . . . I've been having delusions, you see.'

'Get clear, Artemis,' cried Holly, her voice not her own, feeling like her brain was sending signals to someone else's mouth. 'That ship is real. It will crush you.'

'No it won't, you'll see.' Artemis was actually smiling benignly. 'Delusional disorder, that's all this craft is. I simply constructed this vision from an old memory, one of Foaly's blueprints I sneaked a look at. I need to face my dementia.

Once I can prove to myself that this is all in my head, then I can keep it there.'

Holly crawled across the roof, feeling her insides buzz as magic went to work on her organs. Strength was returning, but slowly, and her legs felt like lead pipes. 'Listen to me, Artemis. Trust me.'

'No,' Artemis barked. 'I don't trust any of you. Not Butler, not even my own mother.' Artemis hunched his shoulders. 'I don't know what to believe, or who to trust. But I do know that there cannot be a space probe crash-landing here at this precise moment. The odds against it are just too astronomical. My mind is playing tricks on me and I have to show it who's boss.'

Holly registered about half of that speech, but she'd heard enough to realize that Artemis was referring to his own mind in the third person, which was a warning sign no matter which head doctor's theories you subscribed to.

The spaceship continued to bear down on them, unaffected by Artemis's lack of belief in its existence, shunting shockwaves before it. For a memory it certainly seemed very real, each panel richly textured by the tribulations of space travel. Long jagged striations were etched into the nose cone like scars from lightning bolts, and buckshot dents peppered the fuselage. A ragged semicircular chunk was missing from one of the three fins, as though a deep-space creature had taken a bite from the passing craft, and strangely coloured lichen was crayoned in the square patch vacated by a hull plate.

Even Artemis had to admit it. 'That doesn't seem particularly ethereal. I must have a more vivid imagination than I had thought.'

Two of the ship's silencers blew out in rapid succession and engine roar filled the bowl of grey sky.

Artemis pointed a rigid finger at the craft. 'You are not real!' he shouted, though even he did not hear the words. The ship was low enough now for Artemis to read the message written in several scripts and pictograms across the nose cone.

'I come in peace,' he mumbled, and thought: *Four words. Death.*

Holly was thinking too, images of tragedy and destruction flashing past like the lights of a train carriage, but there was one other notion holding steady through the chaos.

I can't reach him from this rooftop. Artemis is going to die and there's nothing I can do but watch.

And then a hysterical afterthought.

Butler is going to kill me.

CHAPTER 2: THE JADE PRINCESS AND CRAZY BEAR

The night before in Cancún, Mexico

 THE man in the rental Fiat 500 swore loudly as his broad foot mashed the tiny brake and accelerator pedals, stalling the tiny car for the umpteenth time.

It might be a little easier to drive this miniature vehicle if I could sit on the back seat so my knees were not jammed under my chin, the man reasoned. And with that thought he pulled over sharply on to the verge bordering Cancún's spectacular lagoon. In the reflected light of a million twinkling luxury-suite balcony lamps, he performed an act of vandalism on the Fiat which would definitely cost him his deposit and possibly send him rocketing to number one on the Hertz blacklist.

'Better,' grunted the man, and tossed the driver's seat down the verge.

Hertz only have themselves to blame, he thought, on a reasoning roll. *This is what happens when you insist on giving a toy car to a man of my proportions. It's like trying to load fifty-calibre rounds into a Deringer boot gun. Ridiculous.*

He crammed himself into the vehicle and, navigating from the back seat, pulled into the flow of cars, which even at close to midnight were packed together tighter than train carriages.

I'm coming, Juliet, he thought, squeezing the steering wheel as though it were a threat to his little sister somehow. *I'm on my way.*

The driver of this carelessly remodelled Fiat was of course Butler, Artemis Fowl's bodyguard, though he had not always been known by that name. In the course of his career as a soldier of fortune, Butler had adopted many a *nom de guerre* to protect his family from recriminations. A band of Somali pirates knew him as Gentleman George, he had for a time hired himself out in Saudi Arabia under the name Captain Steele (Artemis had later accused him of having a touch of the screeching melodramas) and for two years a Peruvian tribe, the Isconahua, knew the mysterious giant who protected their village from an aggressive logging corporation only as *El Fantasma de la Selva*, the ghost of the jungle. Of course, since becoming Artemis Fowl's bodyguard there was no more time for side projects.

Butler had travelled to Mexico at Artemis's insistence, though insistence had hardly been necessary once Butler had read the message on his principal's smart phone. They had been in the middle of a mixed martial-arts session earlier in the day when the phone rang. A polyphonic version of Morricone's

'Miserere', which signified the arrival of a message.

'No phones in the dojo, Artemis,' Butler had rumbled. 'You know the rules.'

Artemis had delivered one more blow to the pad, a left jab that had little power and less accuracy, but at least his shots were landing on the pad now. Until recently, Artemis's punches were so wide of the mark that in the event of actual combat a passer-by would be in more danger than any assailant.

'I know the rules, Butler,' said Artemis, taking several breaths to get the sentence out. 'The phone is definitely off. I checked it five times.'

Butler pulled off a pad, which in theory protected the wearer's hand from punches, but in this case protected Artemis's knuckles from Butler's spade-like palm. 'The phone is off, and yet it rings.'

Artemis trapped a glove between his knees and tugged his hand free. 'It's set to emergency breakthrough. It would be irresponsible of me not to check it.'

'Your speech seems strange,' noted Butler. 'Stilted some-how . . . Are you *counting* your words?'

'That is patently ridiculous . . . actually,' said Artemis, colouring. 'I am simply choosing carefully.' He hurried to the phone, which was one of his own design with a dedicated operating platform based on an amalgamation of human and fairy technology. 'The message is from Juliet,' he said, consulting the seven-centimetre touch screen.

Butler's pique immediately evaporated. 'Juliet sending an emergency message? What does it say?'

•❨◗▢◒☌▢↻•⊕▢◗•↻☌•⬥⅋⌂•↻◯⌘⬡▢•⊙◯

Artemis wordlessly handed over the phone, which seemed to shrink as Butler's massive hand enfolded it.

The message was short and urgent. Five words only.

In trouble, Domovoi. Come alone.

Butler's fingers squeezed the phone until its casing cracked. The first names of all Blue Diamond bodyguards were closely guarded secrets, and the mere fact that Juliet had invoked his name to summon him was an indicator of how much trouble she was in.

'Naturally I'm coming with you,' said Artemis briskly. 'My phone can trace that call to the nearest square centimetre and we can be anywhere in the world in just less than a day.'

Butler's features belied the struggle between big brother and detached professional that raged inside him. Finally the professional got the upper hand.

'No, Artemis. I cannot put you in harm's way.'

'But . . .'

'No. I must go, but you will return to school. If Juliet is in trouble, I need to move quickly, and caring for you will simply double my responsibility. Juliet knows how seriously I take my job and she would never ask me to come alone unless the situation was dangerous.'

Artemis coughed. 'It's probably not too dangerous. Perhaps Juliet is more *inconvenienced* than in any actual peril. But in any case you should go as soon as . . .'

He plucked the phone from Butler's grasp and tapped the screen.

'Cancún, Mexico, that's your destination.'

Butler nodded. It made sense. Juliet was currently with a Mexican wrestling troupe building a rep for her character, the Jade Princess, and praying for that magic call from the World Wrestling Entertainment group.

'Cancún,' he repeated. 'I've never been. There's not much call for people like me there. Too safe.'

'The jet is at your disposal naturally,' said Artemis, who then frowned, unhappy with the sentence. 'Hopefully this entire thing is nothing but a . . . goose chase.'

Butler glanced sharply at his young charge. Something was wrong with the boy, he felt sure of it, but at the moment there was only room for Juliet in the *concern for others* corner of his brain.

'This is no goose chase,' he said softly, then with considerably more force: 'And whoever caused this message to be sent will regret it.' To drive this point home, Butler allowed his big-brother side to surface for a moment and punched a training mannequin so hard that its wooden head flew off and spun on the practice mat like a top.

Artemis picked up the head and tapped the crown half a dozen times, or thereabouts.

'I imagine they already do,' he said, his voice the rustle of dry leaves.

So now Butler was making agonizingly slow progress through the late-night Cancún traffic, head and shoulders squashed flat against the Fiat's roof. He had neglected to reserve a car and so had been forced to accept whatever the Hertz lady had left in the lot. A Fiat 500. *Très* cool if you were a single teen on the way to the spa, but not so suitable for a hundred-kilogram hulk.

An unarmed hundred-kilo hulk, Butler realized. Generally the bodyguard managed to bring a few weapons with him to whatever party he was about to break up, but in this case public transport was actually quicker than the Fowl jet, so Butler had been forced to leave his arsenal at home, even his beloved Sig Sauer, which almost drew a tear. He had connected through Atlanta, and the marines at customs would not have taken kindly to anyone smuggling hardware into the US, especially someone who looked like he could probably breach the White House with a few belts of ammunition.

Butler had been at something of a loose end since leaving Artemis's side. For more than fifteen years he had spent the vast bulk of his time engaged in Artemis-related activities. Finding himself virtually alone in business class on a trans-Atlantic flight with several hours of enforced down time, he could not sleep for worrying about his sister and so his mind naturally drifted to Artemis.

His charge had changed recently – there was no doubt about it. Since his return from saving endangered species in Morocco last year there had been a definite mood swing. Artemis seemed less open than usual, and *usually* he was about as open as a Swiss vault at night. Also, Butler had noticed that Artemis seemed obsessed with the placement of objects, something Butler himself was very alert to as he was trained to see everything in a building as a potential weapon or shrapnel fragment. Often Artemis would enter a room that his bodyguard had already swept and cleared and start moving things back to where they had been. And Artemis's speech seemed *off* somehow. Artemis generally spoke in sentences that were almost poetic, but lately he seemed to care less about what he said than how many words it took to say it.

As the Boeing began its descent into Atlanta, Butler decided that he would go to Artemis Senior as soon as he made it back to Fowl Manor and make a clean breast of his concerns. While it was undeniably his job to protect Artemis from danger, it was difficult to do that when the danger came from Artemis himself.

I have protected Artemis from trolls, goblins, demons, dwarf gas and even humans, but I cannot guarantee that my skill set will save him from his own mind. Which makes it imperative that I find Juliet and bring her home as soon as possible.

Butler eventually grew tired of the traffic's crawl down Cancún's main strip and decided that he would make better time on foot. He pulled over sharply into a taxi rank and, ignoring the indignant cries of the drivers, set off past the rows of five-star hotels at a brisk jog.

Locating Juliet would not be difficult; her face was splashed all over dozens of downtown banners.

LUCHASLAM! FOR ONE WEEK ONLY AT THE GRAND THEATRE.

Butler did not much care for Juliet's picture on the banners. The artist had twisted her pretty face to make his sister seem more aggressive, and her stance was obviously just for show. It may look good on a poster, but it was all wrong and left her wide open for a hook to the kidneys.

Juliet would never approach an adversary in that way.

His sister was the best natural fighter he had ever seen and too proud to ask for help unless there was no other option available to her, which was why her message was so worrying.

Butler jogged two miles without breaking a sweat, weaving through throngs of revellers, until he arrived at the glass and stucco façade of the Grand Theatre. A dozen or so red-jacketed doormen clustered around the automatic doors, nodding and smiling at the crowd hurrying in for the main event.

Around the back, he decided. *The story of my life.*

Butler skirted the building thinking that it would be nice, just once, to go in the front door. Maybe he would in another lifetime, when he got too old for this business.

How old do I have to be? he wondered. *Come to think of it, with all the time travel and fairy healings, I'm not even sure how old I actually am any more.*

As soon as Butler reached the back door, he put all other thoughts from his mind, apart from the job at hand. Get to Juliet, find out what trouble she was in and extricate her with minimal collateral damage. There were still ten minutes before the show was scheduled to start, so with a little luck he could nab his sister before the room got too crowded.

The only security on the back door was a single surveillance camera. Luckily the Grand was a straight theatre and not the convention room of a resort hotel or there would be a cluster of pools at the back door, along with crowds of tourists, a salsa band and possibly half a dozen undercover private cops. As it was, Butler slid unnoticed into the theatre and simply waved at the camera on the way in, effectively covering his face.

Butler did not meet a shred of opposition on his way through the theatre's backstage area. He passed a couple of costumed wrestlers sharing an electrolytic drink, but they barely spared him a glance, probably assuming he was one of them. Big and dumb by the look of him, the bad guy.

Like most theatres, the Grand had miles of corridors and back passages which did not show up on the blueprints that Butler had downloaded on his smart phone from Artemis's interpedia, which had a dedicated blueprint site containing any plans that had ever been uploaded and quite a few that Artemis had stolen and uploaded himself. After several wrong turns, even Butler's excellent sense of direction was failing him and the big bodyguard was tempted to simply punch through walls and create the shortest route to where he wanted to go: the performers' dressing room.

Butler finally arrived at the dressing-room door just in time to see the tail end of the wrestling squad winding their way through to the stage, looking like sections of a Chinese dragon in all their Lycra and silk. After the last wrestler slipped through, a barrier of meat and muscle in the shape of two enormous bouncers closed across the backstage doors.

I could take them, thought Butler. *That would not be a problem, but it would only leave me seconds to find Juliet and get her out of here and, knowing my sister, she will want to conduct a complicated and ultimately meaningless conversation before she's ready to go. I need to think like Artemis, like the Artemis of old, and play this calmly. Blundering in is likely to get both of us killed.*

Butler heard the howls and whoops of the crowd as the wrestlers entered. The noise was muffled through the double doors, but clearer from the dressing room. He poked his head inside and saw a monitor bracketed to the wall, displaying the action in the ring. Convenient.

Butler stepped close to the screen and searched for his sister. There she was, at the corner of the ring, performing some ostentatious warm-ups that were more for show than actual effect. If Butler could have seen his own normally taciturn features at that moment, he would have been surprised by the fond, almost sleepy, smile that lingered on his face.

It's been too long since I've seen you, little sister.

Juliet did not seem to be in any immediate danger; in fact, she appeared to be relishing the crowd's attention, raising her arms for more applause and whipping the jade ring on her ponytail around in figures of eight. The crowd loved her too. Several young men waved banners bearing Juliet's image, and a few were bold enough to shower her with confetti hearts. Butler frowned. He would definitely be keeping an eye on those particular young gentlemen.

Butler allowed himself to relax a little, a loosening of the fingers that perhaps five people in the world would notice. He was still on high alert, but could admit to himself now that his darkest fear had always been that he would arrive too late.

Juliet is alive. And healthy. Whatever the problem is, we can solve it between us.

He decided then that the most prudent course of action would be to observe from this vantage point. He had a clear view of the wrestling ring and, if necessary, he could be by his sister's side in seconds.

The opening match was started by an old-fashioned ringside bell and Juliet leaped high, landing catlike on the top rope.

'*Princesa! Princesa!*' chanted the audience.

A favourite with the crowd, thought Butler. *Of course she is.*

Juliet's opponent was obviously the villain of the piece. A humongous woman, with buzz-cut bleached hair and a costume of blood-red Lycra.

'Boo!' called the crowd.

Like most wrestlers on the luchador circuit, the huge newcomer wore a mask that covered her eyes and nose and was tied at the back with some nasty-looking barbed wire, which Butler suspected was actually plastic.

Juliet seemed like a doll in comparison, apparently outmatched. A little of the cockiness drained from her masked face and she appealed to her corner for assistance, but was met with shrugged shoulders from a stereotypical flat-capped trainer who could have been recruited from the set of a wrestling movie.

This match is all scripted, Butler realized. *There's no danger here.*

He pulled a chair up to the screen and settled to watch his sister.

The first round was gentle enough on Butler's nerves. Then, in the second round, Juliet strayed a little close to her opponent and was pounced on with surprising speed.

'*Oooh,*' cried most of the crowd.

'Snap her in two, Samsonetta!' called a few less charitable observers.

Samsonetta, thought Butler. *It suits her.*

He was not worried at this point. There were at least a dozen ways for Juliet to break Samsonetta's hold as far as he could see. Most she could do without even using her hands. One would be theoretically possible by combining a fake sneeze with a sudden drop.

Butler started to worry when he noticed a dozen men in trench coats sidling along the far wall towards the ring.

Trench coats? In Cancún? Why would anyone wear a trench coat in Mexico unless they were concealing something?

The picture was too grainy for Butler to garner much detail, but there was something about these guys and the way they moved. Purposeful, devious, sticking to the shadows.

I've got time, Butler reasoned, already putting together his plan. *This could be nothing, but it could be everything. I can't take chances with Juliet's life at stake.*

He glanced around the dressing room to see if there were anything he could use as a weapon. No such luck. All he could find were a couple of chairs, plenty of glitter and mascara, and a barrel of old costumes.

I won't be needing the glitter or mascara, thought Butler, reaching into the costume barrel.

Juliet Butler was feeling a little claustrophobic in the arms of her opponent.

'Come on, Sam,' she hissed. 'You're suffocating me.'

Samsonetta stamped flat-footed on the canvas, sending hollow booms bouncing around the auditorium, while at the same time making a show of squeezing Juliet's neck.

'That's the idea, Jules,' she whispered, her Stockholm accent stretching the vowels. 'I whip up the crowd, remember? And then you take me down.'

Juliet turned her face to the three-thousand-strong crowd, delivering a dramatic howl of pain.

'*Kill her,*' screamed the nice ones.

'*Kill her and then snap her in two,*' screamed the not-so-nice ones.

'*Kill her, snap her in two and stamp on the pieces,*' howled the downright nasty audience members, usually easily identifiable by the violent slogans on their T-shirts, and the drooling.

'Careful, Sam. You're moving my mask.'

'And such a pretty mask too.'

Juliet's entire outfit was pretty enough to make her a crowd favourite. A jade skin-tight leotard, and a small eye-mask, which was actually a gel-pack covered with glitter.

If I have to wear a mask, Juliet had reasoned, *it might as well be good for my skin.*

They prepared for Samsonetta's trademark takedown: an overhead drop, helped along by the power of her amazing arms. Usually if her opponents had so much as a spark of energy left in them after that manoeuvre, Sam simply fell on them and that generally did the trick. But since Juliet was the crowd's favourite, the move was not planned to go as usual. A wrestling audience liked to see their hero as far down as possible without being out.

Sam advertised the move by asking the crowd if they wanted the body slam.

'Do you vant it?' she shouted, playing up her accent.

'*Yes!*' they howled, beating the air with their fists.

'The body slam?'

'Slam!' they chanted. 'Slam! Slam!'

A few chanted other rougher slogans but security soon zoned in on them.

'You vant a slam! I vill slam!' Generally Samsonetta would have said *I shall slam!* But Max, the promoter/manager of LuchaSlam, liked her to use 'v' instead of 'w' wherever possible as for some reason it drove the crowd crazy.

And so she bent backwards and hurled the unfortunate Jade Princess towards the deck, and that would have been the end of it had not the Jade Princess somehow twirled in mid-air to land on her toes and fingertips, and that wasn't even the impressive part. The impressive part was springing back up again and whipping her head around, so the jade ring woven into her blonde ponytail whacked Samsonetta in the jaw, landing the giantess flat on her back.

Samsonetta whined and complained, rubbed her jaw to redden it and rolled like a walrus on a hot rock.

She was quite a performer, and for a moment Juliet worried that the jade ring had really hurt her, but then Sam threw her a secret wink and she knew that they were still playacting.

'Have you had enough, Samsonetta?' asked Juliet, springing nimbly to the top rope. 'Would you like some more?'

'No,' blubbed her supposed opponent, then decided to sneak another 'v' in for Max. 'I vant no more.'

Juliet turned to the audience. 'Should I give her some more?'

Oh no, said an imaginary audience. *No more, that would be barbaric.*

But the real audience said things like:

'Kill her!'

'Take her downtown!' (Whatever that meant – they were already downtown.)

'Show her the pain.' *The* pain being obviously more excruciating than just plain old pain.

I love these people, thought Juliet, and launched herself off the top rope for the coup de grâce.

It would have been a thing of beauty. A lovely double flip rounded off with a nice *oooof*-inducing elbow to the stomach, but someone came out of the shadows and snatched Juliet from the air, tossing her roughly into the corner of the ring. Several other silent, muscled attackers piled on top of Juliet until all that was visible of the girl was one green-clad leg.

In the shadows, where he was watching behind one of the lighting rigs, Butler felt a sour ball of fear drop to the pit of his stomach and muttered: 'That's my cue.'

Which sounded an awful lot more flippant than he felt.

The crowd was still applauding the unexpected arrival of the Ninja Squad luchadores in their trademark black costumes disguised by trench coats, who had doubtless shown up to avenge their master's recent defeat at the hands and feet of the Jade Princess at QuadroSlam in Mexico City. Surprise guests often showed up unadvertised at the slams, but the entire Ninja Squad was an unexpected bonus.

The ninjas were a writhing mass of pumping limbs, each member desperate to land a blow on the Jade Princess, and there was nothing the slight girl could do but lie there and absorb it.

Butler entered the ring quietly. The element of surprise was often the difference between victory and defeat in *against the odds* situations, though if Butler were honest with himself he would admit that secretly he usually felt that the odds were in his favour, even in this case when he was outnumbered twelve to one. Twelve to two if Juliet were still conscious, which was six to one, which was virtually even-stevens. A moment earlier Butler had felt a little self-conscious in the borrowed costume of fake bearskin leotard and mask, but now all embarrassment was forgotten as he clicked his brain into that cold space he called combat mode.

These people are hurting my sister, he thought as a hot trickle of anger cracked his icy shell of professionalism.

Time to go to work.

With a growl that was totally in keeping with his Crazy Bear costume, Butler rolled into the ring under the bottom rope, stepped briskly across the canvas and began laying into the ninjas with blatant economy of movement. There was no threatening monologue, not even a simple foot stamp to herald his arrival, which was hardly courteous. He simply dismantled the ninjas as though they were a Jenga stack.

There followed thirty seconds of flailing limbs and high-pitched screaming that would have done hysterical teenagers at a boy-band concert proud, and then, finally, Juliet was uncovered.

Butler saw that his sister was intact, and smiled behind the mask.

'Hello there. I made it.'

And in response to her life being saved, Juliet jammed four rigid fingers into his solar plexus, driving the air from his body.

'Aarrrk,' he grunted, then, 'Whuueeeech.' Which was supposed to be *What are you doing?*

A couple of the ninjas had recovered and tried a few of their stylized moves on their attacker only to be rewarded with casual open-handed slaps.

'Watch it,' snapped Butler, drawing breath once more and shooting them the evil eye. 'I need a minute of family time.'

Something flickered in the corner of Butler's vision, moving with blurred, jittery speed. His left hand automatically shot out to grab the jade ring that was braided into his sister's blonde ponytail.

'Wow,' said Juliet. 'No one's ever done that before.'

'Really?' said Butler, dropping the jade ring. 'No one?'

Juliet's eyes widened behind her mask. 'No one except . . . Brother, is that you?'

Before Butler could reply, Juliet side-stepped and pole-axed with her forearm a ninja who may have been sneaking up on them, or may in fact have been trying to escape from what had become the ring of real pain as opposed to the ring of convincingly faked agony.

'Didn't you guys hear this man? We need family time!'

The ninjas shrank back against the rope, whimpering. Even Samsonetta seemed a little concerned.

'Brother, I'm in the middle of a grudge match. What are you doing here?' asked Juliet.

It might have taken many people a few more minutes before they realized something was amiss, but not Butler. Years of protecting Artemis Fowl had taught him to catch the penny before it dropped.

'Obviously you didn't send for me. We need to leave so I can figure things out.'

Juliet's bottom lip hung sulkily, transporting Butler ten years into the past when he'd forbidden her to shave her head.

'I can't just go. I've got fans expecting me to do cartwheels and give you the signature move.'

⟨⊗⟩⚬⊙⟨⟩•⟨▯▯⚬⟩⟨⊗⟩•⟨⚬⟨⊙⟨⟩→•⊙•⚬⟨⟩•⟨⟩

It was true. The Jade Princess's camp was bouncing on their benches, baying for Crazy Bear's blood.

'If I just leave, there could be a riot.'

Butler glanced up at the giant screen suspended from the ceiling and saw a close-up of his own head looking up at the screen, which was enough to give anyone a headache.

A voice boomed from four old-fashioned conical speakers wired to the corners of the overhead screen.

'Who is this guy, folks? Is it Crazy Bear come to take down his old enemy, the Jade Princess?'

Juliet stuck out her chin. 'Max. Always looking for the angle.'

'Juliet, we don't have time for this.'

'Whoever it is,' continued Max, 'we're not just going to let him walk out of here with our princess, are we, *amigos*?'

Judging by the loud and sustained reaction, the paying customers did not take to the idea of Crazy Bear simply walking out with the princess. The language was florid and Butler could have sworn that the walls were shaking slightly.

Butler took three quick steps to the side of the ring and wagged his finger at a little man holding a microphone.

He was surprised when the little man jumped up on the table, stamped on his own hat, then shouted into the mike.

'You're threatening me, Crazy Bear? After all I've done for you? When those forest rangers found you living with the grizzlies, who took you in? Max Schetlin, that's who. And this is how you repay me?'

Butler tuned out the rant. 'OK, Juliet. We need to get out

of here now. We do not have time for this. Someone wanted me out of the way. Possibly someone who has a grudge against Artemis.'

'You need to be an awful lot more specific than that, brother. Artemis has more enemies than you, and you have quite a few at the moment.'

It was true. The crowd were turning ugly, a lot of it was fake ugly, but Butler's keen eye spotted scores of wrestling fans in the front rows who looked ready to storm the ring.

I need to make a statement, he thought. *Show these people who's boss.*

'Outside the ring, Jules. Right now.'

Juliet did what she was told without complaint. Butler had that look on his face. The last time she had seen *that* look, her brother had punched his way through the hull of a Somali pirate's stolen yacht, sinking the vessel in the Gulf of Aden.

'Don't hurt Samsonetta,' she ordered. 'We're friends.'

Butler shook his head in disapproval. 'Friends? I knew you two were faking.'

Samsonetta and the ninjas were busy throwing shapes in the far corner of the ring. They stamped, punched and threatened without actually attacking.

When Juliet was safely outside the ropes, Butler turned to his own corner and threw his shoulder into the pad covering the post. The impact rattled the post in its housing.

'Crazy Bear really is crazy,' crowed Max. 'He's beating up the ring. Are you going to stand for that, ninjas? This man is defiling the very symbol of our sporting heritage.'

Apparently the Ninja Squad was prepared to accept a little defiling of their symbol if it meant not being attacked by the man-mountain who had taken their pyramid apart with no more effort than a child knocking down a house of cards.

Butler hit the post again, this time smashing it right out of its socket. He hefted the metal pole, stepped underneath the ropes and began to twist the ring in on itself.

This move was so unprecedented that it was several seconds before anyone could appreciate what they were seeing. In years to come the manoeuvre would become known as *the wringer* and would elevate the real Crazy Bear, who was passed out drunk in the back alley, to the status of luchador superstar.

Even Max Schetlin's tirade dried up as his brain tried to process what was actually going on.

Butler took advantage of the stunned stillness to quickly spin the corner post half a dozen times, popping another two supports from their housings.

This is not as difficult as it looks, mused Butler, catching sight of himself on the giant screen. *This entire ring is little more than an inverted tent. A well-fed teenager could pull it down.*

He gathered the three posts in his arms, twirling them deftly, drawing the ring tighter and tighter.

A couple of the ninjas had enough presence of mind to skip out while they could, but most stood slack-jawed and a couple who believed themselves to be dreaming sat down and closed their eyes.

Butler nodded at Samsonetta. 'Out you go, miss.'

Samsonetta actually curtsied, which was totally out of

character, and ducked under the rope, along with one ninja who was sharp enough to recognize a reprieve when he saw one. The rest of the crew was pressed closer together as Butler wound the rope tight. Every twist brought groans from the coils of old rope and from the people trapped inside. The crowd was beginning to realize what was happening and they began to cheer with every twist. Several were gleefully calling for Butler to squeeze the air from the ninjas' lungs, but the bodyguard was content merely to crush them together like passengers on the London Tube at rush hour. And once they were powerless to move he shuffled them to the side of the ring and planted the pole back in its housing.

'I'm going now,' he said. 'And I advise you all to stay put until I am out of the country, at the very least, because if you don't I will be very unhappy.'

Butler did not have the magical power of the *mesmer*, but his voice was extremely persuasive nevertheless.

'OK, Bear, take it easy,' said the only ninja sporting a white headscarf, possibly the leader. 'You're straying way off script. Max is going to go nuts.'

'You let me worry about Max,' Butler advised. 'You worry about me worrying about you.'

The ninja's frown was obvious through the folds of his scarf. 'What? Who should I worry about?'

Butler ground his teeth. Dialoguing was not as easy as the movies would have a person believe.

'Just don't move until I'm gone. Got it?'

'Yep. You should have said that.'

'I know.'

From a bodyguard's perspective, there were so many things wrong with this situation that Butler almost despaired. He turned to his sister.

'Enough of this. I have to go somewhere and think. Some-where with no Lycra.'

'OK, Dom. Follow me.'

Butler stepped down from the platform. 'If you could stop bandying my name about. It's supposed to be a secret.'

'Not from me. I'm your sister.'

'That may be. But there are thousands of people here and half as many cameras.'

'It's not as if I said the whole name. It's not as if I said Dom-o—'

'Don't!' warned Butler. 'I mean it.'

The stage door was a mere twenty metres away and the familiar rhythms of family bickering warmed Butler's heart.

I think we're going to make it, he thought in a rare moment of optimism.

Which was when the picture on the big screen was replaced by a giant pair of glowing red eyes. And although red eyes are usually associated with nasty things like vampires, chlorine burn and conjunctivitis, these particular red eyes seemed friendly and infinitely trustworthy. In fact, anyone who gazed into the fluid swirling depths of these eyes felt that all their problems were about to be solved, if they just did what the owner of those eyes told them to do.

Butler inadvertently caught sight of the eyes in his peripheral vision but quickly tucked his head low.

Fairy magic, he realized. *This entire crowd is about to be mesmerized.*

'Look into my eyes,' said a voice from every speaker in the room. The voice even managed to invade the cameras and phones of the audience.

'Wow,' said Juliet in a monotone that did not suit the word. 'I really need to look into those eyes.'

Juliet might have been reluctant to do what the silky voice commanded if she'd had any memory of her dealings with the fairy People. Unfortunately those memories had been wiped from her mind.

'Block the exits,' urged the voice. 'Block all the exits. Use your bodies.'

Juliet whipped off her mask, which was impeding her view of the screen. 'Brother, we need to block the exits, with our bodies.'

Butler wondered how things could get much worse as hundreds of enraptured wrestling fans surged down the aisles to physically block the entrances and exits.

Block the exits with your bodies? This fairy was pretty specific.

Butler had no doubt that another command was forthcoming and he doubted it would be *now join hands and sing sea shanties*. No, he was certain that nothing benign would issue from that screen.

'Now kill the bear and the princess,' said the layered voice, a few of the layers taking a moment to catch up, lending a sibilant *sssss* to *princess*.

Kill the bear and the princess. Charming.

Butler noticed a glint of dark intent in his sister's eye as she realized that he was the bear. What would she do, he wondered, when she tumbled to the fact that *she* was the princess?

It doesn't matter, he realized. *We could both be dead long before that happens.*

'Kill the bear and the princess,' droned Juliet in perfect unison with the mesmerized crowd.

'And take your time about it,' continued the magical voice, now infused with a merry note. 'Drag it out a little. As you humans say: no pain no gain.'

A comedian, thought Butler. *It's not Opal Koboi, then.*

'Gotta kill you, brother,' said Juliet. 'I'm sorry. Truly.'

Not likely, thought Butler. On a good day, if he was drugged and blindfolded, maybe Juliet could have inflicted a little damage, but in his experience the *mesmer* made people slow and stupid. A large part of their brains were switched off and the parts left awake were not going to be winning any Nobel prizes.

Juliet tried a spinning kick but ended up twirling off balance and into Butler's arms. Annoyingly, her jade ring spun round and clattered him on the ear.

Even mesmerized, my sister is irritating.

Butler hefted Juliet easily, then tensed his muscles for flight.

'Kill you,' muttered his sister. 'Sorry. Gotta.' Then: 'Fairies? You kidding me?'

Was she remembering the Fowl Manor siege? Butler wondered. Had the *mesmer* accidentally triggered recall?

He could investigate later, if there were a later for them. Butler had considerable faith in his own ability, but he doubted that he could take on a theatre full of zombies, even if they weren't fleet of foot.

'Go to work, my human lackeys,' said the voice that went along with the red eyes. 'Dig deep into the darkest recesses of your brains, such as they are. Leave no evidence for the authorities.'

Leave no evidence? What are they supposed to do with the evidence?

That question really didn't bear thinking about.

Bear? Ha ha ha, thought Butler, and then: *Jokes? I have time for jokes? Is it possible that I am frazzled? Pull it together, man. You've been through worse.*

Although, looking at the dozens of stiff-limbed insta-psychos lumbering down from the upper levels, Butler could not for the life of him remember when.

A pudgy forty-something man sporting an Undertaker T-shirt and a beer hat pointed at Butler from the aisle.

'Beaaaar!' he yowled. 'Beaaaaar and princess!'

Butler borrowed a word from the fairy lexicon.

'D'Arvit,' he said.

CHAPTER 3: ORION RISING

ARTEMIS was jumping between psychoses. 'Not real!' he shouted at the descending ship. 'You are nothing but a delusion, my friend.'

And from there he hopped straight over into paranoia. 'You planned this,' he shouted at Holly. 'Who were your partners? Foaly without doubt. Butler? Did you turn my faithful bodyguard against me? Did you burgle his mind and plant your own truths in there?'

From the rooftop, the directional mike in Holly's helmet picked up no more than every second word but it was enough to tell her that Artemis was not the clinical logistician he used to be.

If the old Artemis could see the new Artemis, the old Artemis would die of embarrassment.

Like Butler, Holly was having a hard time controlling her rebellious sense of humour in this dire hour.

'Get down!' she called. 'The ship is real!'

'That's what you want me to think. That ship is nothing more than a cog in your conspiracy . . .' Artemis paused. If the ship was a cog in the conspiracy, and the conspiracy was real, then the ship must be real. 'Five!' he blurted suddenly, having forgotten all about it for a minute. 'Five ten fifteen.'

He pointed all of his fingers at the ship, wiggling them furiously.

A ten-finger salute. Surely that will vaporize this vision.

And it seemed as though the fingers were having an effect. The four discus-shaped engines, which had been trailing behind the main body like helpless puppies tethered to their spooked master, suddenly flipped and began emitting anti-grav pulses that lolloped towards the ground in fat bubbles, slowing the ship's descent faster than seemed possible for a craft of such inelegant dimensions.

'Hah!' crowed Artemis. 'I control my own reality. Did you see that?'

Holly knew that, far from controlling anything, Artemis was actually witnessing a fairy probe's landing sequence. She had never actually piloted a deep-space probe herself, but nevertheless knew that standing underneath such a behemoth while it was dropping anti-grav bubbles was more than enough to get a person killed, and wiggling fingers like a sideshow magician was not going to change that.

I have to get up, she thought.

But the injury in her legs held her down like a lead blanket.

I think my pelvis is broken, she realized. *Maybe an ankle too.*

Holly's magic had an unusual potency, thanks to a couple of boosts from her friend the demon N⁰1, who was turning out to be the most magical warlock the university had ever enrolled, and it was setting to work on her injuries, but not fast enough. Artemis had a couple of seconds before one of those anti-grav blobs tore him apart or the ship itself actually landed on his head. And you didn't have to be a genius to figure out what would happen then, which was just as well as Artemis didn't seem to be a genius any more.

'Assistance,' she called weakly into her com-set. 'Someone. Anyone?'

There was no one. Anyone who had been inside the shuttle was beyond magic and Foaly was still up-ended in the snowdrift.

Even if there were somebody, it's too late.

Large crack patterns bloomed in the ice like hammer blows as the anti-grav pulses impacted on the surface. The cracks spread across the glacier with a noise like snapping branches, dropping large sink-holes through to the subterranean caverns below.

The ship was as big as a grain silo and seemed to be fighting against the pull of its tethered engines, throwing off waves of steam and jets of fluid. Rocket fuel drenched Artemis, making it difficult to ignore the fact that the rocket was real. But if there was one thing Artemis had not lost it was his stubbornness and so he stood his ground, refusing to yield to his final squeak of good sense.

'Who cares?' he muttered.

‖ ᴚᴑᴚ • ᴁᴃ • ᴚᴜᴑᴃ → • ▢ • ᴑᴚ • ᴈᴑᴚ▢

Holly somehow heard the last two words and thought, *I care*.

Desperate situations call for desperate solutions.

Nothing to lose, thought Holly, flapping at the holster on her thigh.

She swept her pistol from its home in a slightly more erratic arc than usual. The gun was synced with her visor, but even so Holly did not have time to check the settings. She simply held down the command sensor with her thumb then spoke clearly into the microphone at the side of her mouth.

'Gun. [Pause for beep.] Non-lethal. Wide-bore concussive.

'Sorry, Artemis,' she muttered, then fired a good three-second blast at her human friend.

Artemis was ankle-deep in slush and in full rant mode when Holly pulled the trigger.

The beam hit him like a slap from a giant electric eel. His body was lifted and tossed through the air a moment before the probe clattered to a bone-crushing landing, obliterating the spot where he had been standing.

Artemis dropped into a crater like a sack of kindling and disappeared from Holly's sightline.

That's not good, thought Holly, then saw her own magical sparks hover before her eyes like inquisitive amber-tailed fireflies.

Shutdown, she realized. *My magic is sending me to sleep so that I can heal.*

From the corner of her eye Holly saw a door open in the

probe's belly and a gangplank swing down on hydraulics. Something was coming out.

Hope I get to wake up, Holly thought. *I hate the ice and I don't want to die cold.*

Then she closed her eyes and did not feel her limp body roll from the rooftop and thump into a snowdrift below.

Barely a minute later, Holly's eyes fluttered open. Waking up felt jagged and unreal, like documentary footage from a war zone. Holly could not remember standing, but suddenly she was on her feet being dragged along by Foaly who looked extremely dishevelled, possibly because his beautiful quiff had been totally singed and sat balanced on top of his head like a bird's nest. But mostly he seemed depressed.

'Come on, Captain!' Foaly shouted, his voice seeming a little out of sync with his mouth. 'We need to move.'

Holly coughed amber sparks and her eyes watered.

Amber magic now? I'm getting old.

Foaly shook her shoulders. 'Straighten up, Captain. We have work to do.'

The centaur was using trauma psychology. Holly knew this; she could remember the in-service course in Police Plaza.

In the event of battle stress, appeal to the soldiers' professionalism. Remind them of their rank repeatedly. Insist that they perform their duty. This will not have a long-term healing effect on any psychological wounds but it might be enough to get you back to base.

Commander Vinyáya had given that course.

Holly tried to pull herself together. Her leg felt brittle from the knees down and her mid-section buzzed from the post-healing pain known as magic burn.

'Is Artemis alive?'

'Don't know,' said Foaly brusquely. 'I built those things, you know. I *designed* them.'

'What things?'

Foaly dragged her to a glassy droop in the glacier, slicker than any ice-rink.

'The things hunting us right now. The amorphobots. The things that came out of the probe.'

They slid to the bottom of the bank, leaning forward to keep their balance.

Holly seemed to have developed tunnel vision, though her visor was panoramic. The edges of her vision crackled with amber static.

I am still healing. I shouldn't be moving. Gods know what damage I will do myself.

Foaly seemed to read her mind, but more likely it was fairy empathy.

'I had to get you out of there. One of my amorphobots was heading your way, sucking up everything in its path. The probe's gone below, to gods know where. Try to lean on me.'

Holly nodded then coughed again; the spray was instantly absorbed by her porous visor.

They hobbled across the ice towards the crater where Artemis lay. He was extremely pale and there was a speed drip of blood running from the corner of his mouth to his hairline. Foaly dropped to his forelegs and tried to encourage Artemis back into consciousness with a stiff talking-to.

'Come on, Mud Boy,' he said, poking Artemis's forearm. 'No time for lollygagging.'

Artemis's response to this chastising was a barely notice-able jerking of his arm. This was good – at least it told Holly that Artemis was still alive.

Holly tripped over the crater's lip, and stumbled to the bottom.

'*Lollygagging?*' she gasped. 'Is that even a word?'

Foaly poked Artemis one more time. 'Yes. It is. And shouldn't you be killing those robots with your pencil?'

Holly's eyes seemed to light up. 'Really? Can I do that?'

Foaly snorted. 'Certainly. If your pencil has a super-duper demon magic beam inside it instead of graphite.'

Holly was still groggy but, even through a fugue of injury and battle stress, it was obvious that the situation was dire. They heard strange metallic clicks and animalistic whoops chittering through the air, softly at first then rising in tempo and intensity to a frenzy.

The noise grated against Holly's forehead as though her skin was being yanked.

'What is that?'

'The amorphobots are communicating,' whispered Foaly. 'Transferring terabytes of information wirelessly. Updating each other. What one knows, they all know.'

Holly scanned Artemis's vitals through her visor. The

glowing readouts informed her that he had a slight heart murmur and there was some unusual brain activity in the parietal lobe. Other than that the best thing her helmet computer could conclude about Artemis was that he was basically not dead. If she could survive this latest misadventure, maybe Artemis would too.

'What are they looking for, Foaly?'

'What are they looking for?' repeated the centaur, smiling that particular hysterical smile that exposed too much gum.

Holly suddenly felt her senses snap into focus and knew that the magic had finished its overhaul of her injuries. Her pelvis still throbbed and probably would for a few months, but she was operational again, so maybe she could lead them back to fairy civilization.

'Foaly, pull yourself together. We need to know what those things can do.'

The centaur seemed put out that someone would choose this particular moment to ask him questions when he had so many vital issues to consider.

'Holly, really! Do we have time for explanations now?'

'Snap out of it, Foaly! Information, hand it over.'

Foaly sighed, lips flapping. 'They are bio-spheres. Amorphobots. Dumb plasma-based machines. They collect samples of plant life and analyse them in their plasma. Simple as that. Harmless.'

'Harmless,' blurted Holly. 'I think someone has reprogrammed your amorphobots, centaur.'

The blood disappeared from Foaly's cheeks and his fingers

twitched. 'No. Not possible. That probe is supposed to be on its way to Mars to search for micro-organisms.'

'I think we can be pretty sure that your probe has been hijacked.'

'There is another possibility,' suggested Foaly. 'I could be dreaming all of this.'

Holly pressed on with her questions.

'How do we stop them, Foaly?'

It was impossible to miss the fear that flickered across Foaly's face, like a sun flash across a lake. 'Stop them? The amorphobots are built to withstand prolonged exposure to open space. You could drop one of these on to the surface of a star and it would survive for long enough to transmit some information back to its mother probe. Obviously I have a kill code, but I suspect that has been overridden.'

'There must be a way. Can't we shoot them?'

'Absolutely not. They love energy. It feeds their cells. If you shoot them, they'll just get bigger and more powerful.'

Holly laid a palm on Artemis's forehead, checking his temperature.

I wish you would wake up, she thought. *We could really use one of your brilliant schemes right now.*

'Foaly,' she said urgently. 'What are the amorphobots doing right now? What are they looking for?'

'Life,' replied Foaly simply. 'They're doing a grid search now, starting at the drop site and moving out. Any life forms they encounter will be absorbed into the sac, analysed then released.'

Holly peeped over the lip of the crater. 'What are their scan criteria?'

'Thermal is the default. But they can use anything.'

Thermal, thought Holly. *Heat signatures. That's why they are spending so much time by the flaming shuttle.*

The amorphobots were arranged on corners of invisible grid squares, slowly working their way outwards from the shuttle's smoking carcass. They seemed innocuous enough, rolling balls of gel with twin glowing red sensors at their cores. Like slime balloons from a children's party. Maybe the size of a crunchball.

They couldn't be all that dangerous surely. Dozy little blëbers.

Her opinion altered sharply when one of the amorphobots changed colour from translucent green to angry electric blue and the colour spread to the others. Their eerie chittering became a constant shrill whine.

They have found something, Holly realized.

The entire squad of twenty or so bots converged on a single spot, some merging so that they formed larger blobs, which flowed across the ice with a speed and grace heretofore concealed. The bot that had flashed the message to the others allowed a charge to crackle across its skin, which it then discharged into a hillock of snow. An unfortunate snow fox leaped from the steam, tail smoking like a fuse, and made a dart for freedom.

It's almost comical. Almost.

The amorphobots jiggled as though laughing and sent a few bolts of crackling blue energy after the doomed fox, carving black rents in the ground, steering the terror-stricken mammal away from the shelter of the Great Skua. In spite of its natural speed and agility, the bots anticipated its movements with incredible accuracy, sending the animal running in circles, its eyes rolling, tongue dangling.

There was only one possible conclusion to this game of cat and mouse: the largest amorphobot droned an impatient bass command through the almost invisible gel speakers in its body and turned abruptly to continue its search. The others followed, leaving only the original bot to hunt the fox. It quickly tired of the sport and nailed the fox in mid-jump with a bolt of power cast like a spear from its mid-section.

Murderer, thought Holly, more angry than horrified. *Foaly didn't design this.*

Foaly suddenly moved in front of her. 'You've got that look in your eyes, Captain.'

'What look?'

'The one Julius Root always talked about. The *I'm about to do something incredibly stupid* look.'

There was no time for debate. 'I need to get to Artemis's crate.'

'You can't go. What does the LEP manual suggest in these kinds of situations?'

Holly ground her teeth. Her two geniuses were useless; she would have to do this herself.

'The manual, which you helped to write, would advise me to retreat to a safe distance and construct a bivouac, but, with respect, those guidelines are a pile of troll weevils.'

'Wow. Nice respect. Do you know what the word *respect*

actually means? I'm no book professor, but I'm pretty sure comparing my manual to a steaming pile of troll weevils does not constitute respect.'

'I never said steaming,' said Holly, then decided that time was short and she could apologize later. 'Listen, Foaly. I don't have a downlink to Police Plaza. There are murdering blobby robots on our trail and the only people who might be able to come up with a solution are either fast asleep dreaming or, in your case, wide awake dreaming. So I need you to cover me while I make a run for Artemis's crate. Do you think you can do that?'

Holly handed the centaur her back-up weapon. Foaly held the gun gingerly, as though it were radioactive, which to a certain degree it was.

'OK. I know how this thing works, in theory.'

'Good,' said Holly, and slithered on her belly up and on to the ice field before she could change her mind.

Holly felt her torso numb and stiffen as she slid across the glacier. The ice stretched in front of her, carved by the prevailing wind into elegant swoops and whorls, a wind which was to her rear, making progress relatively easy considering she had until recently been suffering from several broken bones.

Saved by magic once more.

But now she had not a spark left in her.

The fox's carcass lay smoking on a bed of snow, melting a grave for itself.

Holly tore her gaze from the pathetic mammal's eyes, still

rolled back in its blackened head, and looked instead at Artemis's crate, which stood disregarded by the bots, but past their search line.

I need to breach the line, unnoticed. Their default sensor is heat. I'll give them a little heat to think about.

Holly switched on the air-conditioning in her suit, which had about five minutes left in it according to her visor readout, then selected the flare package on her Neutrino hand gun. She also accidentally activated the tunes player in her helmet with a series of shivery winks. Luckily the volume was muted and she managed to switch off Grazen McTortoor's metal epic 'Troll Sundown' before the amorphobots detected the vibration.

Grazen McTortoor's music never killed anyone before. He'd probably be thrilled.

Holly flipped on to her back, looking up at a sky of pitch and granite, the bowed cloud bellies licked by flame.

Heat.

Holly steadied her hand and removed the detachable trigger finger section of her glove. She pointed her weapon skywards and sent a wide-arced spray of flares into the air.

Flares. If only someone could see them and come to help.

The amorphobots' relaxed chittering amped up to a whine and she realized that it was time to move.

Holly was up on her feet and running before her good sense had time to kick in. She raced full pelt for Artemis's crate, taking as straight a tack as possible, weapon held along her sightline.

I don't care what Foaly says. If one of those red-eyed monsters comes anywhere near me, I'm going to find out what a plasma grenade does to its innards.

The bots had without exception pointed their sensors towards the descending flares, which fizzled like the sputterings of an oxyacetylene torch cutting through the clouds. The amorphobots' malleable bodies sprouted gel periscopes and they stood following the flares' progress like ill-defined meerkats. They may have noticed an inconsistent heat source jiggling across the glacier, but they were programmed to prioritize.

Not so smart after all.

Holly ran as fast as her brittle bones would carry her.

The terrain was flat but treacherous. The light September snow had dusted the grooves and Holly almost lost her footing in a tractor trail. Her ankle grated but did not crack. Lucky.

> *Lucky little elf*
> *Sat on the shelf*
> *And the silly human boy*
> *Mistook her for a toy.*

A nursery rhyme used to teach children to sit still if they saw a human.

Think like a little tree and that's what the Mud Men will see.

I'm a tree, thought Holly, without much conviction. *A little tree.*

So far so good: the bots were glued to the flares and were showing no interest in her heat signature. She skirted the wreckage of the shuttle, trying not to hear the groan of the chassis or notice the front panel of a flight suit melded with the windscreen. Beyond the shuttle lay Artemis's great experiment. An oversized refrigerator cannon.

Great. More ice.

Holly knelt at the base of what Artemis had called his Ice Cube and quickly located the control panel, which luckily had an omni-sensor so it was a simple matter to sync it with her own helmet. Now the refrigerator cannon would fire when she wanted and at whatever target she chose. She set a timer running and set herself running seconds afterwards, straight back the way she had come.

It occurred to her that the flares were lasting well and she really should congratulate Foaly on the new models, at which point they inevitably began to wink out.

With no more pretty lights in the sky, the amorphobots returned to their methodical searching of the site for signs of life. One was dispatched to check the erratic blob of heat crossing their grid. It rolled across the surface, scanning the ground as it went, sending out gel tendrils to scoop up debris and even whipping out a tongue like a bullfrog's to snag a low-flying black-headed gull. If there had been a soundtrack to its movements it would have been *tum-ti-tum-ti-tum*. Business as usual, no worries. Then its vector crossed Holly's and they virtually collided. The bot's scanner eyes flashed and lightning bolts jittered inside its globulous body.

All I need is a few seconds, thought Holly, and blasted the bot with a narrow beam right in its gut.

The beam sliced through the centre of the blobby body, but was diffused before reaching the hardware nerve centre at the core. The bot bounced backwards like a kicked ball, whining as it did so, updating its friends.

Holly did not slow down to see what the response might be; she did not need to – her keen elfin hearing gave her all the information she needed: they were coming for her. They were all coming. Their semi-solid forms pummelled the ice as they moved like quick bongo rolls, along with that dreadful chittering.

A bot in her path skittered to one side, a temporary Neutrino hole drilled in its top quadrant. Apparently Foaly was taking his job as cover provider seriously, even though he knew his weapon could not kill these things.

Thanks, Mister Consultant.

The bots were converging on her now, trundling from all sides, burping and squeaking as they came.

Like kiddie-cartoon characters.

Which did not stop Holly from blasting as many of the cute critters as she could. She vaguely heard Foaly shouting at her to kindly only shoot when necessary, or to quote him verbatim:

Holly. In the name of all the gods, stop shooting energy into all-energy beings. Just how stupid are you?

The bots quivered and meshed, growing larger and more aggressive.

'*D'Arvit*,' huffed Holly, her breath coming hard now. Her helmet informed her cheerily that her heart rate was over 240 bpm which would be fine for a sprite but not for an elf. Normally a flat-out sprint would not inconvenience Holly, nor indeed any fairy who had passed the LEP physical, but this was a desperate dash immediately after a major healing. She should be in a hospital sipping rejuvenation sludge through a straw.

'Two minutes to cardiac arrest,' said her helmet breezily. 'Ceasing all physical activity would be a really great idea.'

Holly spared a nanosecond to despise the voice of her helmet. Corporal Frond, the glamorous face of the LEP, all blonde hair and tight jumpsuits, who'd recently had her bloodline traced back to Frond the Elfin King and now insisted on referring to herself as Princess.

Foaly emerged from the crater and grabbed his friend's elbow. 'Come on, Holly. We have seconds of life left before those critters that you led right to our hidey-hole kill us all like rodents.'

Holly ran as fast as she could, bones creaking. 'I have a plan.'

They stumbled over the frozen glacier, back to the depression where Artemis Fowl lay unconscious. The amorphobots flowed after them like marbles rolling down the side of a bowl.

Foaly dived into the hole. It was not elegant – centaurs do not make good divers, which is why they do not compete in pool events.

'Whatever your idea was, it's not working,' he cried.

Holly dived into the depression, covering Artemis as well as she could.

'Put your face in the ice,' she ordered. 'And hold your breath.'

Foaly ignored her, his attention attracted by Artemis's Ice Cube, which was swivelling on its base.

'It seems as though Artemis's cannon is about to fire,' he said, his scientific interest piqued in spite of the horrible death approaching them.

Holly grabbed the centaur's mane, roughly dragging him to the ground. 'Face down, hold breath. How hard is that?'

'Oh,' said Foaly. 'I see.'

There must have been a build-up of heat somewhere, because the bots froze for a moment, exchanging curious chitters. The noise was quickly drowned out by a bass heavy thump followed by a descending whistle.

'Ooooh,' chorused the amorphobots, sprouting gel periscopes.

Foaly closed one eye and cocked his ear. 'Mortar,' he proclaimed, and then as the whistling grew louder he decided that it might be a good idea to take a breath and cover as many orifices as possible.

This is really going to hurt, he thought, and for some reason giggled like a four-year-old pixette.

Then the entire indent was submerged in a pancake of densely packed nano-wafers that worked into every crack, coating the occupants of the hole and completely obliterating any heat signatures.

The amorphobots jiggled backwards, away from the mystery substance, searched around for the beings they had been pursuing and then shrugged their blobby shoulders and trundled after their mother ship, which had bludgeoned and melted its way through the surface to the subterranean volcanoes below.

Underneath the gunky quagmire, two fairies and one human lay still, blowing bubbles with their breath.

'It worked,' gasped Holly finally.

'Shut your face,' snapped Foaly.

Holly pulled his head free from the goo strings. 'What did you say to me?'

'Don't take it personally,' said Foaly. 'I just felt like being rude to someone. Do you have any idea what it's going to be like getting this stuff out of my mane? Caballine will shave me for sure.'

'Save you?

'Shave me. What are you, deaf?'

'No. My ears are clogged with stuff.'

Holly flip-flopped herself and Artemis from the indent, using her glove-sensor to check the human's vitals.

Still alive.

She tilted his head back to make sure the airway was clear.

Come back to us, Artemis. We need you.

The amorphobots had gone and the only signs that they had ever been on the Vatnajökull glacier were the grooves in the ice and snow that marked their passage. The air was blessedly chitter free, though maybe a little chittering would have distracted from the crackle of still-burning troop shuttle.

Holly separated from Artemis with a noise like a very big band-aid being slowly pulled from a weeping wound.

What a disaster, she thought, the weight of her coated helmet causing her head to droop. *What a total catastrophe.*

Holly looked around, trying to make some kind of assessment of the situation. Commander Vinyáya was gone, along with the military. An LEP Martian probe had been hijacked by forces unknown and seemed to be heading into the Earth's crust. The probe was blocking their link to Haven and it was only a matter of time before humans came to investigate all the flares and explosions. And she had no magic left to shield herself.

'Come on, Artemis,' she said, desperation creeping into her voice. 'We're in deeper trouble than ever before. Come on, you love this kind of impossible problem. I'm sorry I shot you.'

Holly tugged off a glove and held her fingers high, inspecting them just in case a spark remained.

Nothing. No magic. Perhaps it was just as well. The mind was a delicate instrument and Artemis's dabblings with the fairy arts had probably triggered his Atlantis Complex in the first place. If Artemis wanted to get well, he would have to do it the old-fashioned way, with pills and electro-shock.

I already gave him his first shock, thought Holly, swallowing a guilty chuckle.

Artemis shifted on the ice, trying to blink under a faceful of sloppy nano-wafers.

'Unhhh,' he moaned. 'Ayyy ga breee.'

'Wait,' said Holly, scooping handfuls of gunk away from his nostrils and mouth. 'Let me help.'

Artemis's own inventions dribbled from the corners of his mouth. There was something different about his eyes. They were the same colours as usual, but softer somehow.

You're dreaming.

'Artemis?' she said, half expecting a typical snappy retort as in, *Of course it's Artemis. Who were you expecting?* But instead he simply said:

'Hello.'

Which was fine and Holly was happy enough, until he followed it with:

'And who might you be?'

Ooooh, D'Arvit.

Holly tugged off her helmet. 'It's me, Holly.'

Artemis smiled in delight. 'Of course, yes. Artemis thinks about you all the time. It's embarrassing that I didn't recognize you. First time up close.'

'Uh . . . Artemis thinks about me. But *you* don't?'

'Oh yes, I do constantly, and may I say you look even more bewitching in the flesh.'

Holly felt a feeling of foreboding creep over her like the shadow of a summer storm cloud.

'So, we haven't met before?'

'Not met *per se*,' replied the human youth. 'I have of course been aware of you. Seen you from afar, submerged as I was by Artemis's personality. Thank you for releasing me, by the way.

I had been making inroads in the host consciousness for some time now, since Artemis developed his little number obsession, but that jolt from your weapon was just the thing to give me the boost I needed. It was your weapon, wasn't it?'

'Yes, it was,' said Holly absently. 'And you're welcome. I think.' A sudden idea cut through her confusion. 'How many fingers am I holding up?'

The boy did a quick digit check. 'Four.'

'And that doesn't bother you?'

'No. To me a number is a number. Four is no more a harbinger of death than any other whole number. Fractions, though, they're freakish.'

The youth smiled at his own joke. A smile of such simple saintly goodness that it would have made Artemis retch.

Holly was drawn into the psychosis and had to ask, 'So if you're not Artemis Fowl, then who are you?'

The boy extended a dripping hand straight up. 'My name is Orion. I am so pleased to meet you at last. I am, of course, your servant.'

Holly shook the proffered hand, thinking that manners were lovely, but they really needed someone cunning and ruthless right now, and this kid didn't appear to be very cunning.

'That's great, em . . . Orion. Really. We're in a bind here and I can use all the help I can get.'

'Excellent,' said the boy. 'I have been taking stock of the situation from the rear seat, as it were, and I suggest that we retire to a safe distance and construct some form of bivouac.'

Holly groaned. Of all the times for Artemis to go AWOL inside his own head.

Foaly clambered from the morass of nano-wafers, using his fingers to draw aside curtains of gunk that obscured his vision.

'I see Artemis has woken up. Good. We could do with one of his trademark *apparently ridiculous but actually ingenious* plans.'

'Bivouac,' said the boy in Artemis Fowl's head. 'I suggest a bivouac and perhaps we could gather kindling for a camp-fire and some leaves to make a cushion for the lovely lady.'

'Kindling? Did Artemis Fowl just use the word *kindling*? And who's the lovely lady?'

The wind picked up suddenly, lifting loose surface snow and sending it skittering across the ice. Holly felt flakes settle on her exposed neck, sending a prickling chill trickling down her spine.

Things are bad now, she realized. *And they're about to get worse. Where are you, Butler? Why aren't you here?*

CHAPTER 4: FLOYD'S STAG NIGHT

 BUTLER had an excuse for not being in Iceland that would hold up in any court of law and possibly even on a note for teacher. In fact, he had a number of excuses.

One: his employer and friend had sent him away on a rescue mission that had turned out to be a trap. Two: his sister had been in fake trouble whereas now she was in very real trouble. And three: he was being chased around a theatre hall in Mexico by a few thousand wrestling fans, who at this moment looked very much like zombies, without the rotting limbs.

Butler had read in the entertainment section of his in-flight magazine that vampires *had* been all the rage but this year zombies were in.

They're certainly in here, thought Butler. *Far too many of them.*

Strictly speaking, *zombies* wasn't an accurate description

of the mass of mindless humans milling about in the theatre hall. They were of course *mesmerized*, which is not the same thing at all. The generally accepted definition of a zombie is: a reanimated corpse with a taste for human brains. The mesmerized wrestling fans were not dead and had no desire to sniff anyone's brains, never mind take a bite out of them. They were converging on the aisle from all sides, cutting off any possible escape routes, and Butler was forced to back up over the collapsed ring and on to the wrestling platform. This retreat would not have made the top one hundred on his list of preferred options, but at this stage any action that granted a few more heartbeats was preferable to standing still and accepting one's fate.

Butler slapped his sister's thigh, which was easy as she was still slung over his shoulder.

'Hey,' she complained. 'What was that for?'

'Just checking your state of mind.'

'I'm me, OK? Something happened in my brain. I remember Holly and all the other fairies.'

Total recall, Butler surmised. Her encounter with the fairy mesmerist had watered the seed of memory in his sister's mind and it had sprawled in there, bringing everything back. It was possible, he supposed. That the strength of this mental chain reaction had obliterated the attempted mesmerization.

'Can you fight?'

Juliet swung her legs high then flipped into a fighting stance.

'I can fight better than you, old-timer.'

Butler winced. Sometimes having a sister two decades younger than oneself meant putting up with a lot of ageist comments.

'My insides are not as old as my outsides, if you must know. Those fairy People you are just now remembering gave me an overhaul. They took fifteen years off and I have a Kevlar chest. So I can look after myself, and you if need be.'

As they bantered, the siblings automatically swivelled so they were back to back and covering each other. Butler talked to let his sister know that he was hopeful they could escape from this. Juliet responded to show her big brother that she was not afraid so long as they stood side by side. Neither of these unspoken messages was true exactly, but they gave a modicum of comfort.

The mesmerized wrestling fans were having a little trouble negotiating the wrestling platform and their packed bodies clogged the ringside like sticks in a dam. When one did manage to climb up, Butler tossed him or her back out as gently as possible. Juliet was not so gentle on her first toss and Butler definitely heard something snap.

'Easy, sister. These are innocent people. Their brains are hijacked.'

'Oops, sorry,' said Juliet, not sounding in the least penitent, and rammed the heel of her hand into the solar plexus of someone who was probably a soccer mom when not mesmerized.

Butler sighed. 'Like this,' he said patiently. 'Watch. You pick them up, and just slide them out over the top of their friends. Minimum impact.' He performed the move a few times just to give Juliet the idea.

Juliet jettisoned a drooling teenager. 'Better?'

'Much.' Butler jerked a thumb at the screen overhead. 'That fairy has mesmerized everyone who looked into his eyes and heard his voice. It's not their fault they're attacking us.'

Juliet almost looked upwards, but stopped herself in time. On screen, the red eyes still burned and over the speaker system that soft hypnotic voice flowed through the crowd like warm honey, telling them everything would be all right if they could just kill the princess and the bear. If they could perform that one simple act, all their dreams would come true. The voice affected the Butlers, made their sense of purpose a little mushy, but without eye contact it could not control their actions.

More of the crowd were making it on to the stage now and it was only a matter of seconds before the platform collapsed.

'We need to shut that guy up,' shouted Butler over the rising hubbub of mesmerized moaning. 'Can you reach the screen?'

Juliet squinted, measuring the distance. 'I can reach the gantry, if you give me a little height.'

Butler patted one of his broad shoulders. 'Climb aboard, little sister.'

'Just a sec,' said Juliet, dispatching a bearded cowboy with a roundhouse kick. She climbed up Butler's frame with the agility of a monkey and stood on his shoulders. 'OK, boost me.'

Butler grunted a grunt that any family member could interpret as *hold on a moment*, and with Juliet balanced overhead he punched one of the support wrestlers in the windpipe, and swept another's legs from under him.

Those two were twins, he realized. *And dressed as Tasmanian devils. This is the strangest fight I have ever been in, and I've tangled with trolls.*

'Here we go,' he said to Juliet, side-stepping a man in a hot-dog costume. Butler wiggled his fingers under her toes.

'Can you lift me?' asked his sister, keeping her balance with the ease of an Olympic gymnast, which Juliet might have been if she could have been up in time for the early morning training sessions.

'Of course I can lift you,' snapped Butler, who might have been an Olympic weightlifter if he hadn't been battling goblins in an underground laboratory when the last trials were on.

He sucked in a breath through his nose, tightened his core and then with a burst of explosive power and a growl that would not have sounded out of place in a Tarzan movie, he thrust his baby sister straight up towards the six-metre-high metal gantry supporting the screen and a pair of conical speakers.

There was no time to check if Juliet had made it as the zombies had formed a body ramp and the wrestling fans of Cancún were pouring on to the stage, all determined to kill Butler slowly and painfully.

Right now would have been a prudent time to have activated the jet pack he often wore underneath his jacket, but in the absence of a jet pack, and his jacket, Butler thought it might be an idea to increase the aggression of his defence, enough to buy himself and Juliet a few more seconds.

He stepped forward to meet the throng, using an adapted form of t'ai chi to tumble the front row back into the crowd, building a mountain of bodies the mesmerized fans would have to climb over. Which worked fine for about half a minute until half of the stage collapsed, allowing the unconscious bodies to roll off and form an effective ramp for the wrestling fans to climb. The injured fans seemed not to feel any pain and climbed instantly to their feet, often walking on twisted and swollen ankles. The drones flowed on to the stage with only one desire in their hijacked minds.

Kill Crazy Bear.

It's hopeless, thought Butler, for the first time in his life. *Utterly hopeless.*

He didn't go down easy, but go down he did under the sheer weight of bodies flowing over him. His face was smooshed by back fat and he felt teeth close round his ankle. Punches were thrown but they were badly aimed and weak.

I am going to be crushed to death, Butler realized. *Not beaten.*

This realization didn't make him feel any better. What did make him feel better was the fact that Juliet should be safe on the gantry.

Butler fell back, like Gulliver dragged down by the Lilliputians. He could smell popcorn and beer, deodorant and sweat. His chest was pressed and tight, breath came hard. Someone wrestled with one of his boots for some reason, and suddenly he could not move. He was a prisoner under the sheer weight of bodies.

Artemis is alone. Juliet will know to take my place as his bodyguard.

Lack of oxygen turned the world black and it was as much as Butler could do to shove his arm through the mass of bodies smothering him and wiggle his fingers goodbye to his sister.

Someone bit his thumb.

Then he disappeared utterly and the fairy on screen laughed.

Juliet hooked two fingers of her left hand round the bottom lip of a gantry beam and pressed down so hard that she could almost feel her fingerprints. For ninety-nine per cent of the world's population, two fingers would simply not be enough to bear one's own bodyweight. Most mere mortals would need a strong two-handed grip to keep them up for no more than a minute, and there is a large percentage of people who couldn't hoist themselves aloft with anything short of a winch system and a couple of trained shire horses. But Juliet was a Butler and had been trained at the Madame Ko roving bodyguard academy where there had been an entire semester devoted to bodyweight vectors. In a pinch, Juliet could keep herself off the ground using only a single toe, so long as no passing mischief-maker decided to tickle her in the weak spot under her ribcage.

While it is one thing to hold oneself aloft, it is quite another to hoist oneself upwards, but fortunately Madame Ko had put a few seminars into that too. That is not to say it was easy, and Juliet imagined her muscles screaming as she swung her other hand about for a better grip, then hauled herself on to the beam. On another day, she would have paused to allow her heart to slow down a little, but from the corner of her eye she saw her brother about to be engulfed by wrestling fans and decided that this was not the day for leisurely recuperation.

Juliet popped to her feet and ran the length of the beam with the confidence of a gymnast. A good gymnast that is, not one who slips painfully on the beam, which is exactly what happened to a mesmerized lighting technician who attempted to cut Juliet off before she could reach the screen.

Juliet winced. 'Oooh. That looked sore, Arlene.'

Arlene did not comment, unless turning purple and tumbling flailing into space can be counted as commentary. Juliet knew that she shouldn't have grinned when the technician's fall was comically broken by a cluster of men lumbering towards her brother, but she couldn't hold it in.

Her smile faded when she noticed the mass of bodies swarming along Butler's frame, burying him. Another technician approached her, this one a little smarter than his predecessor; he straddled the beam with his ankles locked below him. As he inched forward, he banged a large spanner on the beam, raising concussive bongs and spark flurries.

Juliet timed the arc of his swing, then planted a foot on

his head and stepped over him as though he were a rock in the middle of a stream. She did not bother to topple the man from his perch. By the time he turned round it should be too late for him to stop her, but he should have a nice bruise on his forehead to wonder about when his senses returned.

The screen was ahead, bracketed by metal tubing, and the red eyes glared at her out of the black background, seeming to emanate pure hate.

Or maybe this guy was up late partying.

'Stop where you are, Juliet Butler!' said the voice, and to Juliet it seemed as though the tones were suddenly those of Christian Varley Penrose, her instructor at the Madame Ko Academy. The only person, besides her brother, whom she had ever considered her physical equal.

'Some students make me proud,' Christian would say in his BBC tones. 'You just make me despair. What was that move?'

And Juliet would invariably answer, 'It's something I made up, master.'

'Made up? Made up? That is not good enough.'

Juliet would pout and think, *It was good enough for Bruce Lee.*

And now Christian Varley Penrose seemed to have a line directly into her brain.

'Stop where you are!' the voice told her. 'And, having stopped, feel free to lose your balance and plummet to the earth below.'

The voice, Juliet felt, was taking hold of her determination and twisting it like a wet towel.

꒰✦•❘▲❘◗❘▤•❯✕◗❙◈✐•◉•⬥•✷⬢⬙•⌐▱◗❒꒱

Don't look. Don't listen.

But she had looked and listened, if only for a second, and it was long enough for the insidious magic to snake a couple of tendrils into her brain. Her legs locked as though clamped with braces and the paralysis spread upwards.

'D'Arvit,' said Juliet, though she wasn't quite sure why, and, with her last spurt of self-control, pin-wheeled her arms wildly, sending her entire body careening into the tubular frame supporting the screen and speakers.

The screen yielded elastically and, for a moment, the little bubble of Juliet's mind that she still held on to believed that the screen would not break, then her elbow, which Butler had told her as a child was sharp enough to open a tin of field rations, punched through the material, sending a jagged rent running down its length.

The fairy's red eyes rolled and the last thing Juliet heard before her outstretched arm snagged the AV cables was an irritated snort, and then she was tumbling through a hole in the suddenly blank screen and falling towards the spasming mass of bodies below.

Juliet used the half-second before impact to curl herself into a ball.

Her very last thought before striking the crowd was: *I hope zombies are soft.*

They were not.

As soon as the fairy had flickered from the screen, the enthralled wrestling enthusiasts gradually regained their senses.

✦ • ⚘ • 🕭 🜚 🜃 ⟊ ◗ 🕿 ⊖ 🜚 🜂 ✦ • ◗◗ ◻ ⟑◗ 🜍 • ⊖ • 🜚 ⚘

Geri Niebalm, a retired beauty therapist from Seattle, found that she had somehow made it all the way from the rear of the hall to the stage itself without the aid of her walking frame. What was more she had a phantom memory of vaulting over several youngsters in her pursuit of that pretty young wrestler with the stone in her ponytail. Two months later Geri would undergo regression therapy at her friend Dora Del Mar's salon to bring that memory to the surface so that she could relish it at her leisure.

Stu 'Cheeze' Toppin, a semi-professional bowler from Las Vegas, woke up to find his mouth somehow stuffed with a foul-smelling nappy and the words *kill bear kill* written across his shirtfront in lipstick. This rather confused Stu as his last memory was of the succulent hot dog he had been just about to bite into. Now, with the nappy aftertaste lingering on his tongue, Stu decided that he might just forget about the hot dog for the time being.

Though Stu had no way of knowing, the nappy in question belonged to little André Price, a baby from Portland who suddenly developed a speed and grace unheard-of in eight-month-old limbs. Most victims of the *mesmer* move in a sluggish fashion but André skipped over the heads of mob members and executed a perfect triple somersault from the ringside commentator's table, managing to sink his only tooth into Butler's thumb before the bodyguard was completely submerged. André Price began speaking a few months later – unfortunately it was in a language which his parents had no way of knowing was actually Gnommish. To their relief, he quickly picked up English too, though he never forgot his strange first language and found that he could sometimes make twigs burst into flame if he thought about it hard enough.

A huge cacophonous moan almost lifted the roof from the theatre as thousands of people realized they were not where they were supposed to be. Though there were miraculously no fatalities, by the time the last cut had been swabbed with antiseptic, there was a final count of 348 broken bones, more than 11,000 lacerations and 89 cases of hysteria that had to be treated with sedatives, which, luckily for the patients, were a lot cheaper in Mexico than they would have been in the USA.

And even though this was the age of amateur video, where most of those attending the event were in possession of at least one camera, there was not a single frame of evidence to prove that the mass mesmerization had ever taken place. In fact, when police flicked through the files on the confiscated cameras and phones, they found that every single instrument had been reset to factory conditions. No photos. In time, the Cancún Event, as it came to be known, would be mentioned in the same breath as Area 51 or Yeti Migration.

Butler did not suffer from hysteria, possibly because he did not have enough air in his lungs for screaming, but probably because he had been in tighter spots (Butler had once shared a chimney in a Hindu temple with a tiger for several hours), but he had suffered over a dozen lacerations of his own, though he did not wait around long enough to have them added to the count.

As for Juliet, she was relatively unmarked in spite of her tumble. The moment she had recovered her breath, she began rolling bodies away from the spot where she had seen her brother submerged.

'Butler!' she called. 'Brother! Are you under here?'

The top of her brother's head appeared, smooth as a lollipop. Juliet knew immediately that her brother was alive because of the vein pulsing at his temple.

There was a chubby semi-naked infant wrapped around Butler's face and chewing on his thumb. Juliet dislodged the boy gently, noticing that he seemed very sweaty for a baby.

Butler drew a deep breath. 'Thank you, sister. Not only did that child bite my thumb but it tried to get a fist up one of my nostrils.'

The baby gurgled happily, wiped its fingers in Juliet's ponytail, then crawled across the piles of humanity towards a crying lady who was waiting with open arms.

'I know you're supposed to like babies,' said Juliet, huffing as she grabbed a banker type by his braces and sprung him from his perch on Butler's shoulders, 'but that guy stank and he was a biter.' She took a firm grip on a middle-aged lady whose blonde hair was sprayed till it shone like a buttercup. 'Come on, missus. Get off my big brother.'

'Oh,' said the lady, eyelids fluttering as she tried to make sense of everything. 'I was supposed to catch the bear. Or something like that. And I had popcorn, a large popcorn that I just paid for. Who's going to compensate me for that?'

Juliet rolled the lady across the bellies of four identically dressed cowboys who all wore FLOYD'S STAG NIGHT T-shirts under their rhinestoned waistcoats.

'This is ridiculous,' she grunted. 'I am a glamorous young lady. I can't be dealing with all this body odour and squidginess.'

There was indeed a lot of body odour and squidginess about, much of it related to Floyd and his stag night, which smelled like it had gone on for about two weeks.

This was confirmed when the cowboy wearing a FLOYD badge awoke from his stupor with the words: 'Dang. I stink worse than a dead skunk wearing a suit of bananer skins.'

Bananer? thought Juliet.

Butler rolled his head, clearing space to breathe.

'We've been set up,' he said. 'Have you made any enemies down here?'

Juliet felt sudden tears plop over her bottom lids. She had been so worried. *So* worried. Big brothers can only be indestructible for so long.

'You big galoot,' she said, sounding very Floyd-like. 'For your information, I am fine. I saved you and everyone else.'

Butler elbowed himself gently from between two luchadores dressed in garish Lycra and leather masks.

'Time for patting yourself on the back later, sister.' He climbed from the tangle of limbs and stood tall in the centre of the stage. 'Do you see all of this?'

Juliet clambered along her brother's frame and stood lightly on his shoulders, and then to show off she stepped with easy balance on to his head. One foot only, the other tucked behind her knee.

Now that she had a second to appreciate the enormity of what had happened, it took her breath away. A sea of confusion spread out all around them, groaning and twisting. Blood ran, bones cracked and tears flowed. It was a disaster area. People pawed at their mobile phones for comfort and sprinklers sent down a fine mist that dusted Juliet's face.

'All this to kill us,' she breathed.

Butler held out his massive palms, and, as she had done so many times in the Fowl dojo, Juliet stepped on to her brother's hands.

'Not just to kill us,' he said. 'Two bolts from a Neutrino could have done that. This was entertainment for someone.'

Juliet somersaulted to the stage. 'Entertainment for who?'

At the rear of the conference hall a section of the stand collapsed, sending up a fresh round of shrieks and misery.

'I don't know,' said the bodyguard grimly. 'But whoever tried to kill us wanted Artemis unguarded. First I change into my own clothes, and then we find out who Artemis has annoyed this time.'

CHAPTER 5: **ONWARDS AND OUTWARDS**

 TURNBALL Root took his entertainment wherever he could get it. Maximum security prisons didn't tend to be brimming with fun and flighty distractions. The guards were gruff and unobliging. The beds were unyielding and not enjoyable to bounce on, and the colour scheme was simply ghastly. Olive green throughout. Disgusting. In surroundings like this, one had to enjoy every modicum of light relief that came one's way.

For months after his arrest by his brother, Commander Julius Root, and that naive, straight-arrow Holly Short, Turnball had simply fumed. He had actually spent weeks on end pacing his cell, bouncing his hatred off the walls. Sometimes he ranted and occasionally he threw fits, smashing his furniture to smithereens. He realized eventually that the only person he was hurting with these displays was himself. This point had been driven home when he'd developed an ulcer, and because he had long since forfeited his magic through abuse and neglect, he had been forced to call in a medical warlock to put his organs right. The young whelp didn't seem much older than Turnball's prison uniform and had been extremely patronizing. Called him *grandpa*. Grandpa! Didn't they remember, these whelps? Who he was? What he had accomplished?

I am Turnball Root, he would have thundered, had the healing not totally sapped his strength. *Captain Turnball Root, nemesis of the LEP. I stripped every ingot of gold from the First Pixie Prudential Bank. I was the one who rigged the Centenary Crunchball Final. How dare you refer to me as grandpa!*

'Youngsters today, Leonor,' muttered Turnball to his absent, beloved wife. 'No respect.'

Then he shuddered as he considered this statement.

'Ye gods, darling. I do sound old.'

And using phrases like *ye gods* wasn't helping any.

Once he'd had enough of self-pity, Turnball had decided to make the best of the situation.

My chance will come eventually to be with you again, Leonor. Until then, why not make myself as comfortable as possible?

It hadn't been too difficult. After months of incarceration, Turnball had opened a dialogue with the warden, Tarpon Vinyáya, a malleable university graduate who had never washed blood from under his manicured nails, and offered him titbits of information to send to his sister in the LEP in return for some harmless comforts. It hadn't bothered Turnball a whit to sell out his old underworld contacts, and for his trouble he was allowed to wear whatever he liked. He chose his old LEP dress uniform, complete with ruffled shirt and three-corner hat, but without insignias. Betraying two visa forgers working out of Cuba got him a computer limited to the prison network. And the address of a rogue dwarf operating as a house breaker in Los Angeles got him a sim-down quilt for his plank of a bed. The warden would not be moved on the bed, however. Something for which his sister would one day pay the price.

Turnball had often passed many a happy hour thinking how he would one day kill the warden in revenge for this slight. But, truth be told, Turnball was not too concerned about the fate of Tarpon Vinyáya. He was far more interested in securing his own freedom, in looking deep into his wife's eyes once more. And to achieve these goals Turnball would have to play the soft, doddery reprobate for a while longer. He had been toadying up to the warden for more than six years now, what did a few more days matter?

Then I will be transformed into my true self, he thought, squeezing his fingers into tight fists. *And this time my baby brother won't be around to apprehend me, unless that young rascal Artemis Fowl has come up with a way to bring the dead back to life.*

The door to Turnball's cell fizzled and dissolved as a nuclear-powered charge precipitated a phase change. In the doorway stood Mister Vishby, Turnball's regular guard for the past four years and the one that he had finally managed to turn. Turnball did not like Vishby, in fact he detested all Atlantean elves with their fish-like heads, slobbering gills and thick tongues, but Vishby had the seeds of discontent in his heart and so had unknowingly become Turnball's slave. Turnball was prepared to tolerate anybody who could help him escape from this prison before it was too late.

Before I lose you, my darling.

'Ah, Mister Vishby,' he gushed, rising from his non-regulation office chair (three mackerel-smuggling sprites). 'You're looking well. That gill rot is really clearing up.'

Vishby's hand flew to the triple stripes below his tiny left ear.

'Do you think so, Turnball?' he gurgled, his voice thick and laboured. 'Leeta says she can't stand to look at me.'

I know how Leeta feels, thought Turnball, and: *There was a day when I would have had you flogged for addressing me by my first name. Captain Root, if you please.*

Instead of voicing these less than complimentary thoughts, he took Vishby by his slick elbow with barely a flinch of revulsion. 'Leeta does not know how lucky she is,' he said smoothly. 'You, my friend, are a catch.'

Vishby did not try to conceal his flinch. 'A c-catch?'

Turnball drew a sharp, guilty breath. 'Ah yes, excuse me, Vishby. Atlantean water elves do not like to think of themselves as catches, or being caught for that matter. What I meant to say was that you are a fine specimen of an elf and any female in her right mind would consider herself fortunate indeed to have you as a mate.'

•▯ ✦⚬⚬ •⚗⚭ ₿ •◊◖Ɑ₿Ϝ→ •◉ ꝝ •⊕▯ ✦⚭⊕ •|Ɑ

'Thanks, Turnball,' muttered Vishby, mollified. 'How's it been going, then? The *plan*?'

Turnball squeezed the water elf's elbow to remind him that there were eyes and ears everywhere.

'Oh, my plan to construct a model of the *Nostremius* aquanaut? That plan? It's going rather well. Warden Tarpon Vinyáya is being most cooperative. We're negotiating over *glue*.' He led Vishby to his computer screen. 'Let me show you my latest blueprint, and can I say how much I appreciate you taking an interest? My rehabilitation depends on interaction with decent individuals like yourself.'

'Uh . . . OK,' said Vishby, uncertain whether or not he had just been complimented.

Turnball Root waved his hand in front of the screen, awakening a v-board on the desk (real wood: identity thieves, Nigeria).

'Here, look. I've solved the problem with the ballast tanks, see?'

Then with a smooth three-finger combination, he activated the scrambler that Vishby had smuggled in for him. The scrambler was an organic wafer, which had been grown in the Atlantis branch of the now-defunct Koboi Labs. The scrambler was a reject lifted from the trash that had merely needed a dab of silicon to get it operational.

There is so much waste in industry, Turnball had sighed to Vishby. *Is it any wonder we're in the middle of a resource crisis?*

The tiny scrambler was vital to Turnball because it made everything else possible. Without it he would have no link to the offsite computer; without it the authorities here in the Deeps would be able to record every stroke of his keyboard and see exactly what he was really working on.

Turnball tapped the screen. It was split into two sections. One showed a recording from a few hours ago: an arena packed with mesmerized humans crawling all over each other. The second a real-time bot's-eye view of a burning shuttle craft on an icy tundra.

'One tank is gone and the other is an indulgence, so I will outsource rather than waste any more time on it.'

'Good thinking,' said Vishby, who for the first time was beginning to understand that land dwellers' phrase *in over one's head.*

Turnball Root rested his chin on one hand in the fashion of an elderly actor posing for his headshot. 'Yes, Mister Vishby. Very soon now my *model* shall be complete. Already one of the major parts is on its way down here, and when that arrives there won't be a fairy left in Atlantis . . . Eh, that is, there won't be a fairy left undazzled by my model.'

It was a feeble cover-up, he knew. Was *undazzled* even a word? But no need for panic as nobody watched him any more. They hadn't for years. He was no longer seen as a threat. The world in general had forgotten disgraced Captain Turnball Root. Those who knew him now found it difficult to believe that this shabby old-timer could really be as dangerous as his file said he was.

It's Opal Koboi this, and Opal Koboi that, Turnball often thought bitterly. *Well, we'll see who breaks out of this place first.*

Turnball banished the screen with a click of his fingers. 'Onwards and outwards, Vishby. Onwards and outwards.'

Vishby smiled suddenly, which with sea elves was accompanied by a slurping noise as they pulled their tongue back to make way for teeth. In fact, smiling was an unnatural expression for sea elves and they only did it to let others know how they were feeling.

'Oh, good news, Turnball. I got my pilot's licence back finally after the Mulch Diggums escape.'

'Good for you, sir.'

Vishby had been one of Mulch Diggums's escorts when he escaped from the LEP. All sub-shuttle crew were required to hold a pilot's qualification, in case the primary pilot became incapacitated.

'Just for emergency trips. But in a year or two I'll be back in rotation.'

'Well, much as I know how you long to pilot a submarine again, let's hope there are no emergency evacuations, eh?'

Vishby approximated a wink, which was difficult as he didn't have any eyelids and would have to give himself a spray soon to wash off the accumulated grit on his lower lid. His version of a wink was to tilt his head jauntily to one side.

'Emergency evacuations. No, we wouldn't want that.'

Eye grit, thought Turnball. *Disgusting.* And: *This fish boy is about as subtle as a steamroller with a siren on top. I'd better change the subject in case someone does happen to glance at the security monitors. It would be just my luck.*

'So, Mister Vishby. No mail for me today, I assume?'

'Nope. No mail for the umpteenth day in a row.'

Turnball rubbed his hands in the manner of one with urgent business. 'Well, then. I must not keep you from your duties and I myself have some modelling to do. I impose a schedule on myself, you see, and that must be adhered to.'

'Right you are, Turnball,' said Vishby, who had long since forgotten that he should be the one doing the dismissing, not the other way round. 'Just wanted to let you know I had my licence back. Because that was in *my* schedule.'

Turnball's smile never wavered and he kept it bright by promising himself that he would dispose of this fool the second he was no longer of any use.

'Good. Thanks for coming by.'

Vishby was almost fully through the hatch before he turned to drop another clanger.

'Here's hoping we don't have an emergency evacuation, eh, Captain Root?'

Turnball moaned internally.

Captain. Now he calls me captain.

Vatnajökull, now

The new guy, Orion Fowl, was checking his hosiery.

'No compression socks,' he declared. 'I have been on several plane journeys over the past few weeks, yet Artemis never wears compression socks. And I know he is aware of deep vein thrombosis; he simply chooses to ignore the risks.'

⊕⊙◊⊘•⊛•⊙ ⊙⊿⊘•⊘⊿⊀⊖⊗⊟⊦•⊀⊦⊀⊙⊟➤

This was Orion's second rant in as many minutes, the last one detailing Artemis's use of non-hypoallergenic deodorant, and Holly was growing tired of listening.

'I could sedate you,' she said brightly, as if this were the most reasonable course of action. 'We slap a pad on your neck and leave you at the restaurant for the humans. End of hosiery discussion.'

Orion smiled kindly. 'You wouldn't do that, Captain Short. I could freeze to death before help arrived. I am an innocent. Also, you have feelings for me.'

'An innocent!' spluttered Holly, and it took an especially outlandish statement to make her splutter. 'You are Artemis Fowl! For years, you were public enemy number one.'

'I am not Artemis Fowl,' protested Orion. 'I share his body and his knowledge of the Gnommish tongue among other things but I have a completely different personality. I am what is known as an alter ego.'

Holly snorted. 'I don't think that defence will stand up in front of a tribunal.'

'Oh, it does,' said Orion happily. 'All the time.'

Holly wormed up the slide of wafer slop to the lip of the crater in which the small band sheltered.

'No signs of hostiles. They appear to have descended into the underground craters.'

'Appear?' said Foaly. 'Can't you be a little more specific?'

Holly shook her head. 'No. I'm on eyes only. All our instruments are out. We have no link outside our own local network. I would guess that the probe is blocking communications.'

Foaly was busy grooming himself, peeling long strings of gluey nano-wafers from his flank. 'It's designed to emit a broad-spectrum jammer if it's under attack, knocking out communications and weapons. I'm surprised Artemis's cannon fired and I would imagine your guns have been isolated by now and shut down.'

Holly checked her Neutrino. Dead as a doornail. There was nothing on her helmet readout either except a slowly revolving red skull icon, which signalled catastrophic systems failure.

'D'Arvit,' she hissed. 'No weapons, no communications. How are we supposed to stop this thing?'

The centaur shrugged. 'It's a probe not a battleship. It should be easy enough to destroy once radar picks it up. If this is some mastermind's plot to destroy the fairy world, then he's not much of a mastermind.'

Orion raised a finger. 'I feel I should point out, correct me if Artemis is misremembering, but didn't your instruments dismally fail to pick up this probe in the first place?'

Foaly scowled. 'I was just starting to like you a little better than the other one.'

Holly stood erect. 'We need to follow the probe. Work out where it's going and somehow get word through to Haven.'

Orion smiled. 'You know, Miss Holly, you look very dramatic like that, backlit by the fire. Very attractive, if I may say so. I know you shared a *moment passionné* with Artemis, which he subsequently fouled up with his typical boorish behaviour. Let me just throw something out there for you to consider while we're chasing the probe: I share Artemis's passion but not his boorishness. No pressure, just think about it.'

This was enough to elicit a deafening moment of silence even in the middle of a crisis, which Orion seemed to be blissfully unaffected by.

Foaly was the first to speak. 'What's that look you have on your face there, Captain Short? What's going through your head right now? Don't think about it, just tell me.'

Holly ignored him, but that didn't stop the centaur talking.

'You had a moment of passion with Artemis Fowl?' he said. 'I don't remember reading that in your report.'

Holly may have been blushing, or it may have been the aforementioned dramatic backlighting. 'It wasn't in my report, OK? Because there was no moment of passion.'

Foaly didn't give up so easily. 'So nothing happened, Holly?'

'Nothing worth talking about. When we went back in time, my emotions got a little jumbled. It was temporary, OK? Can we please focus? We are supposed to be professionals.'

'Not me,' said Orion cheerily. 'I'm just a teenager with hormones running wild. And may I say, young fairy lady, they're running wild in your direction.'

Holly lifted her visor and looked the hormonal teenager in the eye. 'This had better not be a game, Artemis. If you do not have some serious psychosis, you will be sorry.'

'Oh, I'm crazy all right. I do have plenty of psychoses,' said Orion cheerily. 'Multiple personality, delusional dementia, OCD. I've got them all, but most of all I'm crazy about you.'

'That's not a bad line,' muttered Foaly. 'He is definitely not Artemis.'

Holly stamped the slush from her boots. 'We have two objectives. First we need to hide evidence of fairy technology, i.e. the shuttle, from curious humans until such time as we can send a LEP retrieval team to haul it below. And our second objective is to somehow stay on the tail of that probe and get a message through to Police Plaza that it's up here.' She glanced sharply at Foaly. 'Could this be a simple malfunction?'

'No,' said the centaur with absolute certainty. 'And I say that with absolute certainty. That probe has been deliberately reprogrammed, the amorphobots too. They were never meant to be used as weapons.'

'Then we have an enemy. Police Plaza needs to be warned.'

Holly turned to Orion. 'Well, any ideas?'

The boy's eyebrows rose a notch. 'Bivouac?'

Holly rubbed the spot on her forehead where a headache had just blossomed.

'Bivouac. Fabulous.'

From behind came a sudden wrenching noise as the shuttle sank a little lower in the ice like a defeated warrior.

'You know,' mused Foaly, 'that ship is pretty heavy and the rock shelf there is not very –'

Before he could finish, the entire shuttle disappeared into the landscape, taking the restaurant with it as though both had been swallowed by a subterranean kraken.

Seconds later, Artemis's Ice Cube nano-wafer cannon tumbled into the newborn chasm.

'That was incredibly quiet,' said Orion. 'If I hadn't seen it, I would never have known.'

'This terrain is like dwarf cheese. Full of holes,' said Holly, then she was up and gone, racing across the ice towards the new crater.

Orion and Foaly took their time, strolling across the glacier, chatting amiably.

'On the plus side,' said Foaly, 'there's our first objective achieved. The evidence is gone.'

Orion nodded, then asked: 'Dwarf cheese?'

'Cheese made by dwarfs.'

'Oh,' said Orion, relieved. 'They make it. It's not actually . . .'

'No. What a horrible thought.'

'Exactly.'

The hole in the surface of the ice revealed a cavernous under-world. A subterranean river pulsed along, tearing shreds from what was left of the Great Skua restaurant. The water was deep blue and moving with such power that it almost seemed alive. Great chunks of ice, some the size of elephants, sheared away from the banks, tumbled against the current and then submit-ted to its will, gathering speed until they struck the building, pulverizing what was left. The only sound was one of raging water; the building seemed to surrender without a whimper.

The shuttle had become impaled on an ice ridge below a slight bank in the underground river. An ice bank that could not survive the pounding waters for long.

The craft was stripped down by the brute force of nature until only a small section remained, an obsidian arrowhead jammed point down into the ice and rock.

'The shuttle's escape pod,' shouted Holly. 'Of course.'

Objective two, staying on the probe's tail, was now actually possible. If they could board the pod, and if the pod still had any power in it, they would be able to follow the probe and try to get a message to LEP headquarters.

Holly tried to scan the small craft with her helmet, but her beams were still blocked.

She turned to the centaur. 'Foaly? What do you think?'

Foaly did not need her question explained. There was only one thing to think about: the escape pod wedged into the ice below them.

'Those things are damn near indestructible and built to hold the entire crew in a pinch. Also the power source is a solid fuel block, so there aren't many moving parts to go wrong. All the usual modes of communication are on board, plus a good old-fashioned radio, which our secret enemy might not have thought to block, though considering he thought to phase the probe's shield to repulse our own sensors I doubt there's much he didn't think of.'

Holly wiggled forward until her torso hung over the rim, spray from the subterranean river painting a sheen on her visor.

'So, that's our way out, if we can make it down.'

Foaly clopped his front hooves. 'We don't all have to make it down. Some of us are a tad less nimble than others, those with hooves for example. You could hop on down there then fly the pod back up to collect the rest of us.'

'That makes perfect sense,' said Orion. 'But I should be the one to go. Chivalry demands that I take the risk.'

Foaly scowled. 'Come on, Holly. Please sedate this deluded idiot.'

Orion cleared his throat. 'You are not being very sensitive to my illness, centaur.'

Holly seriously considered the sedation, then shook her head. 'Artemis . . . Orion is right. One of us should go.'

Holly unravelled a piton cord from the reel on her belt, quickly wrapping it round one of the exposed steel rods in the restaurant's foundations.

'What are you doing?' asked Orion.

Holly strode briskly to the hole. 'What you were going to do in about five seconds' time.'

'Haven't you read the classics?' shouted Orion. '*I* should go.'

'That's right,' she said. 'You should go.' And she hopped into the underground cavern.

Orion made an animalistic noise, if the animal was a tiger having its tail tied in a knot, and he actually stamped his foot.

'Wow,' said Foaly. 'Foot stamping. You are really angry.'

'It would seem so,' said Orion, peering over the edge.

'Generally the foot stamping is on the other foot as you are usually the one driving Holly crazy. The other you.'

'I can't say I'm surprised,' said Orion, calming somewhat. 'I can be insufferable.'

The youth lay flat on the ice.

'You're on a good line, Holly,' he said, almost to himself. 'You should definitely miss that big wall of ice.'

'I doubt it,' grunted Foaly, and, as it turned out, the centaur was right.

Captain Short went down faster than she would have liked, which was totally due to equipment malfunction. If the reel at her belt had not been damaged during the recent amor-phobot attack, then it would have automatically slowed her descent and Holly could have avoided the impact that was surely to come. As it was, she was more or less falling at full g with nothing to lessen her impact other than a slight tension from the piton line.

A thought flashed through Holly's mind even faster than the ice could flash past her head.

I hope nothing breaks; I have no magic left to fix it.

Then she crashed into the ice wall with her knees and elbows. It was harder than rock and sharper than glass, cutting her uniform as though it were paper. Cold and pain jittered along her limbs and there was a cracking noise, but it was surface ice and not bones.

The wall sloped gradually to the bank of the underground glacier run-off river, and Holly Short slid down helplessly, tumbling end over end, landing feet first through sheer luck. The final gasp of air huffed from her lungs as the shock of impact travelled along her legs. She prayed for a spark of magic but nothing came to take away the pain.

🜚•🝿🝰•🝰🝮🝭🝯🝮🝱🝲🝳•🝴🜚🜚•🝵🝮🝰🝶🝷🝸🝹🜚

Get a move on, soldier, she told herself, imagining Julius Root giving the order.

She scrambled across the ice bank, seeing her own distorted reflection in the ice stare wild-eyed back at her, like a desperate swimmer trapped under a skating pond.

Look at that face. I could use a day in a sludge-immersion tank, she thought.

Usually the idea of spending time in a relaxation spa would horrify Holly, but today it seemed a most attractive prospect.

Regeneration sludge and cucumber eye pads. Lovely.

No point dreaming about it now, though. There was work to be done.

Holly scrambled to the escape pod. The river rushed past, pounding the fuselage, hammering cracks in the ice.

I hate the cold. I really hate it.

Mist rose in freezing clouds from the water, draping a spectral blue tent over the massive stalactites.

Spectral blue tent? thought Holly. *Maybe I should write a poem. I wonder what rhymes with crushed?*

Holly kicked at the ice clustered at the pod's base, clearing the hatch, thankful the doorway wasn't completely submerged, as, without her Neutrino, she would have no way to clear it.

The captain channelled all the day's frustrations into the next few minutes of furious kicking. Holly stamped on that ice as though it had somehow been responsible for blowing up the shuttle, as though its crystals were somehow to blame for the probe's attack. Whatever the source of Holly's strength, her

efforts bore fruit and soon the hatch's outline was visible beneath
a transparent sheath of mashed ice.

A voice floated down from above. 'Helloooo. Holly. Are
you OK?'

There was another phrase at the end. Muffled. Could this
Orion person have called her *fair lady* again? Holly fervently
hoped not.

'I . . . am . . . fine!' she grunted, each word punctuated
with another blow to the shell of ice.

'Try not to become too stressed,' said the echoing voice.
'Do a few breathing exercises.'

Unreal, thought Holly. *This guy has lived in the back of
Artemis's head for so long that he has no idea how to handle the
actual world.*

She wormed her fingers into the recessed handle grip,
flicking away tenacious clots of ice blocking the handle. The
hatch was purely mechanical so there was no problem with
jammers, but that did not necessarily hold for the pod's
controls. The rogue probe could theoretically have fried the
pod's guidance systems just as easily as it had taken out their
communications.

Holly planted a boot on the hull and hauled the hatch
open. A deluge of pink disinfectant gel poured out, pooling
around her second boot, and quickly evaporated to mist.

*Disinfectant gel. In case whatever destroyed the shuttle had been
bacterial.*

She poked her head inside and the motion sensors heated
a couple of phosphorescent plates on the roof panels.

Good. Emergency power at least.

The escape pod was totally inverted, pointed straight down to the centre of the Earth. The interior was Spartan and made with soldiers in mind, not passengers.

Orion is going to love this, she thought, strapping herself into the pilot's harness. There were six separate belts in the harness as this ship had little in the way of gyroscopes or suspension.

Maybe I can shake Artemis out of his own brain. We can count up to five together.

She flexed her fingers, then allowed them to hover above the control panel.

Nothing happened. No activation, no sudden heads-up controls. No icon asking her for a start code.

Stone age it is, thought Holly and leaned forward to the limits of her harness, reaching underneath the console for a good old-fashioned steering wheel and manual propulsion controls.

She pressed the ignition plunger and the engine coughed.

Come on. I have things to do.

One more press and the escape pod's pitiful engine caught and turned over, irregular as a dying man's breathing, but it turned over nevertheless.

Thank you.

Holly thought this just before jets of black smoke blurted through the vents into the cabin, making her splutter.

There's some damage, but we should be OK.

Holly cranked open the for'ard porthole and was alarmed

by the view that was suddenly revealed. She had expected to see the blue waters of a subterranean river splashing across the transparent polymer, but instead she saw an abyss. The pod had punched into a vast underground cavern that seemed to run right through the glacier in a dizzyingly sheer drop towards the bedrock below. Rippling walls of ice stretched below her, illuminated by the distant flickering blue lights of the probe's engines as it made its way into the depths of the cavern.

There it is. Heading down.

Holly hit the thaw button for the fuel block and tapped her fingers impatiently while it heated up.

'What I need now,' she muttered to herself, 'is reverse. And quickly.'

But reverse did not come soon enough. The glacier river worked its tendrils into the ice ridge supporting the escape pod and quickly stripped it back. For a moment the probe hung suspended then it dropped through the hole and fell powerless straight down.

A couple of minutes earlier the boy who wore Artemis Fowl's face had been standing on the surface, peering down at Holly Short. Appreciating her labours and admiring her form.

'She's a feisty one, *n'est-ce pas*? Look at her battling the elements.'

Foaly clopped to his side. 'Come on, Artemis. You can't kid me. What are you up to?'

Orion's face was smooth. On him, Artemis's features

seemed open and trustworthy. This was a neat trick as, on Artemis, these same features seemed conniving and almost sinister, some would say sneaky. Indeed one music teacher did use this term in Artemis's school report, which was quite an unprofessional thing to do, but in fairness Artemis had rewired the man's keyboard so that it would only play 'Jingle Bells' no matter what keys were pressed.

'I am not up to anything,' said Orion. 'I am alive and I am here. That is all. I have Artemis's memories but not his disposition. I believe that I owe my sudden appearance to what fairies would call an Atlantis Complex.'

Foaly wagged a finger. 'Nice try, but Atlantis Complex generally manifests itself through compulsion and delusion.'

'Stage two.'

Foaly took a moment to consult his near-photographic memory.

'Atlantis Complex stage two can result in the subject displaying signs of several completely different and distinct personalities.'

'And?' prompted Orion.

'Stage two can be initiated by either or both mental trauma or physical shock, typically electrocution.'

'Holly shot me. So there we go.'

Foaly scraped the snow with a hoof. 'That's the problem with beings of our intellect. We can argue our points of view all day without either gaining a significant advantage. That's what happens when you're a genius.' The centaur smiled. 'Look, I scraped an F for Foaly.'

⯩⯫⯭⯬⯮⯯ ⬩ ⬚ ⬩ ⯲⯳⯴⯵ ⬩ ⬢⬣⬤ ⬩ ⬥⬦⬧ ⬩ ⬨⬩⬪ ⬫⬬⬭⬮ ⬩

'That is excellent work,' said Orion. 'Such straight lines. That takes hoof control.'

'I know,' said Foaly. 'It's a real talent, but there's no forum for this kind of expression.'

Foaly was well aware that he was babbling about hoof drawings in order to distract himself from the current situation. He had often assisted Holly through one crisis or another. But he had rarely been in the field to actually witness these crises occurring.

The video logs never really capture the emotion, he thought. *I am scared out of my wits right now, but no helmet-cam footage can convey that.*

It scared Foaly that someone had managed to hack his space probe and reprogram the amorphobots. It scared him that this person had no regard for life, fairy, human or animal. And it totally terrified him that if, gods forbid, Holly was injured or worse, then it would be up to him and this simpering alternate Fowl personality to warn Haven, and he hadn't the first idea how he was qualified for this job, unless the talents of smartalecry and rapid v-board manipulation were somehow called for. Artemis would know what to do, but apparently Artemis wasn't at home right now.

Foaly realized with a jolt that the current situation was quite close to being his own worst nightmare, especially if it eventually led to Caballine shaving him. Control was very important to Foaly, and here he was stuck on a glacier with a damaged human, watching their only hope of salvation fighting an underground river.

His current worst nightmare was suddenly relegated to second place as the escape pod, with Holly inside it, was suddenly swallowed whole by the ice. Loose chunks tumbled quickly to fill the hole, and before Foaly had time to gasp in shock it was as if the craft had never been there.

Foaly sank to his fore-knees. 'Holly!' he called desperately. 'Holly.'

Orion was equally distraught. 'Oh, Captain Short. There was so much I wanted to tell you, about how we feel, Artemis and I. You were so young, with so much left to give.' Fat tears rolled down his cheeks. 'Oh, Artemis, poor, foolish Artemis. You had so much and did not know it.'

Foaly felt hollowed out by sudden, wrenching grief. Holly was gone. Their last best chance of warning Haven. How could he hope to succeed aided only by a mooning Mud Boy who began every second sentence with the word 'oh'?

'Shut up, Orion! Shut up. A person is gone. A real person.' The ice was hard beneath Foaly's knees and made their situation seem more desperate.

'I don't have much experience with real people,' admitted Orion, slumping beside the centaur. 'Or feelings that translate to the world. But I think I am sad now. And lonely. We have lost a friend.'

These were words from the heart and Foaly felt he had to be sympathetic. 'OK. It's not your fault. We have both lost someone special.'

Orion sniffed. 'Good. Then, worthy centaur, perhaps you could give me a ride to the village on your back. Then I can make a few pennies with my verses while you build us a shack and perform circus tricks for passers-by.'

This was such a surprising statement that Foaly briefly considered jumping into the hole to get away.

'This isn't Middle Earth, you know. We're not in a novel. I am not noble, neither do I have a repertoire of circus tricks.'

Orion seemed disappointed. 'Can you juggle at least?'

Orion's idiocy was just what Foaly needed to shake him temporarily from his grief. He jumped to his feet and stomped in a circle round Orion.

'What are you? *Who* are you? I thought you shared Artemis's memories. How can you be so stupid?'

Orion was unperturbed. 'I share everything. Memories and movies are as real as each other to me. You, Peter Pan, the Loch Ness monster, me. It's all real, maybe.'

Foaly rubbed his forehead. 'We are in so much trouble. Gods help us.'

Orion brightened. 'I have an idea.'

'Yes?' said Foaly, daring to hope that a spark of Artemis remained.

'Why don't we look for some magic stones that can grant wishes? Or, if that doesn't work, you could search my naked body for some mysterious birthmark that means I am actually the prince of somewhere or other.'

'OK,' sighed Foaly. 'Why don't you get started on the stones thing and I'll scrape some magical runes in the snow.'

Orion clapped his hands sharply. 'Excellent notion, noble

creature.' And he began kicking over stones, to see if any of them were magical.

The complex is progressing, realized Foaly. *He wasn't this deluded only minutes ago. The more desperate the situation becomes the further from reality he gets. If we can't get Artemis back soon, he will be gone forever.*

'I found one!' Orion shouted suddenly. 'A magic stone!' He bent to examine his discovery. 'No. Wait. It's a shellfish of some kind.' He smiled apologetically at Foaly. 'I saw it scuttling and so I assumed . . .'

Foaly thought a thought he had thought he would never think.

I would prefer to be with Mulch Diggums.

This notion caused him to shudder.

Orion yelped loudly and scuttled backwards. 'I found it. Really, this time. Look, Foaly. Look!'

Foaly looked, in spite of himself, and was amazed to see that a stone actually did seem to be dancing.

'That's not possible,' he said, and wondered, *Is he somehow sucking me into his delusion?*

Orion was jubilant. 'Everything is real. I am abroad in the world.'

The stone flipped high into the air, spinning off across the frozen lake. Where it had been, the black hull of the escape pod punctured the ice. It rose and rose above a bass rumbling of engines that set the ice plates vibrating themselves to pieces.

It took Foaly a moment to realize what was happening, but then he too was jubilant.

'Holly!' he called. 'You made it. You didn't leave us.'

The escape pod lurched to the surface, then toppled on its side. The for'ard porthole was winched open and Holly's face appeared in the frame. She was pale and bleeding from a dozen minor cuts, but her eyes were bright and determined.

'Took a while for the fuel block to dissolve,' she explained over the engine noise. 'Get inside, both of you, and buckle up. We have to catch that fire-breathing monster.'

This was a simple order and both Foaly and Orion could obey without their realities clashing.

Holly is alive, thought Foaly.

My princess lives, exulted Orion. *And we're chasing a dragon.*

'Foaly,' he called after the centaur. 'I really think we should search for my secret birthmark. Dragons love that sort of thing.'

ARTEMIS FOWL'S BRAIN, NOW

Artemis was not gone completely. He was confined to a small virtual room in his own brain. The room was similar to his Fowl Manor office, but there were no screens on the situations wall. In fact, there was no wall. Where his selection of gas screens and digital televisions had been mounted, there now floated a window into his body's reality. He could see what the fool Orion saw, and hear the ridiculous sentences dripping from his own mouth, but he could not control the actions of the romantic nincompoop who seemed to be in the driving seat, to use a motor-car reference that Butler and Holly would appreciate.

In Artemis's room there was a desk and a chair. He wore one of his lightweight Zegna bespoke suits. He could see the weave of threads on his arm and feel the material's weight as though it were real, but Artemis knew all these things were illusions constructed by his mind to put some order on the chaos in his brain.

He sat upon the chair.

In front of Artemis, on what he had decided to call his mind-screen, events played out in the real world. He winced as the usurper, Orion, rolled out his clumsy charm.

He will utterly destroy my relationship with Holly, he thought.

Now he appeared to be treating Foaly like some kind of mythical pet.

Orion was right about one thing. He was in the second stage of Atlantis Complex, a mental illness he had brought on himself through a combination of reckless dabblings in fairy magic and feelings of guilt.

I brought the guilt on myself too, exposing my mother to Opal Koboi.

Artemis realized suddenly that while he was trapped in his own mind numbers held no sway over him. Neither did he feel any compulsion to rearrange the objects on his desk.

I am free.

A metaphorical weight lifted from his allegorical chest and Artemis Fowl felt himself again. Vital, sharp, focused, for the first time in months. Ideas fluttered from his mind, like bats from the mouth of a cave.

So much to do. So many projects. Butler . . . I need to find him.

Artemis felt energized and potent. He surged from his chair towards the mind-screen. He would push his way through, force his way out and send this Orion character back to where he came from. Next on his to-do list would be to apologize to Foaly and Holly for his rudeness and then get to the bottom of this space-probe hijack. His Ice Cube had been torn to pieces by the subterranean river, but it could be rebuilt. In months the project could be operational.

And when the glaciers were safe perhaps he would submit to a little regression therapy from one of the People's less flamboyant psychotherapists. Certainly not that Cumulus fellow who had his own talk show.

When Artemis reached the screen, he found it to be less solid than it had first appeared. In fact, it was deep and gloopy, reminding Artemis of the plasma conduit he had crawled through at Opal Koboi's lab all those years ago. Nevertheless he forged ahead and soon found himself submerged in a cold, viscous gel that pushed him backwards with floppy fingers.

'I will not be deterred,' shouted Artemis, finding that he could shout inside the mind-screen. 'I am needed in the wide world.'

And then.

Deterred? Wide world? I am beginning to sound like that idiot Orion.

This thought gave him strength and he tore at the curtains

of gunk that kept him a prisoner. It felt good being active and positive. Artemis felt like the Fowl heir of old. Unstoppable.

Then he spotted something in the air before him. Bright and fizzling like a Halloween sparkler. There were more, dozens, all around him, sinking slowly through the gel.

What were they? What could those things mean?

I made them, thought Artemis. *I should know.*

A moment later he did know. The fizzling sparklers were actually tiny golden numbers. All the same number. All fours.

Death.

Artemis recoiled, but then rallied.

No. I will not be a slave. I refuse.

A tiny number four grazed his elbow, sending a shock through his entire body.

This is a memory, nothing more. My mind is reconstructing the plasma conduit. None of this is real.

But the shocks felt real. Once the tiny fours realized that he was there, they gathered like a shoal of malignant fish, herding Artemis back to the safety of his office.

He fell backwards to the floor, panting.

I need to try again, he thought.

But not yet. The fours seemed to watch him, matching his movements.

Five, thought Artemis. *I need five to stay alive. I will try again soon. Soon.*

Artemis felt a weight settle on his chest that seemed too heavy to be just his imagination.

I will try soon. Hold on, my friends.

CHAPTER 6: TRIMMING THE WEIGHT

 PRISONER 42 checked the LEP's official site and was amused to see that he was no longer on the Top Ten Most Dangerous list.

They forget what I have done, he thought with some satisfaction. *Which is exactly as I planned.*

Turnball sent a quick v-mail to Leonor, one of the dozen he sent daily.

Prepare yourself for travel, darling. I shall be with you soon.

He waited breathlessly for the reply, and it soon came. A single word.

Hurry.

Turnball was cheered by the prompt response, even after all these years they hung on each other's words. But he was a little worried too. Lately all of Leonor's messages had been brief, often no more than a phrase. He did not believe that

his darling wife was not inclined to write more – he believed
that she grew too weak, the effort was too painful.

Turnball sent a second mail to Ark Sool, an LEP turncoat
he had recently employed to make sure his wife and affairs
were well looked after.

*Leonor grows weaker without my fairy magic beside her, Mister
Sool. Take special care.*

Turnball grew suddenly impatient.

Mere hours separate us, my dear. Hold on for me.

The authorities were mistaken, of course. Turnball Root was
extremely dangerous. They had forgotten he was the elf who
had stolen millions from the LEP's own weapons budget.
The elf who had almost managed to destroy half of Haven
City just to get rid of a competitor.

I would have done it too, he thought for the thousandth time.
If not for my holier-than-thou little brother.

He banished this thought. Thinking about Julius would
just get his vitals up and the jailers might notice.

I should give myself a little treat, he thought, sitting down at
his terminal. *It could be the last one before I go. Vishby will come
for me soon and then the LEP will realize their mistake. Too late, of
course.*

He smiled at his reflection on the screen as he typed a
brief message for a certain website.

One is never too old for mischief, Turnball realized as he
pressed SEND.

The Sozzled Parrot, Miami, now

It is a universal law that fugitives flock together. No matter how large the posse on their tail, people on the run always manage to find that one low-down dirty dive, with the cheapest hooch, run by the dodgiest innkeeper, that not even the police know about. These establishments generally have steel doors, paint over their windows, mould in their bathroom stalls and don't serve anything with more than two ingredients. The Sozzled Parrot was such a place.

The owner was a certain dwarf called Barnet Riddles who ruled the roost with a certain wheedling panache that made him a likeable host in a sleazy sort of way. And if wheedling panache was not enough to calm a troublemaker down, then Barnet would follow it with a tap from a stolen LEP buzz baton.

The Sozzled Parrot was a dwarf hangout and the club motto was: *If you are not welcome there, then you are welcome here*, which meant that every exiled, criminal or slumming fairy in North America sooner or later turned up at the Sozzled Parrot. Barnet Riddles made the perfect host as, by some freak of nature, he was one of only a tiny percentage of fairies who were over four feet tall. And so, as long as he wore a bandanna to cover his ears, Barnet was the ideal go-between with the humans, who supplied him with liquor, slightly turned beef for his quesadillas and as much firepower as he could shift out of the back room.

The early hours of this morning in the Sozzled Parrot were

pretty much the same as any other. Dwarfs sat hunched over tankards of ale in one of the booths. A couple of sprites were playing video crunchball on their handhelds and half a dozen elfin soldiers of fortune were trading war stories by the pool table.

Barnet Riddles was deep in conversation with a dwarf at the bar.

'Come on, Tombstone,' he wheedled in a charming way. 'Buy a couple of guns. A grenade at least. All you do is sit there and drink creek water. Isn't there someone you'd like to shoot a couple of times?'

The dwarf grinned, baring his trademark tombstone teeth. 'It's getting that way, Riddles.'

Barnet was not discouraged – then again this particular dwarf was a born optimist. Who else would set up a bar for photosensitive dwarfs in sunny Miami?

It's the last place the Leppers will look for us fugitives from justice, he often explained. *They're up freezing their LEP tails off in Russia, meanwhile we're sinking beers here in luxurious air-conditioned surroundings.*

Luxurious was a stretch. Even *clean* would have been a stretch. But the Sozzled Parrot was somewhere for fairy soldiers of fortune to meet and exchange war stories day or night, and so they were prepared to put up with Barnet's exorbitant prices and his constant sales pitches.

'How about a computer implant?' persisted the innkeeper. 'Everybody has implants these days. How do you keep tabs on the LEP?'

Tombstone pulled down the brim of his felt hat, so that it covered his eyes. 'Believe it or not, Riddles, I'm not on the hot list any more. What you are looking at now is a one hundred per cent legit citizen. Heck, I've even got a visa to be above ground.'

'Groomchunks,' said Barnet doubtfully.

Tombstone slid a plastic square across the bar. 'Read it and weep.'

Barnet squinted at the Gnommish writing and checked the official hologram.

'Looks pretty real,' he admitted.

'That is because it is real, my beer-watering friend.'

Barnet shook his head. 'I don't get it. If you can be anywhere, why are you here?'

Tombstone tossed a handful of beezel nuts into his cavernous mouth, and Barnet swore that after each crunch there was an echo.

'I am here,' said Tombstone eventually, 'because of the clientele.'

Barnet was even more befuddled. 'What? Thieves, mercenaries, extortionists and forgers?'

Tombstone's grin was wide and bright. 'Yep. My kind of people.'

Barnet checked on a pitcher of toad sludge that he was fermenting for the pixies.

'You are a riot, Tombstone. Do you know that?'

Before Tombstone could answer, a plastic parrot on the bar opened its beak and squawked.

'New post,' squawked its animatronic mouth. 'New post on the message board.'

'Excuuuuuse me,' said Barnet Riddles, with exaggerated politeness, 'while I check this extremely handy implant I have in my head.'

'Handy, until you pass a microwave and lose ten years of memory,' commented Tombstone. 'Then again, you spend so much time in here that you probably wouldn't miss the odd decade.'

Barnet was not listening. His eyes fogged over as he checked the illegal implant hotwired directly into his cortex by a disbarred doctor. After a couple of *hmmms* and one *really* he returned to the here and now.

'How are the brain cells?' enquired Tombstone mildly. 'I hope the message was worth it?'

'Don't you worry about it, Mister Hundred Per Cent Legit,' said Barnet briskly. 'This one is for us criminals.' He pounded the bar with his buzz baton, sending sparks rippling across the length of the brass rail.

'Cruik,' he called across the room. 'You have a ship? Right?'

One of the dwarfs at the end booth raised a grizzled head. Beer foam fell in blobs from his beard. 'Yeah. I got a gyro. A bit of a crock but she runs OK.'

Barnet clapped his hands, already counting his commission. 'Good. A job came in on the board. Two humans, kill 'em dead.'

Cruik shook his head slowly. 'No killing dead. We may be criminals but we're not humans.'

'The client will accept a full wipe. Can you stomach that?'

'Full wipe?' interrupted Tombstone. 'Isn't that dangerous?'

Barnet sniggered. 'Not if you keep your fingers away from the electrodes. Two humans, brother and sister by the name of Butler.'

Tombstone twitched. 'Butler? Brother and sister?'

Barnet closed one eye, consulting his implant. 'Yeah. I'm shooting the details across to your gyro, Cruik. This is a rush job. Top dollar, as the Mud Men would say.'

The dwarf called Cruik checked the charge in an old-fashioned blunderbuss Neutrino.

'These Mud Men won't be saying much of anything by the time I'm finished with them.' He pounded the table to summon his warriors. 'Let's go, my fine fellows. We have brains to suck.'

Tombstone stood quickly. 'Do you guys have room for one more?'

'I knew it,' chuckled Barnet Riddles. 'One hundred per cent legit, I don't think so. As soon as I laid eyes on you, this guy has history, I said.'

Cruik was buckling on a belt loaded with spikes, shells and dangerous-looking implements with fuses and capacitors.

'Why should I take you, stranger?'

'You should take me because if your pilot gets killed to death by these Butler humans, then I can take his place.'

An uncharacteristically skinny dwarf looked up from the romance novel he was reading. 'Killed to death?' he said, lip trembling slightly. 'I say, Cruik, is that likely?'

'I've had experience with the Butlers,' said Tombstone. 'They always go for the pilot first.'

Cruik sized up Tombstone, taking in his powerful jaws and muscled legs.

'OK, stranger. You take the co-pilot's chair. You get a junior share and no quibbling.'

Tombstone grinned. 'Why quibble now when we can quibble later?'

Cruik thought about this statement for a moment until his brain ached.

'OK. Whatever. Everybody take a sober pill and mount up. We have some humans to wipe.'

Tombstone followed his new captain across the bar floor. 'How good is your mind-wiping equipment?'

Cruik shrugged. 'Who cares?' he said simply.

'I like your attitude,' said Tombstone. Almost immediately.

Cancún, Mexico, now

The Butlers in question were of course the very same Butlers who had escaped the mesmerized wrestling fans and who were now, thirty minutes after Cruik took on his new co-pilot, taking a moment to catch their breath in the morning sunshine on the shore of Cancún's lagoon. These two were being pursued by Turnball Root more for his own entertainment than the possibility that they could actually interfere with his plans. Though it was possible that opponents as formidable as the Butlers had proved themselves to be could prove troublesome. And Turnball's plans were delicate enough without adding troublesome humans to the mix. Better to wipe them at least. Also, they had escaped the first time, so Turnball was irked, which he did not like.

Juliet squatted just above the waterline, listening to the sounds of party laughter and the tinkling of champagne flutes stream across the water from a passing yacht.

'I have an idea, brother,' she said. 'Why don't we ask Artemis for a million dollars and just retire? Well, I could retire. You could be *my* butler.'

Butler sat beside her. 'Frankly, I don't think Artemis has a million dollars. He's put everything into this latest project. *THE PROJECT*, as he calls it.'

'What's he stealing now?'

'Nothing. Artemis has moved on from crime. These days he's saving the world.'

Juliet's arm froze halfway through the motion of throwing a pebble. 'Artemis Fowl has moved on from crime? Our Artemis Fowl? Isn't that against Fowl family law?'

Butler didn't exactly smile, but his scowl definitely grew less pronounced. 'This is hardly the time for jokes, sister.' He paused. 'But, if you must know, the Fowl statutes actually state that a family member caught straying on to the straight and narrow can have his Doctor Evil manual and suction cups confiscated.'

Juliet snickered. 'Suction cups.'

Butler's customary scowl quickly reasserted itself. 'Seriously, sister. This is a sinister situation we find ourselves in.

Pursued by fairy agents and on the far side of the world from my principal.'

'What are you even doing here? Who sent you on this wild-goose chase?'

Butler had been thinking about this. 'Artemis sent me. He must have been coerced, though it didn't seem so. Perhaps he was tricked.'

'Tricked? Artemis Fowl? He has changed.'

Butler frowned, patting the spot where his shoulder holster would normally hang. 'Artemis has changed. You would barely recognize him now, he is so different.'

'Different? How?'

Butler's frown deepened, a slash between his eyebrows. 'He counts everything. Steps, words, everything. I think five is the big number. Also, rows. He groups all the stuff around him into little rows. Usually five per row, or ten.'

'I've heard about stuff like that. Obsessive compulsive disorder. OCD.'

'And he's paranoid. He doesn't trust anyone.' Butler's head dropped to his chest. 'Not even me.'

Juliet tossed the pebble far into the lagoon. 'It sounds like Artemis needs help.'

Butler nodded. 'How about you? You've had quite a bit sprung on you in the past hour.'

Juliet raked the shoreline with her fingers, gathering pebbles. 'What? You mean little things like being chased by a mesmerized horde? And the fact that fairies do exist? Those tiny things?'

Butler grunted. He had forgotten how much his sister made fun of him and how he for some reason put up with it. 'Yes, those *tiny* things,' he said, elbowing her fondly.

'Don't worry about me, brother. I'm a modern woman. We're tough and smart, hadn't you heard?'

'I get it. You're *coping*, is that it?'

'No, brother. I feel fine. The Butlers are together and nothing can stand against us.'

'The new memories aren't freaking you out?'

Juliet laughed and the sound did Butler's heart good. 'Freaking me out? Where are we, the 1970s? And, no, the memories aren't freaking me out. As a matter of fact, they feel . . .' She thought about her next sentence for a while. 'They feel right in my head. They belong where they are. How could I have forgotten Holly? Or Mulch?'

Butler pulled a pair of sunglasses from his jacket pocket. They were a little clunkier than the current style and had tiny solar panels on the arms.

'With fairies on our tail, we may need these.'

Juliet plucked them from his fingers, and the stimulus from the contact brought memories flooding back.

Artemis made these from disassembled LEP helmets, so we could see through fairy shields. The LEP are sneaky but Artemis is sneakier.

'I remember those glasses. Why did you even bring them?'

'Boy scout rule number one. Be prepared. There are fairies around us all the time. I don't want to accidentally shoot one, or miss one for that matter.'

Juliet hoped her brother was being funny.

'You wouldn't shoot a fairy,' said Juliet, slipping the glasses on to her face.

Immediately something appeared in her vision as though it had popped out of a toaster. The *something* was certainly not human. It hung suspended from a harness and was aiming a bulbously barrelled weapon at her head. Whatever it was wore a bodysuit that seemed to be made of a viscous tar-like substance, which clung to its wobbling torso and coated every hair of its shaggy beard.

'Shoot the fairy!' she yelped, shocked. 'Shoot it.'

Most people might have assumed that Juliet was joking. After all, what were the chances that a fairy would show up the very moment she donned fairy filters? Not to mention the fact that Juliet was well known for her inappropriate sense of humour and regularly spouted witticisms in moments of mortal danger.

For example, when Christian Varley Penrose, her sous instructor at the Madame Ko Academy, lost his grip on the north face of Everest and went plummeting earthwards with only a skinny girl between him and certain death, Juliet braced herself and called to her sensei as he pin-wheeled past: 'Hey, Penrose. Surely saving you is worth some extra credit.'

So it would be quite reasonable to assume that when Juliet yelled *Shoot the fairy* she was actually joshing her big brother, but Butler did not assume this for a second. He was trained to recognize stress registers, but even if Artemis hadn't forced him to listen to that MP3 lecture in the car he knew the difference between *genuinely shocked* Juliet and *having a laugh* Juliet. So when Juliet cried *Shoot the fairy* Butler decided on a course of aggressive action in the time it would take a hummingbird to flap its wings.

No gun, so no shooting, he thought. *But there are options.*

The option Butler chose was to grasp his sister's shoulder firmly and push her sideways so that she actually skidded along the pebbled beach, her shoulder ploughing a furrow in the stones.

Scratched shoulder. I'll be hearing about that for weeks.

Butler swung both arms forward and used the momentum to pull himself up and forward into a full-tilt launch at whatever had spooked Juliet. At this point he could only hope that the *whatever* was close enough to grapple, otherwise there was a fairy somewhere laughing into his facemask and calmly aiming a weapon.

His luck held. Butler made contact with something squat and lumpy. Something that struggled and bucked like a pig in a blanket, and exuded a particular odour which a person might experience if that person were unfortunate enough to somehow end up face down in a medieval swill patch.

I know that smell, Butler realized, holding on grimly. *Dwarf.*

Whatever was holding the dwarf up whined and dipped, dunking Butler and his wriggling captive into the lagoon's waist-high water. For Butler, the dunking was harmless enough, he was virtually clamped around the invisible dwarf and in fact the cool water felt quite refreshing, but for the shimmer-suited fairy the sudden dip was catastrophic. Abrasive contact with the sharp scree on the lagoon bed punctured his camouflage suit, breaking the skin, releasing the charge.

The dwarf, Cruik, was suddenly visible.

'Aha,' said Butler, hauling Cruik from the surf. 'Dwarf head. Good.'

Cruik had forfeited his gift of tongues along with the rest of his magic, but he had been living among the humans for long enough to pick up a smattering of several languages and Butler's simple statement was terrifyingly easy to misinterpret.

Dwarf head? This Mud Man is going to eat my head.

Butler was actually glad to see the dwarf's head because dwarf heads are disproportionately large and this particular dwarf's head was even more bulbous than most. It was almost Butler-sized and there was a helmet perched on top of it.

With a fairy helmet, I can see what this little guy sees.

It was the helmet Butler was after, not the meaty noggin inside.

'C'mere, slippy,' grunted the bodyguard, intuitively snapping the helmet's seals and popping it off. 'Did you just try to shoot my sister?'

Recognizing the word *shoot* Cruik glanced down at his own hands and was dismayed to find them empty. He had dropped his gun.

Cruik was a career criminal and had lived through many close calls without losing his nerve. He had once faced down a gang of drunken goblins armed with only a jar of burn lotion and three bottle tops, but this bloodthirsty giant with a face of fury and a thirst for brains finally sent him over the edge.

'Nooooo,' he screamed shrilly. 'No brain biting.'

Butler ignored the tantrum and the musty helmet pong and gripped the protective hat one-handed as a basketball player might grip a basketball.

Cruik's skull was now totally exposed and the dwarf swore he could feel his brain trembling.

When a dwarf finds himself unnerved to this extent, one of two things is likely to happen. One: the dwarf will unhook his jaw and attempt to eat its way out of trouble. This option was not available to Cruik because of his suit's hood. And two: the terrified dwarf will *trim the weight*. Trimming the weight is an aviators' trick, which involves jettisoning as much unnecessary cargo as possible to keep the ship in the air. Dwarfs are capable of shedding up to a third of their bodyweight in less than five seconds. This is obviously a last resort and can only be performed once a decade or so. It involves a rapid expulsion of loose-layered *runny fat*, ingested mining dirt and gases through what dwarf mummies politely refer to as the nether tunnel.

Trimming the weight is mostly an automatic response and will be engaged when the heart rate nudges past two hundred beats per minute, which happened to Cruik the moment Butler enquired whether Cruik had tried to shoot his sister. At that moment, Cruik more or less lost control of his bodily functions and had just time to scream '*No brain biting!*' before his body decided to trim the weight and use the resulting propulsion to get the heck out of there.

Of course, Butler was not aware of these biological details.

All he knew was that he was suddenly flying backwards, up high through the air, holding on to a jet-powered dwarf.

Not again, he thought, possibly the only human who would have this thought in this situation.

Butler saw Juliet shrinking into the distance, her mouth a shocked dark circle. And to Juliet it seemed as though her brother had suddenly developed the power of flight while wrestling a dwarf clad in a shiny hooded leotard.

I'll worry about Juliet worrying about me later, thought Butler, trying not to think about the glossy, bubbled stream pushing them further into the sky and closer to whatever craft they were suspended from. *Look out below.*

Butler had a more urgent problem than Juliet worrying about him, which he realized upon jamming Cruik's helmet on to his own head. He and Cruik were coming up on the gyro fast with no control over their approach. All Cruik could do was yell something about his brain, so it was up to Butler to see them through this alive. Altitude wasn't the problem. They weren't high enough to sustain any real damage, especially with a watery mattress below. The problem was the gyro's rotor blade, which would slice them both into fine strips if they passed through it, then doubtless the gyrocopter would explode and incinerate the slices. The engine was whisper quiet but a couple of bodies passing through the blade would soon blow the mufflers.

My last act on Earth could be to expose the fairy People and there is nothing I can do to prevent it.

Up they went, whooshing backwards, wind snagging their

clothes, chilling their skin. The dwarf's eyes were wide and rolling and his flesh hung in loose flaps.

He was chubby before. I'm sure of it.

The gyro blade was metres away as they whiplashed over the top of the craft and hung suspended for a nanosecond as Cruik finally ran out of nether-tunnel steam.

'Nice timing,' snarled Butler, then down they went directly towards the rotors.

Still, thought Butler. *Killed saving my sister from a murderous dwarf. It could be worse.*

At the last possible moment, the gyro's rotor swivelled ninety degrees, tilting the craft dramatically, allowing Butler and Cruik to slot into it neatly on the leeward side.

Butler barely had a moment to thank his lucky stars when he was thrust into yet another perilous situation.

There seemed to be some serious in-fighting going on among an entire dwarf gang. The passenger bay was littered with unconscious fairies while the three remaining dwarfs were slugging it out, two against one. The *one* had a bloody nose and a sooty star on his shoulder where someone had tagged him with a Neutrino, but still he seemed quite cheery.

'It's about time you got here,' he said to Butler from the side of his mouth. 'These guys are quite angry that I flipped their gyro.'

'Tombstone, you collaborator!' howled one of the remaining dwarfs.

'Tombstone?' said Butler, managing to groan and speak at the same time.

'Yeah,' said Butler's old friend Mulch Diggums. 'It's my *out-and-about* name. And lucky for you I do go out.'

The gyro's stabilizers steadied the craft and Butler took advantage of the moment's peace to disentangle himself from Cruik, whom he tossed out of the bay door.

'Ah, Cruik,' said Mulch. 'Rarely does one meet someone with such a phonetically appropriate name.'

Butler wasn't even listening. If there were a time to engage with Mulch's ramblings, he hadn't reached it yet. Instead he turned to the remaining hostile dwarfs.

'You two,' he said, treating them to his fiercest expression, an expression which had once made a troll think that maybe he had bitten off a little more than he could chew.

The two in question quailed under Butler's gaze and wondered anxiously what this giant would order them to do.

Butler jerked a thumb towards the bay door.

'Jump,' he said, keeping it simple.

The dwarfs looked at each other and the look spoke volumes.

Should we actually jump into daylight, thought the dwarfs, *or should we stay and fight this terrifying man-mountain?*

They held hands and jumped.

It took mere moments for Mulch to get control of the flight systems and drop the gyro down to scoop up Juliet.

'Hi ho, Jade Princess,' he called from the pilot's chair. 'How's the wrestling career going? I have an alter ego now too. Tombstone, they call me. What do you think?'

'I like it,' said Juliet, kissing Mulch's cheek. 'Thanks for rescuing us.'

Mulch smiled. 'There was nothing on the TV. Except pay-per-view and I refuse to buy programmes, on principle. Except that chef guy with the foul mouth. I love him and what he can do with a turkey crown and a couple of string beans.'

Juliet's newfound memories reminded her of Mulch's obsession with food.

'So you just happened to be in a bar when the call came in to these guys?' said Butler doubtfully, throwing some emergency field packs to the stranded dwarfs below.

Mulch tugged the virtual joystick, quickly pulling the gyro into the clouds.

'Yes. It's fate, my friends. I went against my own kind for you. I hope you appreciate it. Or rather I hope your rich master appreciates it.'

Butler closed the hatch, shutting out the rush of air. 'The way I remember it, I did most of the saving.'

'All you did was mess up my plan,' snorted the dwarf. 'I was going to let them stun you both, winch you aboard and then make my move.'

'Brilliant plan.'

'As opposed to throwing yourself into the gyro rotor blade?'

'Point taken.'

There was silence for a moment, the kind of silence you would definitely not get in a human flying machine. Also the kind of silence you get when a small group of people wonder just how long they can keep emerging from certain death situations with a reasonable amount of life in their bodies.

'We're off again, I suppose?' said Mulch eventually. 'Off on another save-the-world, nick-of-time, seat-of-the-pants adventure?'

'Well, in the space of one night we have been attacked by zombie wrestling fans and invisible dwarfs,' said Butler glumly. 'So it certainly looks like it.'

'Where to?' asked Mulch. 'Nowhere too sunny, I hope. Or too cold. I hate snow.'

Butler found that he was smiling, not with fondness exactly, but not with wolfish menace either.

'Iceland,' he said.

The gyro dipped sharply as Mulch momentarily let go of the v-joystick. 'If you're kidding, Butler, that's not funny.'

Butler's smile disappeared. 'No,' he said. 'It isn't.'

CHAPTER 7: HOW DO I LOVE THEE?

 ORION Fowl chose to strap himself into the emergency evac harness directly behind Holly and spoke into her ear as she piloted the escape pod through the glacial wormhole excavated by the rogue probe.

Having a person talk directly into one's ear is irritating at the best of times, but when that person is spouting romantic nonsense while the owner of the ear is attempting to wrestle with the controls of a twenty-year-old escape pod in a high-speed pursuit, then it's a little more than annoying – it's dangerously distracting.

Holly scrubbed the porthole with the sleeve of her suit. Outside a single nose beam picked out the wormhole's path.

Straight, she thought. *At least it's straight.*

'How do I love thee?' wondered Orion. 'Let me see. I love

thee passionately and eternally . . . obviously eternally – that goes without saying.'

Holly blinked sweat from her eyes. 'Is he serious?' she called over her shoulder to Foaly.

'Oh, absolutely,' said the centaur, his voice juddering along with the pod's motion. 'If he asks you to look for birthmarks, say *no* immediately.'

'Oh, I would never,' Orion assured her. 'Ladies don't look for birthmarks; that is work for jolly fellows, like the goodly beast and myself. Ladies, like Miss Short, do enough by simply existing. They exude beauty and that is enough.'

'I am not exuding anything,' said Holly, through gritted teeth.

Orion tapped her shoulder. 'I beg to differ. You're *exuding* right now, a wonderful aura. It's pastel blue with little dolphins.'

Holly gripped the wheel tightly. 'I'm going to be sick. Did he just say pastel blue?'

'And dolphins, little ones,' said Foaly, happy enough to be distracted from the fact that they were now chasing the probe that had blown up their shuttle, which was a bit like a mouse chasing a cat, a giant mutant cat with laser eyes and a belly-ful of smaller spiteful cats.

'Be quiet, *goodly beast*. Be quiet, both of you.'

Holly could not afford to be distracted, so to shut out the babbling Orion, she talked herself through what she was doing, recording it all on the ship's log.

'Still going through the ice, an incredibly thick vein. No radar, or sonar, just following the lights.'

•◈⬡◐)⚙◉⧉•)⬦⬡∆⫯•)∪⬟)⬀⬡⬢⌒⫯⟶•

The lightshow on display through the porthole was both eerie and colourful. The probe's engines shot beams along the carved ice, sending rainbows flickering across the flat planes. Holly was sure she saw an entire school of whales preserved in the glacier, and maybe some kind of enormous sea reptile.

'The probe maintains its course, a diagonal descent. We are transitioning from ice to rock now with no discernible delay.'

It was true; the increased density seemed to have no effect on the probe's laser cutters.

Foaly could not resist a smug comment. 'I know how to build 'em,' he said.

'But not how to control 'em,' Holly rejoined.

'You have displeased the princess,' cried Orion, thrashing in his harness. 'Were it not for these accursed bonds . . .'

'You would be dead,' said Foaly, completing the sentence for him.

'Good point,' Orion conceded. 'And the princess is calm now, so no harm done, goodly fellow. I must mind my knight's temper. Sometimes I rush to battle.'

Holly's ears itched, which was purely from stress, she knew, but that didn't stop them itching.

'We need to cure Artemis,' she said, wishing for a free hand to scratch. 'I can't take much more of this.'

The rock face flashed by outside in a confusing meld of greys and deep blue. Ash, pulverized stone and chunks of debris spiralled down the tunnel wall, further impairing Holly's vision.

She checked the escape pod's communications station without much hope.

'Nothing. No contact with Haven; we're still blocked. The probe must have seen us by now. Why no aggressive action?'

Foaly squirmed in a harness built for two-legged creatures. 'Oh yes, why no aggressive action? How I long for aggressive action.'

'I live for aggressive action!' thundered Orion squeakily, which was unusual. 'Oh, how I pray that dragon will turn round that I may smite it.'

'Smite it with what?' wondered Foaly. 'Your secret birthmark?'

'Don't you mock my birthmark, which I may or may not have.'

'Shut up, both of you,' snapped Holly. 'The light's changed. Something is coming.'

Foaly smooshed his cheek against the rear porthole. 'Ah yes. I expected that.'

'What did you expect?'

'Well, we must be below sea level by now, so what's coming would be a great big bit of ocean. Now we'll see just how well I did design that probe.'

The light bouncing off the tunnel wall had suddenly become dull and flickering and a huge booming *whoomph* vibrated through the pod's walls. Even Orion was struck dumb as a solid tube of water surged upwards towards them.

Holly knew from her training that she should relax her

muscles and ride the impact, but every cell in her body wanted to tense up before contact.

Keep the nose straight, she told herself. *Cut through the surface. Underneath is calm.*

The water closed around them like a malevolent fist and shook the pod, battering its occupants. Everything that was not bolted down became a missile. A toolbox gave Foaly a nasty welt and Orion's forehead was punctured by a fork that left tiny wounds where it had struck.

Holly swore like a sailor as she battled to keep the nose down, fighting the fury of nature, talking to the pod as though it were an unbroken bronco. A rivet pinged from its housing and ricocheted around the cabin, knocking a sliver from the viewscreen, sending a web of shining cracks crackling across the glass.

Holly winced. 'D'Arvit. Not good. Not good.'

Orion placed a hand on her shoulder. 'At least we take the great adventure together, eh, maiden?'

'Not just yet, we don't,' Holly said, levelling out the rear flaps and punching the craft through the turmoil into the wide, calm ocean.

The viewscreen held, for the moment, and Holly glared through it, searching for the probe's telltale engine glare. For several moments she saw nothing out of place in the Atlantic Ocean, but then south-south-west, down ten fathoms or so, she noticed four glowing blue discs.

'There!' she cried. 'I see it.'

'Shouldn't we head for the nearest shuttle port?' wondered Foaly. 'Try to make contact with Haven?'

'No,' replied Holly. 'We need to maintain a visual and try to work out where this thing is going. If we lose it, then thanks to *your* stealth ore, it's lost, with plenty of water to hide in.'

'That's another jibe, young lady,' said Foaly sulkily. 'Don't think I'm not counting.'

'Counting,' said Orion. 'Artemis used to do that.'

'I wish we had Artemis now,' said Holly grimly. 'Fives and all. He would know what to do.'

Orion pouted. 'But you have me. I can help.'

'Let me guess. Bivouac?' Orion's face was so desolate that Holly relented. 'OK. Listen, Orion, if you really want to help, keep an eye on the coms screen. If we get a signal, let me know.'

'I shall not fail you, fair maiden,' vowed Orion. 'This coms screen is now my holy grail. I shall wish a signal from its cold heart of wire and capacitors.'

Foaly was about to interject and explain how the communications screen had neither wires nor capacitors, but when he saw the poisonous look Holly was shooting him the centaur decided to keep his mouth closed.

'And you,' said Holly, in a tone to match her look, 'try to figure out how the great Foaly was circumvented so completely, and maybe then we can get control of that probe before anyone else gets hurt.'

That's another jibe, thought Foaly, but he was wise enough not to say this aloud.

*

Down and down they went into deeper and darker blue. The probe stuck rigidly to its course, turning aside for neither rock nor reef, seemingly unaware of the tiny escape pod on its tail.

They must see us, thought Holly, pushing the pod to its limits just to keep up. But if the probe had spotted them it gave no sign, just ploughed through the ocean at a constant rate of knots, unswervingly drawing closer to its goal, wherever that was.

Holly had a thought. 'Foaly. You have a communicator, don't you?'

The centaur was sweating in the oxygen-depleted atmosphere, light blue shirt now mostly dark blue. 'Of course I do. I already checked for a signal. Nothing.'

'I know, but what kind of mini-programs do you have on there? Anything for navigation?'

Foaly pulled out his phone and scrolled through the mini-programs. 'I do have a nav mi-p. All self-contained, no signal needed.' The centaur did not need to be told what to do; he unstrapped himself from the harness and laid his phone on an omni-sensor on the dash. Its screen was instantly displayed on a small screen in the porthole.

A 3D compass appeared, and spent a few seconds plotting the pod's movements, which Holly made sure were mirroring the probe's course.

'OK,' said the centaur. 'We are locked in. I designed this mi-p, by the way. I earn more from this little wonder than all my LEP work.'

'Just tell me.'

Foaly dragged a little ship icon along its straight line on the screen until it reached the ocean floor. There was a pulsing red circle at the point of impact.

'That circle is pretty,' said Orion.

'Not for long,' said Foaly, paling.

Holly took her eyes off the probe for half a second. 'Tell me, Foaly. What's down there?'

The centaur suddenly felt the full weight of his responsibility. Something he had been repressing since the probe's . . . *his* probe's attack.

'Atlantis. My gods, Holly, the probe is headed directly for Atlantis.'

Holly's eyes swivelled back to the four circles of light. 'Can it break through the dome?'

'That's not what it was designed to do.'

Holly gave him a moment to think about what he had just said.

'OK, I admit it's doing a lot of things it wasn't designed to do.'

'Well, then?'

Foaly made a few calculations on the screen, calculations that Artemis might have understood had he been present.

'It's possible,' he said. 'Nothing of the probe would remain intact. But at this speed it might put a crack in the dome.'

Holly coaxed a little more speed from the pod. 'We need to warn Atlantis. Orion, do we have anything on the communications?'

The pod's human passenger looked up from the screen. 'Not a twitter, princess, but *this* light is flashing rather urgently. Does it have a special significance?'

Foaly peered over his shoulder. 'The hull must have been breached in the tunnel. We're running out of oxygen.'

For a second Holly's shoulders slumped. 'It doesn't matter. We keep going.'

Foaly cupped both hands around his cranium, holding in the thoughts. 'No. Now we try to get outside the probe's jamming corona. We should run for the surface.'

'What if it changes course?'

'Then it won't hit Atlantis and nobody will drown or be crushed. And even if it does swing back round they'll be ready for it.'

It went against Holly's instincts to run. 'I feel like we're deserting those people down there.'

Foaly pointed at the screen. 'At that speed, the probe will reach Atlantis in three hours. We'll run out of oxygen in five minutes. We'll be unconscious in six, dead in twelve, and no use to anybody.'

'I feel a little dizzy,' said Orion. 'But also wonderfully elated. I feel that I am on the verge of finding a rhyme for the word "orange".'

'Oxygen deprivation,' said Foaly. 'Or perhaps it's just him.'

Holly closed down the throttle. 'Can we make it?'

Foaly tapped out a complicated equation. 'If we go in the opposite direction right now. Maybe. If whoever is doing this has somehow boosted the jammer, then no.'

•◈▣◻•◈⅋•◭◙♦•◻▥•⧓◊⚮⅃⅃⚮•⊙◈⬡•◭♭•◈

'Maybe is the best you can do?'

Foaly nodded wearily. 'The absolute best.'

Holly swung the pod round with three deft manoeuvres. 'Best odds I've had all day,' she said.

It was a race now, but an unusual one where the competitors were running away from each other. The goal was simple: now that they knew where the probe was headed, Holly had six minutes to pilot the pod out of the jamming corona. Also it would be nice to have some oxygen to breathe. Luckily the probe was on a steep descent so the pod should go on a steep ascent. If they managed to break the surface before the six minutes ran out, then brilliant. They'd broadcast until Haven picked up the signal. If not, then the pod wasn't equipped with automatic pilot or broadcast facilities so the probe would be on top of the Atlantis security towers before they even noticed it, and another little negative was that they would be dead.

It's funny, thought Holly. *I don't think my heart rate is up that much. These life-or-death situations have become almost normal for me ever since meeting Artemis Fowl.*

She glanced sideways at the romantic who was wearing Artemis's face, and he caught the look.

'Penny for your thoughts, princess. Though they are worth a king's ransom.'

'I was wishing that you would go away,' said Holly bluntly. 'And return Artemis to us. We need him.'

Orion hmmed. 'That thought is not as valuable as I had

imagined. Why do you want Artemis back? He is nasty and mean to everyone.'

'Because Artemis could get us out of this alive and save the people of Atlantis and possibly find out who murdered all those LEP officers.'

'I grant you that,' said Orion, miffed. 'But his sonnets are heartless and that opera house he designed was totally self-indulgent.'

'Yep, that's what we need now,' Foaly chimed in. 'Opera-house designing skills.'

'Oh yes, traitorous steed,' said Orion testily. 'Probe-designing skills would be much more useful.'

Holly sounded a quick burst on the klaxon for attention. 'Excuse me, gentlemen. All this arguing is consuming oxygen, so could we all *please* be quiet?'

'Is that a command, beloved?'

'Yes,' whispered Holly ominously. 'It is.'

'Very well. Then quiet it shall be. I would rather cut out my own tongue than utter one more word. I would sooner behead myself with a butter knife than speak a single –'

Holly gave in to a baser instinct and jabbed Orion in the solar plexus.

That was wrong, she thought to herself as the boy drooped in his harness, gasping for breath. *I am going to feel guilty about that later.*

If there was a later.

There was plenty of power in the fuel block, just no air in the tanks and no recycling facility to scrub the carbon dioxide from the exhaled air. The pod was supposed to be a short-term option only. It hadn't been designed for actual missions; the hull could crack under the pressure of steep ascent long before the fuel ran out.

So many ways to die, thought Holly. *Eventually one of them is going to get us.*

The digital depth gauge was spinning backwards from 10,000 metres. They were in an Atlantic trench, never before seen by human eyes. Shoals of strange luminous fish swarmed around them, easily keeping pace, butting the hull with the fleshy glowing bulbs in their transparent bellies.

Then the light changed and the fish were gone, darting away so quickly it was as though they had simply dematerialized. In their place were seals and whales and fish like silver arrowheads. A chunk of blue ice rolled past and Holly saw her mother's face in its planes and shadows.

Oxygen deprivation, she told herself. *That's all it is.*

'How long?' she asked Foaly.

The centaur checked the oxygen levels. 'Based on three conscious beings, nervous conscious beings I might add, rapidly consuming the air, we're going to be short a minute or two.'

'You said we could make it!'

'The hole in the tank is expanding.'

Holly beat her fist on the dash. 'D'Arvit, Foaly. Why does it always have to be so hard?'

Foaly spoke calmly. 'Holly, my friend. You know what you have to do.'

'No, Foaly. I don't.'

'Yes, you do.'

Holly did know. There were three conscious people breathing hard. Foaly alone took in more oxygen than a bull troll. It only took one person to steer the ship and send the message.

It was a tough choice, but there was no time to agonize over it. She felt for a squat metal cylinder in one of the rings on her belt and pulled it out.

'What's that, sweetness?' asked Orion, who had just recovered from the belly jab.

Holly answered the question with one of her own. 'Would you do anything for me, Orion?'

The boy's face seemed to light up. 'Of course. Absolutely anything.'

'Close your eyes and count to ten.'

Orion was disappointed. 'What? No tasks? Not even a dragon to slay?'

'Close your eyes if you love me.'

Orion did so immediately and Holly prodded him in the neck with a battery-powered Shokker. The electrocuted boy slumped in the harness, two electrode burns smoking gently on his neck.

'Nicely done,' said Foaly nervously. 'Not in the neck for me if you don't mind.'

Holly checked the Shokker. 'Don't worry. I only had enough charge for one.'

Foaly could not suppress a sigh of relief and when he glanced guiltily across at Orion, knowing that really he should be the unconscious one, Holly hit him in the flank with the second charge.

Foaly did not even have time to think *you sneaky elf* before slumping in the corner.

'Sorry, guys,' said Holly, then made a silent vow not to speak again until it was time to send the message.

The pod powered towards the surface, its prow slicing through the water. Holly steered through a vast underwater canyon which had developed its own ecology completely safe from human exploitation. She saw huge undulating eels that could crush a bus, strange crabs with glowing shells and some kind of two-legged creature that disappeared into a crevice before she could get a proper look at it.

She took the most direct line she could through the canyon, finding a rock chimney that allowed her to exit into open sea.

There was still nothing on the communications array. Solidly blocked. She needed to get further away.

I could really do with some warlock magic right now, Holly thought. *If Number One were here he could wiggle his runes and turn carbon dioxide into oxygen.*

Water, fish and bubbles flashed past the window and could that be a shaft of light from the surface? Had the craft reached the photic zone?

Holly tried the radio again. She heard static this time, but maybe with some chatter inside it.

Good, she thought, but her head was fuzzy. *Did I imagine that?*

No, you heard it all right, said the unconscious Foaly. *Did I ever tell you about my kids?*

Oxygen deprivation. That's all it was.

Why did you shoot me, sweetness? wondered passed-out Orion. *Did I displease you?*

It's too late. Too late.

Holly was shaking now. She filled her lungs but was not satisfied with the foul air. The pod walls became suddenly concave, bending in to crush her.

'It's not happening,' she called, breaking her vow of silence.

She checked the coms again. Some signal now. There were definitely words among the static.

Enough to transmit?

One way to find out.

Holly tapped through her options on the dashboard read-out and selected TRANSMIT only to be informed that the external antenna was not available. The computer advised her to check the connection. Holly pressed her face to the starboard porthole and saw that the connection was pretty well defunct as the entire thing had been knocked out of its housing by one impact or another.

Why doesn't this tug-bucket, stone-age piece of junk have an internal antenna? Even glooping phones have internal antennae.

Phones! Of course.

Holly punched the harness-release button on her chest and dropped to her knees. She slid along the deck, moving towards Foaly.

It smells bad down here. Stale air.

For a second one of the handrails grew a snake's head and hissed at her.

Your time is running out, it said. *Your odds are short, Short.*

Don't listen to the snake, said Foaly, without moving his lips. *He's just bitter because his soul is stuck in a handrail because of some stuff that happened in a previous life.*

I still love you, said sleeping Orion, breathing slow and steady, using hardly any oxygen.

I am really going insane this time, thought Holly.

Holly pulled herself along Foaly's frame, reaching into his shirt pocket for his phone. The centaur never went anywhere without his precious phone and was proud of its modified clunkiness.

I love that phone, said Foaly proudly. *Over five hundred mi-p's. All my own design. I did a nice one called Offspring. Say you find the love of your life, all you need to do is take a photo of you and your beloved, and Offspring will show you what your potential kids will look like.*

Fascinating. I hope we get to talk about it for real sometime.

The phone was switched on, so there was no need for a password, although knowing Foaly as she did Holly supposed that his password would be some version of his own name. His screen was a crazy jumble of mi-p's that probably made sense if you were a centaur.

The problem with all these applications is that sometimes a person just wants to make a quick call. Where's the phone icon?

Then the icons started waving at her.

) ᴖ ✦ • ᴙ • ⬡) ᴃ ⍑ (☎ ⬡ ᴃ ᴥ ✦ •) (▢ ᴙ) ᴖ • ◉ •

'Pick me,' they chorused. 'Over here.'

That's not a hallucination, said passed-out Foaly proudly. *Those little guys are animated.*

'Phone,' Holly shouted into the communicator's microphone, hoping for voice control. To her relief a blurry old-fashioned cone phone icon expanded to fill the screen.

It's not actually blurry. My eyesight's fading.

'Call Police Plaza,' she ordered the icon.

The phone ticked for a minute then asked, 'Do you wish to call Phil's Pizza?'

'No. Call Police Plaza.'

The water rushing by was definitely more azure now, shot through with bubbles and bending streaks of light.

'Do you wish to call Police Plaza?'

'Yes,' gasped Holly. 'Yes, I do.'

There was more jostling as the pod passed through the surface disturbance and was flipped by the waves.

'Connecting you with Police Plaza.'

The phone hummed gently as it tried to connect, then said in a comically sad voice: 'Boo hoo. You don't have a strong enough signal. Would you like to record a message for me to send just as soon as the signal is strong enough?'

'Yes,' croaked Holly.

'Did you say *yikes*? Because *yikes* is not an appropriate response in this situation.'

Holly composed herself. 'Yes. I would like to compose a message.'

'Great,' said the phone brightly. 'Start recording after the bell, and remember good manners don't cost anything, so always introduce yourself and say goodbye.'

Say goodbye, thought Holly. *Funny.*

Holly recorded a concise message containing as few coughs and splutters as possible, identifying herself as the phone had suggested and also identifying the threat heading towards Atlantis. Almost as soon as she had finished, Holly collapsed on her back, flopping weakly like a stranded fish. There were spots before her eyes, which grew larger and became pale circles, crowding together, obscuring her vision.

She did not see the colours outside the porthole change from blue to green to the dull, pearlescent white of a northern sky.

She did not hear the pressure vents pop or feel cool air flooding the cabin, and Captain Holly Short did not know that fifteen minutes after the pod surfaced her message to Police Plaza would finally be transmitted and be acted upon almost immediately.

It would have been acted upon immediately had not the sprite on the switchboard, a certain Chix Verbil, initially believed that the message was a prank call from his poker buddy, Crooz, made to make fun of his nasally voice. Chix only decided to pass the message on to Commander Trouble Kelp when it occurred to him that there could be a career downside to ignoring the warning that could have saved Atlantis.

Trouble Kelp held an emergency video conference with

the People's Council and an evacuation was immediately approved.

THE DEEPS, ATLANTIS, NOW

Turnball Root was busy pretending to be busy working on his model of the *Nostremius* aquanaut, so that he would appear all the more innocent when they came to get him, which he was certain they would very shortly.

Pretending to be busy takes more energy than simply being busy, Turnball realized, and this cheered him tremendously, as it was a witty observation and just the kind of thing that his eventual biographers would pick up on. But witty observations must now take a back seat to the plan. After all, witty observations would be far more enjoyable when he had someone else besides Vishby to listen to them. Leonor adored his little comments and often wrote them in her diary. Turnball's eyes lost their focus and his hands froze in space as he remembered their first summer together on that beautiful island in the Pacific. She, boyish in her vest and jodhpurs, he handsome and rakish in his LEP dress jacket.

'This can never work, Captain. How can it possibly work? I am human after all and you are most certainly not.'

And quick as a flash he had taken her hands in his and said: 'Love can break down any barriers. Love and magic.'

That was when he had made her love him.

Leonor had jumped a little but not removed her hands.

'I felt a spark, Turnball,' she had said.

He joked, 'I felt it too,' then explained, 'Static electricity, that always happens to me.'

Leonor believed it and fell for her captain.

She would have loved me soon enough, anyway, *thought Turnball crossly.* I simply hurried the process.

But he knew in his heart that he had bolstered Leonor's emotions with magic, and now that she was so far beyond her natural end his hold on her was slipping.

Without magic, will she love me as I love her? *he wondered a thousand times a day, and knew that he was terrified to find out.*

To keep his vital signs steady, Turnball turned his thoughts once more to his thrall, Mister Vishby.

Vishby was undeniably a repulsive dolt, and yet Turnball Root had a soft spot for the lad and would perhaps even decide to let him live when this was all over, or at least kill him quickly.

Of all the great schemes and impossible heists that Turnball had been involved in as a crooked cop, fugitive or inmate, the simple-sounding act of turning Vishby had been the most ambitious. It had required perfect timing, audacity and months of grooming. Turnball often thought of this plan which he had set into motion almost four years previously . . .

It wasn't as if Vishby were a human with an already treacherous and self-serving nature. Vishby was a fairy and most fairies, with the exception of goblins, were just not inclined towards the criminal life. Common lawbreakers, like that Diggums character, were common enough, but intelligent, foresighted criminals were rare.

Vishby's downfall was that he was a moaner, and as the months had rolled by he'd gradually let down his guard with Turnball Root and told him all about his demotion following Mulch Diggums's escape. He also expressed a bitterness towards the LEP for the reprimand and wished he could do something to get back at them.

Turnball saw his chance – his first real chance of escape since his arrest. He'd formulated a plan to recruit Vishby.

The first stage was to feign sympathy for the water elf, whereas in reality, had he been in charge, he would have flushed him out of an airlock for his performance in the Diggums episode.

I so enjoy our chats, he had said. *How I wish we could talk more freely.*

Vishby had clammed up immediately, remembering that every word was on tape.

On his next visit, Vishby had entered with a smug tilt to his fishy head and Turnball knew his plan would succeed.

I switched off your mike, the prison warder had said. *Now we can talk about whatever we like.*

And then Turnball knew that he had him. All it would take was a little Turnball Root magic to make Vishby his slave.

Except that Turnball Root didn't have magic. That was the one irrevocable price that criminals paid: loss of magic, forever. This was one forfeit that there was no coming back from, and exiled criminals had been trying for centuries. They bought potions, tried spells, chanted in the moonlight, slept upside down, bathed in centaur dung. Nothing worked.

Once you had broken the fairy rules, your magic was gone. It was partly a psychological thing, but mostly it was the result of age-old warlock hexes that successive administrations did not feel like unlocking.

This denial of his basic fairy rights had always irked Turnball, and during his years as a fugitive he had spent a fortune on dozens of witchdoctors and quacks who all claimed they could have him running hot, brimful of magic, if only he would take this potion or recite that spell backwards in the dead of night while holding a grumpy frog. Nothing worked. Nothing until, a century ago, Turnball found an exiled sprite living in Ho Chi Min City who had somehow managed to maintain a tiny spark of power, just enough to remove the occasional wart. For a huge price, which Turnball would have paid a million times over, she revealed her secret:

Mandrake root and rice wine. It won't bring the sweet magic back, Captain, but each time you partake of these two, they'll give you a spark. One hot spark at a time and that is all. Use this little trick wisely, my Captain, or the spark won't be there when you most need it.

This pearl from an alcoholic sprite.

It was a trick he'd used in the past, but not since his arrest. Until now. And so for his birthday that year Turnball had requested a dinner of puffer fish with fo-fo berries and mandrake shavings, followed by a carafe of rice wine and sim-coffee. This request was accompanied by the revelation of the whereabouts of a notorious group of arms smugglers, which would be quite a feather in the warden's cap. Tarpon

Vinyáya agreed to the request. When Vishby arrived with the meal, Turnball invited him to stay and talk. And while they chatted, Turnball picked at his meal, eating only the mandrake shavings and drinking only the wine, all the time subtly reinforcing Vishby's opinion of the LEP.

Yes, my dear Vishby, they are unfeeling louts. I mean, what were you to do? That thug Diggums left you no option but to flee.

And when the moment was right, when Turnball felt a single spark of magic coalesce in his gut, he rested his hand lightly on Vishby's shoulder, allowing his little finger to touch the water elf's bare neck.

Usually neck touching is no big deal. Wars have rarely been fought over a neck touch, but this touch was malicious. For on the pad of his finger, Turnball had painted, in his own blood, a black-magic thrall rune. Turnball was a great believer in runes. Ideally, for maximum effectiveness, the person having the spell cast on them would be spread-eagled on a granite plinth, doused in oil fermented from the tears of unicorns and tattooed from head to foot with symbols, and then given at least three minutes of magic full in the face, but you make do with what you have and hope for the best.

So Turnball touched Vishby on the neck and transferred his single spark of magic through the contact.

Vishby slapped his neck as if stung. 'Ow! Hey, what was that? I felt a spark, Turnball.'

Turnball quickly withdrew his hand. 'Static electricity. That always happens around me. My mother was afraid to kiss me. Here, Vishby, have some of this wine, to make up for the shock.'

Vishby eyed the contents of the carafe greedily. Alcoholic beverages were not usually allowed in the prison, as with prolonged use it causes the magical receptors to atrophy. But some fairies, much like humans, cannot resist what is bad for them.

'I'm your fairy,' he said, eagerly accepting a cup.

Yes, Turnball thought. *Yes, you are now.*

Turnball knew it would work. It had before, on stronger minds than Vishby's.

And so Vishby found that he could never say no to Turnball Root. It started out with simple harmless requests: an extra blanket, some reading material not in the prison system. But soon Vishby found himself inextricably bound up in Turnball's escape plans, and, what was more, he didn't seem to mind being involved. It seemed the sensible thing to do.

Over the following four years Vishby had gone from guard to accomplice. He had made contact with several inmates who were still loyal to Turnball and prepared them for the great escape. He made several raids on what was then Koboi Laboratories and used his security code to access their sensitive recycling plant, where he found among other things the scrambler wafer and the infinitely more valuable control orb for the Mars probe. Somewhere in the back of his mind Vishby knew that eventually someone would find out about these thefts, but he couldn't seem to make himself care.

Most of what he had found at Koboi Labs was of absolutely no use or was too far gone to be fixed, but the control orb needed only a slight descaling and the insertion of a new omni-sensor. These were such simple tasks that Turnball had Vishby do them at home, with a little web-cam supervision, naturally.

Once he had a working original control orb in his possession, it was a relatively simple matter for Turnball to sync with the Mars probe before take-off and begin the arduous task of reprogramming its mission parameters. This was not a task he could complete before the spacecraft actually left the Earth, but off the top of his head he could think of a dozen ways a rogue spaceship might prove useful. But not on Mars.

Mars? Oh no, no, Leonor. That's too far away and of no use to me. Let's wait until it takes off on its mission and then turn this big fellow round.

His original plan for the probe had been simplicity itself: use it as a very big and very loud distraction on its return from Mars. But, as Leonor's communications became terser and somehow colder, Turnball realized that he would have to accelerate his schedule and refine his plot. It was vital that he escape, but it was even more important that he strengthen his hold over Leonor before her humanity completely reasserted itself. Her ageing was now so rapid that it would take some very special magic to reverse it. And there was only one place to get such magic. If Julius had been alive, Turnball would have worried about his little brother tumbling to his deception, but even with Julius gone there was still the entire

LEP to worry about. He needed to damage the force, cut off the head of the snake and maybe its tail too.

And so Turnball monitored Warden Vinyáya's communications, using the password Vishby had stolen for him. He was especially interested in the calls to the warden's sister, Commander Raine Vinyáya of the LEP.

The snake's head.

Commander Vinyáya was a hard fairy to kill, especially if your weapon was a blunt instrument in space, and the commander seemed reluctant to go topside where she was vulnerable.

And then, only last month, she had made a video call to her brother informing him, in giddy tones that she would never allow anyone else to hear, of her trip to Iceland to meet the Mud Whelp Artemis Fowl. Apparently the boy was planning to save the world.

The infamous Artemis Fowl, Commander Vinyáya and Holly Short too, together in one place. Perfect.

Turnball activated his control orb and fed an entirely new set of mission parameters to the Mars probe, parameters which the probe never even questioned because they came from its own orb. To paraphrase: come back to Earth and crush the commander and as many of her elite team as possible. Crush them, then burn them, then electrocute the cinders.

What fun.

Then there was Artemis Fowl. He had heard of the boy and by all accounts this particular human was a little brighter than most. Better to study up a little just in case the human had a little treachery planned himself. Turnball used the warden's code to access the LEP surveillance feed from more than two hundred camera bugs planted in Fowl Manor and found to his utter delight that Artemis Fowl seemed to be developing Atlantis Complex.

Atlantis is the magic word for this mission, he thought.

Turnball was equally concerned about the Mud Boy's gigantic bodyguard, who seemed just the kind of person to hunt down and kill his master's murderer.

The famous Butler. The man who took down a troll.

Luckily Artemis himself took Butler out of play when his paranoia flared up and he invented a reason to send the bodyguard to Mexico.

Even though it complicated his plans a little, Turnball decided to have a little fun with the Butlers, just to cut off any vengeful loose ends.

I know you would not approve of all these deaths, Leonor, Turnball thought as he sat at his computer, sending instructions through to Vishby's terminal. *But they are necessary if we are to be together forever. Those people are unimportant compared to our eternal love. And you will never know the price of our happiness. All you will know is that we are reunited.*

But in truth Turnball knew that he enjoyed all the machinations tremendously and was almost sorry to send the kill orders. Almost but not quite. Even better than scheming would be all the time to be spent with Leonor and it had been too long since he had seen his wife's beautiful face.

•ᘓᎠᏮ•ᏒᚠᏒᎧᏮᘖᛞ•ᛞᏯ▢•ᘖᎠᎭᎧ•ᏒᏴ

So he'd sent the kill orders to the probe and loaded up on mandrake and rice wine.

Luckily it only took the barest spark of magic to mesmerize humans.

Because they are weak-willed and stupid. But funny, like monkeys.

When Vishby arrived on that final day in prison, Turnball was sitting on his hands, trying hard to contain his excitement.

'Ah, Mister Vishby,' he said when the door dissolved. 'You're early. Is there some irregularity I should be concerned about?'

Vishby's impassive fish face was a little more emotional than usual. 'The warden's sister is dead. Commander Vinyáya and a whole shuttle of LEP blown apart. Did we do that?'

Turnball licked the blood rune on his finger. 'Whether we did or not is unimportant. You shouldn't be concerned.'

Vishby absently fingered his neck, where a faint outline of the rune still glowed. 'I'm not concerned. Why should I be? It was nothing to do with us.'

'Good. Fabulous. I imagine we have bigger fish to fry.'

Vishby flinched at the fish reference.

'Oh. Oops, sorry, Mister Vishby. I should be more sensitive. Come now, tell me, what news?'

Vishby flapped his gills for a moment, getting the sentences together in his head. Captain Root did not like stammering.

'There's a space probe heading directly for Atlantis, so we have to evacuate the city. It's likely that the craft won't actually penetrate the dome, but the Council can't take the chance. I've been called up to pilot a shuttle and you're one of my . . . eh . . . p-passengers.'

Turnball sighed, disappointed. 'Oh . . . p-passengers? Really?'

Vishby rolled his eyes. 'Sorry, Captain. Passengers, of course, one of my passengers.'

'It's so unprofessional, the stammering.'

'I know,' said Vishby. 'I'm working on it. I bought one of those . . . eh . . . au-audio books. I'm nervous now.'

Turnball decided to go easy on Vishby; there would be plenty of time for discipline later when he was killing the water elf. The ultimate punishment.

'It's only natural,' he said magnanimously. 'First day back in the pilot's chair. Then there's this mysterious probe, plus you have to transport all of us dangerous prisoners.'

Vishby seemed even more nervous. 'Exactly. Well, the thing is . . . I don't want to do this, Turnball, but . . .'

'But you have to cuff me,' completed Turnball. 'Of course. I understand completely.' He thrust out his hands with wrists upturned. 'It's not as if you have to fasten the cuffs, is it.'

Vishby blinked and touched his neck. 'No. Why would I fasten them? That would be barbaric.'

The water elf laid a set of standard ultra-light plastic polymer cuffs across Turnball's wrists.

'Comfy?' he asked.

Again, Turnball was feeling generous. 'I'll be fine. Don't worry about me. You concentrate on the shuttle.'

'Thanks, Captain. This is a big day for me.'

⚶⊕☉♊♌•⚭ ☉ ♋☽• ♌♙⚸♖⚭♉♭♄⚶•♄♭♄

As Vishby dissolved the door, Turnball was struck by how the guard's subconscious dealt with betraying all that he believed in. Vishby simply pretended that everything was as it should be, until the moment when it was not. The water elf somehow managed to keep two lives running simultaneously side by side.

Amazing what a person will do to avoid guilt, thought Turnball, following Vishby through the doorway and taking his first breath of free recycled air in years.

Atlantis was small by human standards. With barely ten thousand residents, it wouldn't even qualify as a city to the Mud Men, but to the fairies it was their second centre of government and culture, the first being the capital, Haven City. There was a growing lobby to demolish Atlantis altogether as the upkeep cost a fortune in taxpayers' money and it was only a matter of time before the humans sank one of their submarine drones in the right spot and got a shot of the dome. But the budget for such a massive relocation and demolition project was so huge that continued maintenance always seemed the more attractive option to the politicians. It was more expensive in the long term, but the politicians reasoned that by the time the *long term* came round somebody else would be in office.

Vishby led Turnball Root along a corridor tube with perspex walling through which he could see dozens of craft queuing at the various dome pressure-lock toll gates, waiting to swipe their credit chips for exit. There didn't seem to be any panic. And why would there be? The Atlanteans had been preparing for a dome breach ever since the last one, more than eight thousand years ago, when an asteroid had super-heated a two-mile-long tube of ocean before spending its last gasp of energy knocking a crunchball-sized chunk out of the dome, which in those days had not been shatterproof. In less than an hour the entire city had been submerged with more than five thousand casualties. It had taken a hundred years or so to build the new Atlantis on top of the foundations supplied by the ruins of the old Atlantis and this time an evacuation strategy had featured large in the city blueprints. All of which meant that in case of emergency every male, female and child fairy could be out of the city in less than an hour. Drills were held every week and in nursery school the first rhyme every student learned was:

> The blue dome
> Protects our home;
> If it should crack,
> Prepare for evac.

Turnball Root recalled this ditty as he followed Vishby along the corridor.

Crack, evac? What kind of rhyme was that? Evac wasn't even a real word, just a military contraction. Exactly the kind of word Julius might have used.

I am so glad Leonor never had to endure meeting my boorish brother. If she had, no amount of magical persuasion could have enticed her to marry me.

A part of Turnball knew that he kept Leonor away from the People in general because a ten-minute conversation with any fairy under the world would have shown Leonor that her husband was not quite the noble revolutionary that he pretended to be. Luckily this was a part of himself that Turnball had become quite adept at ignoring.

Other prisoners were shambling from their cells across narrow bridges on to the main walkway. Each was shackled and dressed in a lime-green Deeps prison jumpsuit. Most were laying on the bravado, rolling swaggers and obvious sneers, but Turnball knew from experience that it was the ones with the placid gazes you had to worry about. Those ones were beyond caring.

'Come on now, convicts,' called a particularly Cro-Magnon-looking jumbo pixie, a breed that sometimes popped up in Atlantis due to the pressurized environment. 'Keep moving there. Don't make me buzz you.'

At least I am wearing my full dress uniform, thought Turnball, ignoring the guard, but he did not feel much consoled. Uniform or no, he was being paraded down this walkway like a common prisoner. He soothed himself with the decision that he would definitely kill Vishby as soon as possible and maybe send an e-mail to Leeta, congratulating Vishby's sweetheart on her new single status. She would probably be delighted.

Vishby raised a fist, bringing the procession to a halt at an intersection. The prisoners were forced to wait like cattle while a large metal cube, secured with titanium bands, was floated past them on a hover trolley.

'Opal Koboi,' explained Vishby. 'She's so dangerous they're not even letting her out of her cell.'

Turnball bristled. *Opal Koboi*. People down here spent their days gossiping about Opal Koboi. The current rumour was that there was another Opal Koboi around somewhere who had come out of the past to rescue herself in the present. People might get more done if they stopped obsessing over Opal blooming Koboi. If anyone should be concerned about Koboi, it was him. After all she had murdered his little brother. Then again better not – dwelling on the past could cause his ulcer to return.

It took the cube an age to float by and Turnball counted three doors on the side.

Three doors. My cell has a single door. Why does Koboi need a cell so big that it has three doors?

It didn't matter. He would be out of here soon enough and then he could treat himself like royalty.

Leonor and I shall return to the island where we first met so dramatically.

As soon as the intersection was clear, Vishby led them on towards their shuttle bay. Through the clear plastic, Turnball noticed crowds of civilians walking briskly but without apparent panic towards their own rescue pods. On the upper levels, groups of Atlantis's more affluent citizens strolled to private evacuation shuttles that probably cost more than Turnball could steal in a week.

Ruffles are back in, Turnball noted with some pleasure. *I knew it.*

The corridor opened out into a loading bay where groups of prisoners were waiting impatiently by airlocks which opened directly on to the sea.

'This is all so unnecessary,' said Vishby. 'The water cannons are going to blast this probe thing to smithereens. We'll all be back here in a few minutes.'

Not all of us, thought Turnball, not bothering to conceal a smile. *Some of us are never coming back.*

And he knew in that instant that it was true. Even if his plan failed, he was never coming back here. One way or another, Turnball Root would be free.

Vishby beeped the shuttle door with his keys and the manacled prisoners filed inside. Once they were seated, Vishby activated carnival-ride-style safety bars, which also acted as very effective restraints. The convicts were pinned to their seats and still cuffed. Totally helpless.

'You got 'em, Fishby?' asked the Cro-Magnon pixie.

'Yes, I got 'em. And the name's Vishby!'

Turnball smirked. Office bullying, another reason he had been able to turn Vishby so easily.

'That's what I said, Frisbee. Now, why don't you pilot this bucket out of here and let me keep watch on these scary convicts?'

Vishby bristled. 'Just you wait a minute . . .'

Turnball Root did not have time for a showdown. 'That's an excellent idea, Mister Vishby. You put that pilot's licence to good use and let your colleague here watch over us scary convicts.'

Vishby touched his neck. 'Sure. Why not? I should get us out of here like I'm supposed to.'

'Exactly. You know it makes sense.'

'Go on, Fishboy,' scoffed the big guard, whose name tag had been altered to read K-MAX. 'Do what the convict tells you.'

Vishby sat at the controls and ran a brisk pre-launch, whistling softly through his gills to shut out K-Max's jibes.

This K-Max fellow doesn't realize how much trouble he's in, thought Turnball, the idea pleasing him tremendously. He felt *empowered*.

'Excuse me, Mister K-Max, is it?'

K-Max squinted in what he thought was a threatening fashion, but the actual effect was to make him seem short-sighted and perhaps constipated. 'That's right, prisoner. K to the Max. The king of maximum security.'

'Oh, I see. A sobriquet. How romantic of you.'

K-Max twirled his buzz baton. 'There ain't nothing romantic about me, Root. You ask my three ex-wives. I am here to cause discomfort and that is all.'

'Oops,' said Turnball playfully. 'Sorry I spoke.'

This little exchange gave Vishby a chance to get the shuttle out of the dock and one of the shuttle's other occupants a moment to orientate himself and realize that his old leader was about to make his move. In fact, of the twelve rough and ready specimens locked down behind the shuttle's security bars, ten had served under Turnball at one time or another and most had done very nicely by it, until their capture. Once Vishby had been reactivated, he had easily ensured that these prisoners were allocated seats.

It will be nice for the Captain to have friends around him in a time of crisis, he reasoned.

The most important *friend* was the sprite Unix B'lob who sat directly across the vulcanized walkway from Turnball. Unix was a grounded sprite with cauterized nubs where his wings should be. Turnball had dragged Unix out of a troll pit, and the sprite had served as his right-hand fairy ever since. He was the best kind of lieutenant as he never questioned orders. Unix did not justify or prioritize; he was equally prepared to die fetching Turnball a coffee as he was stealing a nuclear warhead.

Turnball winked at his subordinate to let him know that today was the day. Unix did not react, but then he rarely did, icy indifference being his attitude towards pretty much everything.

Cheer up, Unix, old man, Turnball longed to call. *Death and mayhem will shortly follow.*

But he had to content himself with the wink for the moment.

Vishby was nervous and it showed. The shuttle sputtered forward in lurchy hops, scraping a fender along the docking jetty.

'Nice going, Vishby,' snarled K-Max. 'Are you trying to crush us before the probe does it?'

Vishby flushed, and gripped the rudder stick so tightly his knuckles glowed green.

'It's OK. I've got it now. No problems.'

The shuttle edged from the shelter of the massive curved fins that funnelled the worst of the underwater currents away from the dome and Turnball enjoyed the receding view of new Atlantis. The cityscape was a murky jumble of traditional spires and minarets alongside more modern glass and steel pyramids. Hundreds of slatted filter pods sat at the corners of the giant polymer pentagons that slotted together to form the protective dome over Atlantis.

If the probe hit a filter pod, the dome could go, thought Turnball, and then: *Oh, look, they used schoolchildren's designs to decorate the fins. How fun.*

Out they went, past the water cannons, which were erect in their cradles, just waiting for co-ordinates.

Farewell, my probe, thought Turnball. *You have served me well and I shall miss you.*

A flotilla fled the threatened city: pleasure craft and city shuttles, troop carriers and prisoner transporters, all flitting towards the ten-mile marker where the brainiacs assured them the shockwave would dissipate to the merest ripple. And though the flight seemed chaotic it was not. Each and every craft had a marker to dock with at the ten-mile circle.

Vishby was growing in confidence and quickly navigated the gloomy depths towards their marker only to find a giant squid had latched on to the pulsing buoy, pecking at its glowing beacon.

The water elf turned the shuttle's exhaust on the creature and it scooted off in a flurry of rippling tentacles. Vishby let the auto-dock take over, lowering the shuttle on to its magnetic docking buoy.

K-Max laughed scornfully. 'You shouldn't shoot at your cousins, Fishboy. You won't get invited to family functions.'

Vishby pounded the dash. 'I have had enough of you!'

'Me too,' said Turnball, and reached out, casually pinching K-Max's buzz baton from his belt. He could have shocked the jumbo pixie immediately, but he wanted him to realize what was going on. It took a while.

'Hey,' said K-Max. 'What are you –? You just took my . . .' And then the light-bulb moment. 'You aren't cuffed.'

'What a bright boy,' said Turnball, and thrust the buzz baton into K-Max's gut, sending 10,000 volts crackling through the pixie's body. The guard jittered on point like a possessed classical dancer, then collapsed in a boneless-looking heap.

'You shocked my fellow officer,' said Vishby dully, 'which should upset me, but I am OK with it, more than OK actually, even though you can't tell by my tone of voice.'

Turnball shot Unix another wink that said, *Watch your genius boss at work.*

'You don't need to feel anything, Mr Vishby. All you need to do is release bars three and six.'

'Just three and six? Don't you want to release all your friends? You have been lonely for so long, Turnball.'

Bars three and six popped up and Turnball rose, luxuriously stretching his legs, as though he had been seated for an age.

⑪⑱⑧⑫⑥⑭⑬⑫●⑆⑥●⊕⑦⑨⑯⑬⑤⑧⑥●⑨●⑤⑳⑥●➤

'Not just yet, Mister Vishby. Some of my friends may have forgotten me.'

Unix was also freed and went immediately to work, stripping K-Max of his boots and belt. He shrugged off the top half of his own jumpsuit and tied it off at his waist, so the scar tissue of his wing nubs could get a little air.

Turnball felt a twinge of unease. Unix was a disturbing fellow, loyal unto death, but strange beyond strange. He could have had those wing nubs carved down by a plasti-doc but he preferred to wear them like trophies.

If he ever shows the smallest sign of disloyalty, I will have to put him down like a dog. No hesitation.

'Everything all right, Unix?'

The pale sprite nodded curtly, then continued to frisk K-Max's person.

'Very well,' said Turnball, taking centre stage for his big speech. 'Gentlemen, we are on the brink of what the press often refers to as *an audacious prison break*. Some of us will survive and unfortunately some won't. The good news is that the choice is yours.'

'I choose to survive,' said Ching Mayle, a gruff goblin with bite marks on his skull and muscles up to his ears.

'Not so fast, Mayle. A leap of faith is involved.'

'You can count on me, Captain.'

This from Bobb Ragby, a dwarf fitted with an extra restraint in the form of a mouth ring. He had fought at Turnball's behest in many a skirmish, including the fateful one on the Tern Islands where Julius Root and Holly Short had finally arrested Turnball.

Turnball flicked Bobb's mouth ring, making it ping.

'Can I, Mister Ragby, or has prison made you soft? Do you still have the gumption?'

'Just take this ring off and find out. I will swallow that guard whole.'

'Which guard?' asked Vishby, nervous in spite of the thrall rune that pulsed at his throat.

'Not you, Vishby,' said Turnball soothingly. 'Mister Ragby didn't mean you, did you, Mister Ragby?'

'I did actually.'

Turnball's fingers flew to his mouth. 'How troubling. I am conflicted, Mister Vishby. You have done me no little service, but Bobb Ragby there wants to eat you and that would be entertaining, plus he gets grumpy if we don't feed him.'

Vishby wanted to be terrified, to take some radical action, but the rune on his neck forbade any emotion stronger than mild anxiety. 'Please, Turnball, Captain. I thought we were friends.'

Turnball Root considered this. 'You are a traitor to your people, Vishby. How can I take a traitor for a friend?'

Even a magic-doped Vishby could see the irony in this. After all, had not Turnball Root betrayed his kind on numerous occasions, even sacrificing members of the criminal fraternity for creature comforts in his cell?

'But your model parts,' he objected weakly. 'And the computer. You gave the names of –'

Turnball did not like how this conversation was going and so took two quick steps and buzzed Vishby in the gills. The water elf fell sideways on the pilot seat and hung in his harness, arms dangling, gills rippling.

'Jabber jabber jabber,' said Turnball brightly. 'All these guards are the same. Always sticking it to the cons, eh, my boyos?'

Unix spun Vishby's chair round and began a thorough search, taking anything of potential use, even a small pack of indigestion tablets, because you never knew.

'Here's the choice, gentlemen,' said Turnball to his captive audience. 'Step outside with me now, or stay and wait for an assault charge to be added to your sentence.'

'Just step outside?' said Bobb Ragby, half chuckling.

Turnball smiled easily, charming as a devil. 'That's it, lads. We step outside into the water.'

'I read something about there being pressure underwater.'

'I heard that too,' said Ching Mayle, licking an eyeball. 'Won't we be crushed?'

Turnball shrugged, milking his moment. 'Trust me, lads. It's all about trust. If you don't trust me, stay here and rot. I need men with me I can rely on, especially with what I've got planned. Think of this as a test.'

There were several groans. Captain Root had always had a thing for tests. It wasn't enough to be a murderous marauder – a person had to pass all these tests. Once he had made the entire group eat raw stinkworms just to prove that they were prepared to obey any order, however ludicrous. The hide-away's plumbing had taken quite a battering that weekend.

Ching Mayle scratched the bite marks on his crown. 'Those are our choices? Stay here or step outside?'

'Succinctly put, Mister Mayle. Sometimes a limited vocabulary can be an advantage.'

'Can we think about it?'

'Of course, take all the time you need,' said Turnball magnanimously. 'So long as your cogitations do not take more than two minutes.'

Ching frowned. 'My cogitations can take hours, especially if I have red meat.'

Most fairies found animal flesh disgusting, but every enclave had its omnivorous faction.

'Two minutes? Seriously, Captain?'

'No.'

Bobb Ragby would have wiped his brow if he could have reached it. 'Thank goodness.'

'It's one hundred seconds now. Come on, gents. Tick tock.'

Unix rose from his search and stood wordlessly at Turnball's side.

'That's one. Who else is willing to place their lives in my hands?'

Ching nodded. 'I reckon, yes. You did good by me, Captain. I never even smelled fresh air till I cast my lot with you.'

'Count me in,' said Bobb Ragby, rattling his bar. 'I'm scared, Captain. I won't deny it, but I would rather die a pirate than go back to the Deeps.'

Turnball raised an eyebrow. 'And?'

Ragby's voice was guttural with fear. 'And what, Captain? I said I'd step outside.'

'It's your motivation, Mister Ragby. I need more than a reluctance to go back to prison.'

Ragby banged his head on the restraining bar. 'More? I want to go with you, Captain. Honest I do. I swear it. I never met a leader like you.'

'Really? I don't know. You seem reluctant.'

Ragby was not the sharpest spine on the hedgehog, but his gut told him that going with the captain was a lot safer than staying here. Turnball Root was famous for dealing with evidence and witnesses in a severe fashion. There was a legend going around the fairy fugitive bars that the captain had once burned down an entire shopping complex just to get rid of a thumbprint that he may have left behind in a booth at Falafel Fabulosity.

'I ain't reluctant, Captain. Take me, please. I'm your faithful Ragby. Who was it that shot that fairy on Tern Mór? It were me. Good old Bobb.'

Turnball wiped an imaginary tear from one eye. 'Your pathetic pleadings move me, dear Bobby. Very well, Unix, release Misters Ragby and Ching.'

The mutilated sprite did so, then popped Vishby's harness and hoisted him upright.

'The turncoat?' said Unix.

Turnball started at the sound of Unix's reptilian voice. He realized that in all their time together he probably hadn't heard the sprite speak more than a hundred words.

'No. Leave him. Rice wine turns my stomach.'

Other lieutenants might have requested an explanation

on this point, but not Unix who never wanted to know stuff he didn't need to know and even that information was ejected from his brain as soon as it outlived its usefulness. The sprite simply nodded then tossed Vishby aside like a sack of refuse.

Ragby and Ching stood quickly, as though repulsed by their seats.

'I feel funny,' said the goblin, worming his little finger into one of the tooth marks on his bald skull. 'Good cos I'm free, but a little bad too cos I might be about to die.'

'You never did have much of a filter between your brain and mouth, Mister Mayle,' moaned Turnball. 'Never mind, I'm the one paid to think.' He faced the remaining prisoners. 'Anybody else? Twenty seconds left.'

Four hands went up. Two belonging to the same person, who was desperate not to be left behind.

'Too late,' said Turnball, and gestured for his three chosen acolytes to stand by him. 'Come closer, we need a group hug.'

Hugging was not a habit anyone who knew Turnball Root would ever associate with him. The captain had once shot an elf for suggesting a high five, and so it was an effort for Bobb and Ching to keep the shock from their faces. Even Unix raised a jagged eyebrow.

'Oh, come now, gentlemen, am I as scary as all that?'

Yes, Bobb wanted to scream. *You are scarier than a dwarf mum with a long-handled spoon.* But instead he twisted his mouth into something approximating a smile and stepped into Turnball's embrace. Unix drew close too, as did Ching.

'Aren't we the strange bunch?' said Turnball cheerily.

'Honestly, Unix. It's like hugging a plank. And you, Mister Ragby, you really smell very bad. Has anyone ever told you that?'

Ragby mumbled an admission. 'A few. Me dad, all those who were my mates.'

'I'm not the first, then, thank goodness. I don't mind confirming bad news but I hate to break it.'

Bobb Ragby wanted to cry; for some reason this inane chatter was terrifying.

A rumble rolled through the metal skin of the shuttle. The noise grew rapidly louder until it filled the small space. From nothing to everything in five seconds.

'Two minutes are up,' shouted Turnball. 'Time for the faithful to go outside.'

The hull above the small group's heads glowed red suddenly as something melted it from the outside. Several alarms pulsed into life on the viewscreen's heads-up display.

'Wow,' shouted Turnball. 'Total chaos all of a sudden. What could be going on?'

The section overhead was molten now and it should have dripped down on the group, searing their flesh, but somehow it was siphoned off. Blob by white-hot blob a large circle of the roof was sucked away until there was nothing holding the sea out except some kind of gel.

'Should we hold our breath?' asked Bobb Ragby, trying not to sob.

'Not much point really,' answered Turnball, who loved toying with people.

It's nice to know more than everybody else, he thought, then four amorphobots, who had merged into one large gelatinous blob, dropped a fat tentacle into the shuttle's interior and sucked up Captain Root and his gang, clean as a dwarf sucking a snail from its shell. One second they were there, and the next nothing remained but a slight smear on the deck and the echo of slobbering slurp.

'I am so glad I stayed where I am,' said one of the remaining prisoners who had never served with Turnball. He had, in fact, earned his six-year sentence for making clever copies of collectable cartoon-character spoons. 'That blobby thing looked creepy.'

None of the others spoke as they had immediately realized what catastrophe would result from the blobby thing breaking its seal round the large hole in the hull.

As it happened, the expected catastrophe never got a chance to occur, because as soon as the amorphobots vacated the space the hole was filled by the rogue probe, which had deviated suddenly from its course to plough through the shuttle, bearing it deep into the bedrock of the ocean floor, mashing it completely. As for the people inside the shuttle, they were mostly liquefied. It would be months before any remains were found and even longer before those remains could be identified. The impact crater was more than fifteen metres deep and at least the same across. The whiplash shock rippled across the seabed, decimating the local ecology and stacking half a dozen rescue craft on top of each other like building blocks.

The giant amorpho-blob bore Turnball and his cohorts

swiftly from the impact site, perfectly mimicking the motion of a giant squid, even sprouting gel-tacles, which funnelled the water in a tight cone behind it. Inside the main body of gel, two fairies were perfectly calm: Turnball could fairly be called serene and Unix was as unperturbed by this latest marvel as he was by anything that he had seen in his long life. Bobb Ragby on the other hand could in truth be called terrified out of his tiny mind. While Turnball had summoned the amorphobots and had a fair idea of what to expect, as far as Ragby was concerned they had been swallowed by a jelly monster and were being carried off to its lair to be consumed during the long cold winter. All Ching Mayle could think was one sentence over and over again: *I'm sorry I stole the candy cane*, which more than likely referred to an incident that was significant to him and to whomever he'd stolen the candy cane from.

Turnball reached into the jumble of electronics in the amorphobots' belly and pulled out a small cordless mask, which he slipped over his face. It was possible to speak through the gel, but the mask made it infinitely easier.

'Well, my brave lads,' he said. 'We are now officially dead and free to take a shot at stealing the LEP's most powerful natural resource. Something truly magical. '

Ching snapped out of his candy-cane loop. He opened his mouth to speak, but realized quickly that while the gel some-how fed oxygen to his lungs it didn't support speech so well without a mask.

He gargled for a moment, then decided to pose his question later.

'I can guess what you were about to say, Mister Mayle,' said Turnball. 'Why in heavens would we want to tangle with the LEP? Surely we should stay as far away from the police as possible.' An amber light in the belly of the bot cast sinister shadows across the captain's face. 'I say no. I say we attack now and steal what we need from right under their noses, and while we're about it spread a little destruction and mayhem to cover our tracks. You have seen what I can do from a prison cell – imagine what might be possible from the freedom of the wide world.'

It was difficult to argue with this point, especially when the fairy making the point controlled the gel robot thing that was keeping everyone alive and no one else knew if they could speak or not. Turnball Root always knew how to pick his moment.

The amorphobot dropped quickly behind a jagged reef, escaping the worst of the shockwave. Slivers of rock and lumps of coral tumbled down through the murky water but were rejected by the gel. A squid ventured too close and was treated to a lick with an electrified gel-tacle. And as the walls of a towering undersea cliff flashed by in stripes of grey and green, Turnball sighed into his mask, the sound amplified and distorted.

I am coming, my love, he thought. *Soon we will be together.*

He decided against saying this aloud, as even Unix might think it a little melodramatic.

Turnball realized with a jolt that he was completely happy, and the cost of that happiness bothered him not a jot.

CHAPTER 8: RANDOMOSITY

 ARTEMIS observed and considered from the confines of his own brain, watching through the booby-trapped wall in his imagined office. The scenario was interesting, fascinating, in fact, and almost distracted him from his own problems. Someone had decided to hijack Foaly's Mars probe and aim it directly at Atlantis. And it could not be coincidence that the probe had stopped off in Iceland to take care of Commander Vinyáya and her finest troops, not to mention the fairy People's wiliest, and only, human ally: Artemis Fowl.

There is an elaborate plan being played out in front of us, not just a series of coincidences.

It wasn't that Artemis didn't believe in coincidences – he just found a *series* of them hard to swallow.

There was one main question as far as Artemis could see: who benefits?

Who benefits if Vinyáya dies and Atlantis is threatened?

Vinyáya was well known for her zero-tolerance approach to crime – so many criminals would be delighted to have her out of the way – but why Atlantis?

Of course, the prison! It must be Opal Koboi; this was her bid for freedom. The probe triggers an evacuation that gets her outside the dome.

Opal Koboi, public enemy number one. The pixie who had incited the goblins to revolution and murdered Julius Root.

It must be Opal.

Artemis corrected himself: *It is probably Opal. Don't leap to conclusions.*

It was infuriating to be stuck inside his own brain when there was so much going on in the world. His nano-wafer prototype, the Ice Cube, had been destroyed and, more urgently, there was a probe headed for Atlantis that could potentially destroy the city or at the very least allow a homicidal pixie to effect her escape.

'Let me out, won't you?' Artemis shouted at the mind-screen, and the shimmering fours marshalled themselves into squares and sent a lattice of glittering wire flashing across the screen.

Artemis had his answer.

I was put in here by electricity and now it's barring my way.

Artemis knew that there were many reputable institutes

around the world that still used electro-shock therapy to deal with various psychotic illnesses. He realized that when Holly had blasted him with her Neutrino the charge had boosted the Orion personality, making it the dominant one.

It's a pity Holly wouldn't shoot me again.

Holly shot him again.

Artemis imagined two jagged forks of white lightning skittering through the air and turning the screen white.

I shouldn't feel any pain, reasoned Artemis hopefully, *as technically I am not conscious at the moment.*

Conscious or not, Artemis felt just as much agony as Orion.

Typical of the way my day has been going, he thought as his virtual legs collapsed underneath him.

THE NORTH ATLANTIC OCEAN, NOW

Artemis woke some time later with the smell of singed flesh in his nostrils. He knew he was back in the real world because of the harness digging into his shoulders and the choppy motion of the sea, which was making him nauseous.

He opened his eyes and found himself looking at Foaly's rump. The centaur's back leg was kicking spasmodically as he battled sleep demons. There was music playing somewhere. Familiar music. Artemis closed his eyes and thought, *That music is familiar because I composed it. 'Siren Song' from my unfinished Third Symphony.*

And why was it important?

It is important because I set it as my ring-tone for Mother. She is calling me.

Artemis did not pat his pockets searching for his phone, because he always kept his phone in the same pocket. Indeed, he always had his tailors sew a leather-flapped zip into his right breast pocket so that his phone could not be mislaid. For if Artemis Fowl mislaid his modified phone it would be a little more serious than if Johnny Highschool happened to lose the latest touch-screen model, unless Johnny Highschool's phone happened to have enough tech inside it to easily hack any government site, a nice little laser pointer that could be focused to burn through metal and the first draft of Artemis Fowl's memoirs, which did a little more than kiss and tell.

Artemis's fingers were cold and numb, but after a few attempts he managed to paw the zip open and fumble out his phone. On screen the phone was playing a photo slideshow of his mother while the opening bars of 'Siren Song' soared through the tiny speakers.

'Phone,' he said clearly, holding in a button on the casing to activate voice control.

'Yes, Artemis,' said the phone in Lily Frond's voice, a voice which Artemis had picked simply to annoy Holly.

'Accept the call.'

'Of course, Artemis.'

A moment later the connection was made. The signal was weak but that did not matter as Artemis's phone had speech auto-fill software which was ninety-five per cent accurate.

'Hello, Mother. How are you?'

'Arty, can you hear me? I've got an echo.'

'No. No echo on this end. I can hear you perfectly.'

'I can't get the video to work, Artemis. You promised we would be able to see each other.'

The video-call option was available, but Artemis rejected it as he did not think his mother would be heartened by the view of her dishevelled son hanging from a harness in a crippled escape pod.

Dishevelled? Who am I kidding? I must look like a refugee from a war zone, which is what I am.

'There's no video network in Iceland. I should have checked.'

'Hmm,' said his mother, and Artemis knew that syllable well. It meant that she suspected him of something, but didn't know what exactly.

'So you *are* in Iceland?'

Artemis was glad there was no video feed as it was more difficult to lie face to face.

'Of course I am. Why do you ask?'

'I ask because the GPS puts you in the North Atlantic Ocean.'

Artemis frowned. His mother had insisted on a GPS function on the phone if she were to allow him to go off alone.

'That's probably just a bug in the program,' said Artemis as he quickly tapped into the GPS application and manually set his location to Reykjavik. 'Sometimes the locater is a little off. Give it another try.'

➤ • ᚱᚩᚠᚪᛒ • ᚻᛁ • ᚢᚪᛒᚱ ᚳᛄ ⊗ ᚱᛒ⊗ • ᚱᛒ ᚫ •

Silence for a moment, but for the tapping of keys, then another *hmmm*.

'I suppose it's redundant to ask whether or not you're up to something? Artemis Fowl is always up to something.'

'That's not fair, Mother,' protested Artemis. 'You know what I'm trying to achieve.'

'I do know. My goodness, Arty, it's all you can talk about. *THE PROJECT*.'

'It is important.'

'I know that, but people are important too. How's Holly?'

Artemis glanced at Holly who was curled around the leg of a bench snoring quietly. Her uniform looked very battered and there was blood leaking from one ear.

'She's . . . em . . . fine. A little tired from the journey, but totally in control of the situation. I admire her, Mother, really I do. The way she handles whatever life throws at her and never gives up.'

Angeline Fowl drew a surprised breath. 'Well, Artemis Fowl the Second, that is about the longest non-scientific speech I have ever heard you make. Holly Short is lucky to have a friend like you.'

'No, she isn't,' said Artemis miserably. 'No one is lucky to know me. I can't help anyone. I can't even help myself.'

'That's not true, Arty,' said Angeline strictly. 'Who saved Haven from the goblins?'

'A few people. I suppose I had a part in it.'

'And who found his father in the Arctic when everyone else had given him up for dead?'

'That was me.'

'Well, then, never say you can't help anyone. You've spent most of your life helping. Yes, you've made a few mistakes, but your heart is in the right place.'

'Thank you, Mother. I feel better now.'

Angeline cleared her throat, a little nervously Artemis thought.

'Is everything all right?' he asked.

'Yes, of course. There's just something I need to tell you.'

Artemis felt suddenly nervous. 'What is it, Mother?'

A dozen possible revelations ran through his head. Had his mother found out about some of his shadier operations? She knew all about his various fairy-related schemes, but there was plenty of human stuff he hadn't confessed to.

That's the problem with being a semi-reformed criminal: you are never free from guilt. Exposure is always just a phone call away.

'It's about your birthday.'

Artemis's shoulders drooped with relief. 'My birthday. Is that all?'

'I got you something . . . different, but I want you to have them. It would make me happy.'

'If they make you happy, I am sure they will make me happy.'

'So, Arty, you have to promise me you'll use them.'

Artemis's nature made it hard for him to promise anything. 'What are they?'

'Promise me, honey.'

Artemis glanced out of the porthole. He was stuck in a

burnt-out escape pod in the middle of the Atlantic Ocean. Either they would sink or some Scandinavian navy would mistake them for aliens and blow the tub out of the water.

'Very well, I promise. So, what did you get for me?'

Angeline paused for a beat. 'Jeans.'

'What?' croaked Artemis.

'And a T-shirt.'

Artemis knew that he shouldn't really be upset, in the circumstances, but he couldn't help himself. 'Mother, you tricked me.'

'Now, I know you don't really do casual.'

'That's hardly fair. Last month at that cake sale I rolled up both sleeves.'

'People are afraid of you, Arty. Girls are terrified of you. You're a fifteen-year-old in a bespoke suit, and nobody died.'

Artemis took several breaths. 'Does the T-shirt have any writing on it?'

A rustling of paper crackled through the phone's speakers. 'Yes. It's so cool. There's a picture of a boy who for some reason has no neck and only three fingers on each hand, and behind him in a sort of graffiti style is the word RANDOM-OSITY. I don't know what that means, but it sounds really current.'

Randomosity, thought Artemis, and he felt like weeping. 'Mother, I . . .'

'You promised, Arty. That's what you did.'

'Yes. I did promise, Mother.'

'And I want you to call me Mum.'

'Mother! You're being unreasonable. I am who I am. T-shirts and jeans are not me.'

Angeline Fowl played her trump card. 'Well, you know, Arty dear, sometimes people are not who they think they are.'

This was a none-too-subtle dig at Artemis for mesmerizing his own parents, something Angeline had only become aware of when Opal Koboi had occupied her body and all the secrets of the fairy world had become known to her.

'That's hardly fair.'

'Fair? Wait, let me call the gentlemen of the press. Artemis Fowl just used the word *fair*.'

Artemis realized that his mother was not quite over the mesmerizing thing yet.

'Very well. I consent to wearing the jeans and T-shirt.'

'Excuse me?'

'Very well. I will wear the jeans and T-shirt . . . Mum.'

'I am so happy. Tell Butler to put by two days a week. Jeans and Mums. Get used to it.'

What's next? Artemis wondered. *Baseball hats worn back to front?*

'Butler is taking good care of you, I trust?'

Artemis coloured. More lies. 'Yes. You should see his face at this meeting. He is bored out of his mind with all the science.'

Angeline's voice changed, became warmer, more emotional.

'I know it's important, Arty, what you're doing. Important for the planet, I mean. And I believe in you, son. Which is why I am keeping your secret and letting you gallivant across the globe with fairy folk, but you have to promise me that you're safe.'

Artemis had heard the expression *to feel like a real heel* but now he actually understood it.

'I am the safest human in the world,' he said jauntily. 'I have more protection than a president. I'm better armed too.'

Yet another *hmmm*. 'This is the last solo mission, Arty. You promised me. I just have to save the world, you said, then I can spend more time with the twins.'

'I remember,' said Artemis, which wasn't really agreeing.

'See you tomorrow morning, then. The dawn of a new day.'

'See you tomorrow morning, Mum.'

Angeline hung up and her picture disappeared from Artemis's screen. He was sorry to see it go.

On the deck, Foaly suddenly flipped on his back.

'Not the stripy ones,' he blurted. 'They're just little babies.' Then he opened his eyes and saw Artemis watching him.

'Did I say that out loud?'

Artemis nodded. 'Yes. Something about the stripy ones being babies.'

'Childhood memory. I'm pretty much over it now.'

Artemis stretched out a hand to help the centaur to his hooves.

'No help from you,' Foaly moaned, slapping at the hand

as though it were a wasp. 'I have had enough of you. If you even think the phrase *goodly beast*, I am going to kick you straight in the teeth.'

Artemis slapped the buckle on his chest, opening the harness, stretching his hand out further.

'I am sorry about all of that, Foaly. But I'm fine now. It's me, Artemis.'

Now Foaly accepted the steadying hand. 'Oh, thank the gods. That other guy was really getting on my nerves.'

'Not so fast,' said Holly, appearing fully conscious between the two.

'Whoa,' said Foaly, rearing. 'Don't you moan and groan a bit when you regain consciousness?'

'Nope,' said Holly. 'LEP ninja training. And this guy isn't Artemis. He said *Mum*. I heard him. Artemis Fowl doesn't say Mum, Mummy, Mom or Momsy. This is Orion trying to pull a fast one.'

'I realize how it sounded,' said Artemis. 'But you have to believe me. My mother extorted that term of endearment from me.'

Foaly tapped his long chin. 'Extorted? Endearment? It's Artemis all right.'

'Thanks for shooting me, the second time,' said Artemis, touching the burn marks on his neck. 'The charge set me free from the fours for the time being. And I'm sorry about all that rubbish Orion was spouting. I have no idea where that came from.'

'We need to talk about that at great length,' said Holly,

brushing past him to the dashboard. 'But later. First let's see if I can raise Haven.'

Foaly tapped a button on his phone's screen. 'Already on it, Captain.'

After all the drama of the previous few hours, it seemed impossible that they could simply phone Haven and get a connection just like that, but that's exactly what happened.

Commander Trouble Kelp picked up on the first ring and Foaly put the video-call on speaker.

'Holly? Is that you?'

'Yes, Commander. I have Foaly with me, and Artemis Fowl.'

Trouble grunted. 'Artemis Fowl. Why am I not surprised? We should have sucked that Mud Whelp's brain out through his ear when we had the chance.'

Trouble Kelp was famous for his gung-ho attitude, that and the fact that he had chosen *Trouble* as his graduation name. There was an honest-to-gods true story going around the Academy that, as a lowly street cop, young Officer Kelp drove his riot scooter down an alley in Boolatown during the solstice and PAed to a dozen or so scrapping goblins the immortal line: *If you're looking for trouble, you've come to the right place.* After the goblins had finished laughing, they gave Trouble a hiding he would not soon forget. The scars made him a little more cautious, but not much.

Trouble sat at his desk in Police Plaza, ramrod straight in his blue commander's jumpsuit, acorn cluster glittering on his chest. His dark hair was close cropped over impressive pointed ears, and deep purple eyes glared out from under brows that jinked like lightning bolts as he spoke.

'Hello, Commander,' said Artemis. 'Nice to be appreciated.'

'I appreciate armpit lice more than I'm ever likely to appreciate you, Fowl. Get over it.'

Artemis could think of half a dozen withering responses to this comment off the top of his head, but he kept these put-downs to himself for the greater good.

I am fifteen now, time to behave maturely.

Holly cut through the male posturing. 'Commander, is Atlantis safe?'

'Most of it,' said Trouble. 'Half a dozen evac ships took a pasting. One shuttle suffered a direct hit, buried deeper than hell itself. It's going to take months to put the pieces together.'

Holly's shoulders drooped. 'Casualties?'

'Definitely. We don't know how many yet, but dozens.' Trouble's brow was heavy with the weight of command. 'It's a dark day for the People, Captain. First Vinyáya and her troops, now this.'

'What happened?'

Trouble's gaze shifted to a point off screen as his fingers tapped a v-board. 'One of Foaly's brainers did a simulation. I'm sending it to you now.'

Seconds later a message icon pulsed on the screen of Foaly's phone. Holly selected it and a simple 2D video played, depicting an outlined probe entering the Earth's atmosphere over Iceland.

'Can you see that, Captain?'

•)♭)꙰)♋♌→•꙰)⊕♐⚬꙰•⊙♌♑♌•⚬꙰•

'Yes, it's up.'

'Good. Let me talk you through it. So, Foaly's Martian probe shows up just below the Arctic Circle. We're taking your word for this since we didn't detect it thanks to our own cloaking technology. Shields, stealth ore, all turned against us. I don't have to tell you what happened next.'

On screen the probe sent a laser burst into a small target on the surface, then jettisoned a few bots to deal with survivors. The craft barely slowed down before ploughing through the ice, taking a south-westerly course towards the Atlantic.

'Again, this part of the simulation was done without computer data. We took what you told us and also extrapolated backwards from our own readings.'

Artemis interrupted. 'You had readings? At what point did you start to get readings?'

'It was the strangest thing,' said Trouble, frowning. 'We heeded Captain Short's warning and ran a scan. Nothing. Then, five minutes later, up the probe pops on our screens. No shields, nothing. In fact, she was blowing heat out the vents, so we couldn't miss her. She even blew her engine plates off. The thing was shining brighter than the North Star. And, just in case we missed it, we got a tip-off from a bar in Miami of all places. We had time enough to evacuate.'

'But not enough to reach her,' mused Artemis.

'Exactly,' said Trouble Kelp, who wouldn't have agreed if it had occurred to him that he was agreeing with arch-criminal Artemis Fowl. 'All we could do was pump up the water cannons, empty the city and wait until the probe came into range.'

'And then?' prompted Artemis.

'Then I authorized a few practice shots along the trajectory before the probe was really in range. There shouldn't have been enough power in them to cause any damage – the water shells dissipate over distance – but one must have held on to a bit of punch because the probe spun off course and nose-dived straight into the seabed, taking a shuttle down with it.'

'Opal Koboi was on that shuttle, wasn't she?' said Artemis urgently. 'This is all her doing. This *reeks* of Opal.'

'No, Fowl, if it reeks of anyone, it reeks of you. This all started with your conference in Iceland and now some of our best people are dead and we have an underwater rescue mission on our hands.'

Artemis's face was red. 'Forget how you feel about me. Was Opal on the shuttle?'

'She was not,' thundered Trouble, and the pod's speakers vibrated. 'But you were in Iceland, and now you're here.'

Holly stepped in to defend her friend. 'Artemis had nothing to do with this, Commander.'

'That may be but there are too many coincidences here, Holly. I need you to detain the Mud Boy until I can get a rescue bird up to you. It could be a few hours so take on some ballast in the tanks and drop your buoyancy a little. You shouldn't be spotted below the surface.'

Holly was not happy with this course of action. 'Sir, Commander, we know *what* happened. But Artemis is right – we need to think about *who* made it happen.'

'We can talk about that in Police Plaza. For now my priority is to keep people alive, simple as that. There are fairies still trapped in Atlantis. Everything watertight we have is headed there right now. We can discuss the Mud Boy's theories tomorrow.'

'Maybe we can construct a bivouac while we're at it,' muttered Holly.

Trouble Kelp was not one to swallow insubordination. He leaned close to the camera, his forehead stretching wide in the pinhole lens.

'Did you say something, Captain?'

'Whoever did this is not finished,' said Holly, doing a little leaning in herself. 'This is part of a bigger plan, and detaining Artemis is the worst possible thing you could do.'

'Oh, really,' said Trouble, chuckling unexpectedly. 'Odd you should say that, because in the message you sent earlier, you commented that Artemis Fowl had lost it. Your exact words were –'

Holly glanced guiltily at Artemis. 'No need for the exact words, sir.'

'*Sir* now, is it? Your *exact* words were, and I quote – obviously since they are your exact words – you said that Artemis Fowl was crazier than a saltwater-drinking troll with ringworm.'

Artemis shot Holly a recriminating look that said: *Ringworm? Really?*

Holly brushed the comment aside with a hand. 'That was earlier. I have shot Artemis twice since then and he's fine now.'

Trouble grinned. 'You shot him twice. That's more like it.'

'The point is,' Holly persisted, 'we need Artemis to help figure this out.'

'Like he *figured out* Julius Root and Commander Raine Vinyáya.'

'That is not fair, Trouble.'

Kelp was unrepentant. 'You can call me *Trouble* in the officers' club on the weekend. Until then it's Commander. And I order you, no, I *command* you to detain the human Artemis Fowl. We're not arresting him – I just want him down here for a little chat. What I certainly do not want is for us to act on any of his notions. Understood?'

Holly's face was wooden and her voice dull. 'Understood, Commander.'

'Your pod has enough juice to power the locator, no more, so don't even think about making for the shore. You look a shade paler than death, Captain, so I'm guessing you don't have any spare magic for shielding.'

'Paler than death? Thanks, Trubs.'

'Trubs, Captain? *Trubs?*'

'I meant Trouble.'

'That's better. So all I want you to do is sit on the Mud Boy. Got it?'

Holly's words were so honeyed that they could have charmed a bear. 'I've got it good, Trouble. Captain Holly Short, babysitter extraordinaire, at your service.'

'Hmmm,' said Trouble, in a tone that Angeline Fowl's son understood very well.

'Hmmm, indeed,' said Holly.

'I'm glad we understand each other,' said Trouble, with a flicker of one eyelid that could be interpreted as a wink. 'I, as your superior, am telling you to stay put and not make any attempt to get to the bottom of what's really going on here, especially not with the help of a human, *especially* especially not that particular human. Do you read me?'

'I read you loud and clear, Trouble,' said Holly, and Artemis understood that Trouble Kelp was not forbidding Holly to investigate further – he was actually covering himself on video in case Holly's actions resulted in a tribunal, which they often did.

'I read you loud and clear too, Commander,' said Artemis. 'If that makes any difference.'

Trouble snorted. 'Remember those armpit lice, Fowl? Their opinions make more difference to me than yours.'

And he was gone before Artemis could trot out one of his pre-prepared retorts. And in years to come when Professor J. Argon published the bestselling Artemis Fowl biography, *Fowl and Fairy*, this particular exchange would be deemed significant as one of the few times anyone got the last word over Artemis Fowl II.

Holly made a sound that was a little like a shriek but not as girly and with more frustration.

'What's the matter?' asked Foaly. 'I thought that went pretty well. It seemed to me that Commander Trouble Kelp, aka your boyfriend, gave us the green light to investigate.'

Holly turned her mismatched eyes on him. 'First of all, he's not my boyfriend – we went on one date and I told you that in confidence because I thought you were a friend who wouldn't trot it out at the first opportunity.'

'It's not the first opportunity. I held it back the time when we had that lovely tea.'

'Irrelevant!' shouted Holly, through funnelled hands.

'Don't worry, Holly, it stays in this room,' said Foaly, thinking it would be a bad time to mention that he had posted the gossip on his website www.horsesense.gnom.

'And secondly,' continued Holly, 'maybe Trouble did give me the backhanded go-ahead, but what good is that to us in the middle of the Atlantic in a dead lump of metal?'

Artemis glanced skywards. 'Ah, you see, I might be able to help you there. Any second now.'

Several seconds passed by without any significant change in their situation.

Holly raised her palms. 'Any second? Really?'

Artemis couldn't help being a little peeved. 'Not literally. It might take a minute or so. Perhaps I should call him.'

Fifty-nine seconds later something bonged against the pod's hatch.

'Aha,' said Artemis in a way that made Holly feel like punching him.

OVER THE ATLANTIC, TWO HOURS EARLIER

'This is not a bad ship as it happens,' said Mulch Diggums, pushing a couple of buttons on the stolen mercenaries' ship just to see what they did. When one caused the contents of the sewage recycler to be dumped on an innocent Scottish deep-sea trawler below, the dwarf decided to stop pushing.

(One of the fishermen happened to be making a video of gulls for his university media course and caught the entire descending blob of waste matter on film. It seemed to anyone who saw the tape as though the ponging mass just appeared in the sky then dropped rapidly on to the unfortunate sailors. Sky News ran the video with the headline: Panic on the Poop Deck. The segment was largely dismissed as a student prank.)

'I should have guessed that one,' Mulch said without a trace of guilt. 'There's a little picture of a toilet on the button.'

Juliet sat hunched over on one of the passenger benches that ran along one side of the cargo bay, her head tipping the ceiling, and Butler lay flat on the other one as it was the most practical way for him to travel.

'So Artemis has been shutting you out?' she asked her brother.

'Yes,' replied Butler dejectedly. 'I'd swear he doesn't trust me any more. I'd swear he doesn't even trust his own mother.'

'Angeline? How could anyone not trust Mrs Fowl? That's ridiculous.'

'I know,' said Butler. 'And I'll go one better. Artemis doesn't trust the twins.'

Juliet started, bumping her head on the metal ceiling. 'Oww. *Madre de dios*. Artemis doesn't trust Myles and Beckett? That's just ridiculous. What terrible acts of sabotage are three-year-olds supposed to commit?'

⊕⬡⊗⊖♀♋•⬟♌⚡•⬚⊖♀♋•⬤♌♋⊘♌•♌⬟♌⬓♋•

Butler grimaced. 'Unfortunately, Myles contaminated one of Artemis's Petri dishes when he wanted a sample for his own experiments.'

'That's hardly industrial espionage. What did Beckett do?'

'He ate Artemis's hamster.'

'What?'

'Well, he chewed on its leg for a bit.' Butler shifted in the cramped space. Fairy crafts were not built to accommodate giant, shaven-headed, human bodyguards. Not that the shaved head made much difference.

'Artemis was livid, claimed there was a conspiracy against him. He installed a combination lock on his lab door to keep his brothers out.'

Juliet grinned though she knew she shouldn't. 'Did that work?'

'No. Myles stayed at the door for three days straight tapping away until he came across the correct combination. He used several rolls of toilet paper writing down the possibilities.'

Juliet was almost afraid to ask. 'What did Beckett do?'

Butler grinned back at his sister. 'Beckett dug a bear trap in the garden and when Myles fell in he swapped him a ladder for the code.'

Juliet nodded appreciatively. 'That's what I would have done.'

'Me too,' said Butler. 'Maybe Beckett will end up as Myles's bodyguard.' The light moment didn't last long. 'Artemis isn't taking my calls. Imagine that. I think he's changed his SIM, so I can't track him.'

'But we are tracking him, right?'

Butler checked his touch-screen phone. 'Oh yes. Artemis isn't the only one with Foaly's phone number.'

'What did that sneaky centaur give you?'

'An isotope spray. You just spray it on a surface then track it with one of Foaly's mi-p's.'

'Meepees?'

'Mini-programs. Foaly uses it to keep an eye on his kids.'

'Where did you spray it?'

'Artemis's shoes.'

Juliet giggled. 'He does like 'em shiny.'

'Yes, he does.'

'You're starting to think like a Fowl, brother.'

Mulch Diggums called back from the cockpit. 'Gods help us all. That's what the world needs, more Fowls.'

They all shared a guilty laugh at that.

The mercenaries' gyro tracked the Gulf Stream north to the coast of Ireland, moving at slightly more than twice the speed ever achieved by Concorde, then swung in a long north-westerly arc into the North Atlantic as its computer zeroed in on Artemis's footwear.

'Artemis's shoes are walking us right to him,' said Mulch, chortling at his own joke. The Butlers did not join in the mirth, not from any loyalty to their employer, who enjoyed the occasional joke, but because Mulch's mouth was packed with the contents of the shuttle's cooler box and they had no idea what he had just said.

'Please yourselves,' said Mulch, spattering the inside of

the windscreen with chewed sweetcorn. 'I make the effort to speak in humanese and you two joke snobs won't even laugh at my efforts.'

The shuttle rocketed along, two metres above the wave tops, its anti-grav pulses burrowing periodic cylinders into the ocean's surface. The engine noise was low and could have been mistaken for a whistling wind, and to any smart mammals below who could see through the shields the shuttle could be mistaken for a very fast humpback with an extra-wide tail and a loading bay.

'We really lucked out with this bucket,' commented Mulch, his mouth mercifully empty. 'She's more or less flying herself. I just put your phone into the dock, opened the mi-p and off she went.'

The craft behaved a little like a tracker dog, suddenly coming to a dead stop whenever it lost the scent, then casting its prow about furiously until the isotope showed up again. At one point it had plunged into the ocean, burrowing straight down until pressure cracked the fuselage plates and they lost a square metre of shielding.

'Don't worry, Mud Men,' Mulch had reassured them. 'All fairy craft have sea engines. When you live underground, it makes sense to build watertight ships.'

Juliet had not ceased to worry; from what she remembered, reassurance from Mulch Diggums was about as reliable as a cocktail from the Pittsburgh Poisoner.

Fortunately, the underwater jaunt hadn't lasted too long and soon they were flitting across the wave tops once more without incident, except for the time when Mulch forgot his promise not to press mysterious buttons and almost crashed them into the sun-flecked seas by releasing the emergency-brake mini-parachute cluster.

'It was calling me, that button,' he offered as his excuse. 'I couldn't resist.'

The jolting stop had shunted Butler along the bench. He slid the entire length of the fuselage into the cockpit divider. Only his lightning reactions stopped him getting his head jammed in the railings.

Butler rubbed his crown, which he had clipped on a bar. 'Take it easy, or there will be consequences. You said it yourself: we don't need you to fly the ship.'

Mulch guffawed, giving a nasty view of his cavernous food pipe. 'That's true, Butler, my freakishly large friend. But you certainly need me to land it.'

Juliet's laugh was high and sweet and seemed to ricochet off the curved metal walls.

'You too, Juliet?' said Butler reproachfully.

'Come on, brother. That was funny. You'll laugh too when Mulch plays back the video.'

'There's video?' said Butler, which just set the other two laughing again.

All of this laughing did nothing to delay Butler's reunion with his principal, Artemis Fowl. A principal who no longer trusted him and who had probably lied to him, sending Butler to another continent and using Juliet to ensure that he would travel.

I believed that my own baby sister was in danger. Artemis, how could you?

There would be tough questions asked when he finally caught up with Artemis. And the answers had better be good or, for the first time in the history of their families' centuries-long relationship, a Butler might just walk away from his duties.

Artemis is ill, Butler rationalized. *He's not responsible.*

Maybe Artemis was not responsible. But he soon would be.

The mercenaries' shuttle finally jerked to a halt over a spot of open ocean just above the sixtieth parallel. It was a spot that seemed no different from the square-grey miles that stretched away on all sides, until the anti-grav pillar ploughed through two metres of water below, revealing the arrowhead escape pod.

'I love this ship,' Mulch crowed. 'It makes me look smarter-er than I am.'

The surrounding waters churned and boiled as the invisible pulses tested the surface and compacted the waves enough to keep the ship hovering in place. Down below, the pulses would sound like bell clappers on the pod's skin.

'Hello,' called Mulch. 'We're up here.'

Butler stuck his head and shoulders into the cockpit, which was about all of him that could fit.

'Can't we radio them?'

'Radio?' said the dwarf. 'You don't know much about being a fugitive, do you? The first thing you do when you steal an LEP ship is strip out anything that could carry a signal to Police Plaza. Every wire, every fuse, every lens. All gone. I've known guys who got caught because they left the sound system in. That's an old Foaly trick. He knows bad boys love their loud music, so he installs a set of speakers to kill for in every LEP bird, each one loaded with tracer gel. There's hardly any tech left in here.'

'So?'

'So what?' said Mulch, as if he had no idea what they were talking about.

'So how do we communicate with that ship down there?'

'You have a phone, don't you?'

Butler's eyes dropped to the floor. 'Artemis is not taking my calls. He's not himself.'

'That's terrible,' said Mulch. 'But do you think they have food? Some of those escape pods have emergency rations. A little chewy, but OK with a nice bottle of beer.'

Butler was wondering whether this change of subject warranted a clip on the ear when his phone rang.

'It's Artemis,' he said, seeming a little more shocked than when he'd been surrounded by luchador zombies.

'Butler?' said Artemis's voice in his ear.

'Yes, Artemis.'

'We need to talk.'

'You'd better make it good,' said Butler, and severed the connection.

It took mere moments to winch down a bucket seat to the pod below and another few minutes for the pod's occupants to clamber into the mercenaries' shuttle. Holly was the last up as she pulled the scuttle cord and opened the escape pod's ballast tanks wide before she left, sinking the craft.

As soon as her elbow crabbed over the doorway's lip, Holly began giving orders.

'Monitor LEP channels on the radio,' she barked. 'We need to find out how the investigation is proceeding.'

Mulch grinned from the pilot's chair. 'Aha, you see that might be a problem, this being a stolen ship and all. Not much in the way of communications. And hello, by the way. I'm fine, still alive and all that. Happy to be able to save your life. Also, what investigation are we talking about?'

Holly pulled herself all the way inside, glancing regretfully down at the sinking pod with its – until recently – functional communications array.

'Ah well,' she sighed. 'You work with whatever limited resources you have.'

'Thanks a bunch,' said Mulch, miffed. 'Did you bring any food? I haven't eaten for, wow, it must be minutes.'

'No, no food,' said Holly. She hugged Mulch tightly, one of perhaps four people in the world who would voluntarily touch the dwarf, then pushed him out of the pilot's chair, taking his place. 'That will have to do for niceties. I'll buy you an entire barbecue hamper later.'

'With real meat?'

Holly shuddered. 'Of course not. Don't be disgusting.'

Butler sat up and spared a moment to nod at Holly,

then turned his full attention on Artemis, who carried himself like the Artemis of old but without the customary cockiness.

'Well?' said Butler, the single syllable laden with implication. *If I do not like what I hear, it could be the end of the road for us.*

Artemis knew that the situation merited at least a hug, and some day in the future after years of meditation he might feel comfortable spontaneously hugging people, but at this moment it was all he could do to lay a hand on Juliet's shoulder and another on Butler's forearm.

'I am so sorry, my friends, to have lied to you.'

Juliet covered the hand with her own, for that was her nature, but Butler raised his as though he were being arrested.

'Juliet could have died, Artemis. We were forced to fight off a horde of mesmerized wrestling fans and a shipload of dwarf mercenaries. We were both in grave danger.'

Artemis pulled away, the moment of emotion past. 'Real danger? Then someone has been spying on me. Someone who knew our movements. Possibly the same someone who sent the probe to kill Vinyáya and target Atlantis.'

Over the next few minutes, while Holly ran a systems check and plotted a course for the crash site, Artemis brought Butler and Juliet up to speed, saving the diagnosis of his own illness for last.

'I have a disorder which the fairies call an Atlantis Complex. It is similar to obsessive compulsive disorder but also manifests as delusional dementia and even multiple personality.'

•⏝⊖⏝⏝⏞⏜∂♈⏜•▢♋⏞•⊖♭•⌖▢•⏝♭⌖⏜∂ →

Butler nodded slowly. 'I see. So when you sent me away, you were in the grips of this Atlantis Complex.'

'Exactly. I was in stage one, which involves a large dose of paranoia as one of its symptoms. You missed stage two.'

'Lucky for you,' Holly called back from the cockpit. 'That Orion guy was a little too friendly.'

'My subconscious built the Orion personality as my alter ego. Artemis, I'm sure you remember, was the goddess of the hunt, and legend has it that Orion was Artemis's mortal enemy so she sent a scorpion to kill him. In my mind Orion was free from the guilt I harboured from my various schemes, especially the guilt of mesmerizing my parents, kidnapping Holly and, crucially, seeing my mother possessed by Opal. Perhaps had I not dabbled in magic I might have developed a slight personality disorder, maybe even Child Genius Syndrome, but with my neural pathways coated with stolen magic I know now that it was inevitable I would succumb to Atlantis.' Artemis dropped his eyes. 'What I did was shameful. I was weak and I will carry regret for the rest of my life.'

Butler's face softened. 'Are you well now? Did the electrocution do the trick?'

Foaly was getting a little tired of Artemis doing all the lecturing so he cleared his throat and volunteered some information. 'According to my phone's mi-p almanac, shock treatment is an archaic treatment and rarely permanent. Atlantis Complex can be cured, but only through extended therapy and the careful use of psychoactive drugs. Soon,

Artemis's compulsions will return and he will feel an irresistible urge to complete his mission, to number things and to avoid the number four, which I believe sounds like the Chinese word for death.'

'So, Artemis is not cured?'

Artemis was suddenly glad that there were five other people in the shuttle. A good omen for success.

'No. I am not cured yet.'

Omens? It begins again.

Artemis actually wrung his hands, a physical sign of his determination.

I will not be beaten by this so soon.

And, to prove it, he deliberately composed a sentence with four words.

'I will be fine.'

'Oooh,' said Mulch, who always had trouble grasping the gravity of situations. 'Four. Scary.'

The first thing was to get them down to the crash site as it seemed obvious to everyone except Mulch that the space probe did not navigate its way through the atmosphere with pinpoint accuracy just to accidentally crash into a prison shuttle. With Holly at the controls, the stolen ship was soon slicing through the Atlantic depths, trailing intertwining streams of air bubbles.

'There's something afoot here,' mused Artemis, gripping the fingers of his left hand tightly to stop them shaking. 'Vinyáya was taken out to hobble the LEP, then the probe gives up its own position, and someone phones in a tip allowing the Atlantis authorities just enough time to evacuate, and then the probe lands on a shuttle. Bad luck for the occupants?'

'Is that one of those rhetorical questions?' wondered Mulch. 'I can never get the hang of those. Also, while we're on the subject, what's the difference between a metaphor and a simile?'

Holly snapped her fingers. 'Somebody wanted everybody in the shuttle dead.'

'Somebody wanted us to think that everyone in the shuttle was dead,' corrected Artemis. 'What a way to fake your own death. It will be months before the LEP can put the pieces together, if ever. That's a nice head start for a fugitive.'

Holly turned to Foaly. 'I need to know who was on that prison shuttle. Do you have an inside guy in Police Plaza?'

Butler was surprised. 'Inside guy? I thought you guys were the inside guys?'

'We're a little on the outside at the moment,' admitted Holly. 'I'm supposed to be detaining Artemis.'

Juliet clapped her hands. 'Have you ever actually obeyed an order?'

'It was kind of a non-order and anyway I only obey orders when they are sound. In this case, it would be ridiculous to sit around for an hour in a burnt-out pod while our enemy, whoever it is, gets on with phase two.'

'I agree,' said Artemis, keeping his voice level.

'How can we be sure there is a phase two?' wondered Butler.

Artemis smiled grimly. 'Of course there is a phase two. Our opponent is fiendish and clever – there will never be a better time to drive home his advantage. It's what I would have done, a few years ago.' His normal calm shattered for a moment and he snapped at Foaly. 'I need that list, Foaly. Who was on that prison shuttle?'

'OK, OK, Mud Boy. I'm working on it. I need to go the long way round so my enquiries don't land on Trouble's desk. This is technical, complicated stuff.'

What the centaur would never admit was that he was actually asking his gifted nephew, Mayne, to hack into the police live site and text him the list in return for an extra-large ice-cream cone when he returned home.

'OK. I have it, from my . . . eh . . . source.'

'Just tell me, Foaly.'

Foaly projected a screen from his phone to the wall. Beside each name there was a link to a data charge that would tell you everything about the prisoner right down to the colour of his underpants, if that's what you really wanted to know, and fairy psychologists were becoming more and more convinced that undergarment colouring was a vital part of a person's development.

Mulch spotted a name he knew, and it wasn't a criminal.

'Hey, look. Old Vishby was piloting. They must have given him his licence back.'

'Do you know him, Mulch?' asked Holly sharply.

For such a hardened ex-criminal, Mulch had a soft centre. 'Hey, why so crabby? I'm trying to help out here.

Of course I know him. It would be pretty weird me saying *Hey, look, old Vishby, they gave him his licence back* if I didn't know him.'

Holly took a breath, reminding herself how Mulch had to be handled. 'You're right, of course. So how do you know *Old Vishby?*'

'Funny story really,' replied Mulch, smacking his lips, wishing he had a chicken leg to go along with the story. 'I escaped from him a few years ago when you were in the frame for murdering Julius. He never got over it. He still hates me, hates the LEP too for taking his licence. Sends me abusive mails occasionally. I send him back little vid boxes of myself laughing. Drives him crazy.'

'Someone with a grudge,' said Artemis. 'Interesting. The perfect inside man. But who's running him?'

Holly turned to study the projected list.

'This sprite, Unix. I took him in. He's one of Turnball Root's boys. A cold-blooded killer.' Holly paled. 'Bobb Ragby is on here too. And Turnball himself. *All* these guys are Turnball's. How in the name of the gods did he get his entire gang on one shuttle? This would have raised a dozen flags on the computer.'

'Unless . . .' said Artemis, scrolling down the list on Foaly's screen. He tapped the data charge beside Bobb Ragby. His picture and file opened on a separate window and Artemis quickly scanned it. 'Look, there's no mention of Turnball Root. According to this, Ragby was arrested for mail fraud and has no known affiliations or accomplices.' He tapped another link and read aloud. 'File updated by . . . Mister Vishby.'

Holly was in shock. 'It's Turnball Root. He set this up.'

Holly herself had been responsible for the capture of Julius's brother during her Recon initiation exercise. It was a story she had told Foaly many times.

'It would appear that Turnball is our adversary, which is not good news. But even taking his intellect and his hold over this Vishby person into account we still don't know how he commandeered a space probe.'

'It's just not possible,' said Foaly, adding an equine harrumph to lend weight to a statement that even he did not believe.

'Possible or not, we'll have to talk about it later,' said Holly, levelling the craft to just off horizontal. 'We're at the crash site.'

Everyone was relieved that the stolen ship had made it down in one piece. The mercenaries had probably stripped out much of what they didn't need to save weight, and they were more than likely a little reckless with the crowbars as they were about it. One loose rivet or cracked weld line would have been enough to allow a few atmospheres to squirt out and the ship would have been crushed like a soda can in the hand of a giant who was immensely strong and didn't like soda cans.

But the ship held its integrity in spite of an ominous rippling along the fuselage, which appeared suddenly.

'Who cares?' said Mulch, as usual failing to see the big picture. 'It's not even our ship. What are those mercenaries going to do, sue?' But even as he spoke, Mulch's humour was tinged with loss.

I can never go back to the Sozzled Parrot again, he realized. *And they served great curry. Real meat too.*

Outside and below, Atlantis rescue ships buzzed around the distressed shuttles, working hard to build a pressure dome so the crews could get some magic to the injured. Sea workers in pressure exo-armour hammered through rocks and debris on the seabed to lay a foam seal to build the dome upon. Nobody was too concerned about the crash site itself for the time being. The living came first.

'I should call in this Turnball Root theory,' said Holly. 'Commander Kelp will act on it.'

'We have to act first,' said Artemis. 'Haven won't have its ships here for at least an hour. By then it will be too late. We need to find evidence so that Trouble can make a case to the Council.'

Holly's fingers hesitated over Foaly's phone. There wasn't time to get into a strategy discussion with the commander. She knew Trouble's mind well; it didn't take that long to get to know. If she called him now, he would suggest a strategy that involved them waiting until he arrived and possibly some form of bivouac.

So instead of making a vid-call, she sent a brief text highlighting Turnball Root's name on the passenger list they weren't supposed to have and switched off the phone.

'He's bound to call back,' she explained. 'I'll switch it on again when we have something to tell him.'

Foaly glowered at her. 'I'm going to miss my crunchball

league updates,' he said, then: 'I know that sounds petty, but I pay a subscription.'

Artemis was concentrating on a problem to take his mind off the wall of sparkling fours that had followed him from his mind-screen and seemed to be hovering all around.

Not there, he told himself. *Focus on the Houdini act.*

'How did Turnball get out of the ship alive?' he wondered aloud. 'Foaly, can we access local cctv?'

'Not with this ship. This was once a beautiful emergency vehicle. I helped design the model. Talk about high spec – you could run an entire disaster-site clean-up from this beauty, once upon a time. Now there's barely enough tech in here to stop us crashing into a wall.'

'So there's no way of telling if any ships rendezvoused with the prison shuttle?'

'Not from here,' said Foaly.

'I need to know how Turnball escaped,' shouted Artemis, losing his cool again. 'How else am I supposed to find him? Doesn't anyone else see this? Am I alone in the universe?'

Butler shifted until he sat hunched over Artemis, almost enfolding him with his bulk. 'You're the one who sees, Artemis. That's your gift. We're the ones who get there eventually.'

'Speak for yourself,' said Mulch. 'I usually never get there. And when I do I never like it, especially when Artemis is involved.'

A bead of sweat lodged in the frown wrinkle between Artemis's eyes. 'I know, old friend. I just need to work – that is the only thing that can save me.' He thought hard for a moment. 'Can we run a scan to detect the ion trail of another ship?'

'Of course,' said Foaly. 'Even this stripped-back tub can't do without an omni-sensor.' He opened a program on the screen and a dark blue filter dropped over their view. The ion trails of the rescue ships showed up as spectral beams following behind their engines like glow-worms. One such beam led to the impact site from the direction of Atlantis, and another far more substantial column of light had ploughed down from above.

'There's the prison shuttle and there's the probe. Nothing else. How did he do it?'

'Maybe he didn't do it?' suggested Juliet. 'Maybe his plan went wrong. A lot of geniuses have been totally screwing up lately, if you see what I am trying to say, Artemis.'

Artemis half-smiled. 'I see what you are trying to say, Juliet. Mainly because you are saying it clearly and bluntly with no attempt to spare my feelings.'

'In fairness, Artemis,' said Juliet, 'we were almost crushed to death by mesmerized wrestling fans so I feel you can put up with a little ribbing. Also, I don't work for you, so you can't order me to shut up. You could dock Butler's salary, I suppose, but I can live with that.'

Artemis nodded at Holly. 'I don't suppose you two could be related?' Then he jumped to his feet, almost bashing his head on the ship's low ceiling. 'Foaly. I need to go down there.'

Holly tapped the depth gauge. 'No problem. I can come

around behind that ridge and keep us hidden from the rescue ships. Even if they do see us, they'll assume we've been sent by Haven. Worst-case scenario, they order us to back away from the crime scene.'

'I meant I need to go outside,' clarified Artemis. 'There's a pressure suit in that cubby and I need to take Foaly's phone and search for clues the old-fashioned way.'

'The old-fashioned way,' repeated Mulch. 'With a futuristic pressure suit and a fairy phone.'

A raft of vocal objections followed:

'You can't go – it's too dangerous.'

'I shall go in your place.'

'Why does it have to be my phone?'

Artemis waited until the clamour had died down then dealt with the protests in his usual terse, patronizing manner.

'I must go because the next stage of Turnball's plan obviously involves further loss of life and the lives of many are more important than the lives of the few.'

'I saw that on *Star Trek*,' said Mulch.

'It must be me,' continued Artemis. 'Because there is only one suit and it appears to be approximately my size. And, if I'm not mistaken, and it would be highly unusual that I would be, a correct fit is vital where pressure suits are concerned unless you want your eyeballs popping out of their sockets.'

If someone else had said this, it might be considered a joke to lift the atmosphere, but from the mouth of Artemis Fowl it was simple statement of fact.

'And finally, Foaly, it has to be your phone because, knowing your build standards as I do, it is made to withstand great pressures. Am I correct?'

'You are,' said Foaly, accepting the compliment with a nod of his long face. 'About the fit of the suit too. These things won't even seal properly if they don't like your dimensions.'

Butler was not pleased, but in the end he was the employee, though Artemis did not play that card. 'I must go, Butler,' said Artemis firmly. 'My mind is eating me alive. I think the guilt is the main problem. I must do whatever I can to atone.'

'And?' said Butler, unconvinced.

Artemis held his arms out so that Foaly could drape the suit sleeves over them.

'And I will not be beaten by that jackass.'

'Jackass?' said Foaly, wounded. 'My favourite uncle is a jackass.'

The pressure suit was actually two suits. The inner layer was a one-piece membrane threaded with life support and the outer shell was a body armour with a volatile surface that absorbed the water pressure and used it to power the servo mechanisms. Very clever, as you would expect from Koboi Laboratories.

'Koboi,' muttered Artemis, dismayed, when he saw the logo. Even a person not obsessed with omens would be a little put out by his nemesis's signature etched into the suit that was supposed to save his life. 'I am not buoyed by that.'

'You are not supposed to be buoyed,' said Foaly, lowering the transparent helmet bubble. 'You are supposed to be equalized.'

'I'm pretty sure that both of you just made really horrible jokes,' said Mulch, who was chewing something he had found somewhere. 'But I'm not sure because I think you broke my funny bone.'

At this point, Mulch's comments were like background chatter and were almost soothingly constant.

Foaly fixed his phone to an omni-sensor at the front of the helmet. 'It would take a swipe from a whale's tail to knock this loose. It's good for any depths or pressure you are likely to encounter and will even pick up the vibrations of your speech and convert them to soundwaves. But do try to enunciate.'

'You stick close to the rock face,' said Butler, cradling the helmet to make sure Artemis was paying attention. 'And at the first sign of trouble, *I'm* making the call to reel you in, not *you*. Do you understand, Artemis?'

Artemis nodded. The suit was connected to a dock on the ship's hull by a signature electromagnetic beam, which would zap it back to base in case of emergency.

'Just have a quick look around the site with Foaly's phone, and back you come. Ten minutes is all you get, then you'll have to follow another lead. Got it?'

Another nod from Artemis, but it seemed more like he was shutting out something than actually listening to Butler's words.

Butler snapped his fingers. 'Focus, Artemis! Time enough for your Atlantis Complex later. We have the Atlantis *Trench* outside that door and six miles of water above it. If you want to stay alive, you need to stay alert.' He turned to Holly. 'This is ridiculous. I'm pulling the plug.'

Holly's mouth was a tight line as she shook her head. 'Navy rules, Butler. You're on my boat, you follow my orders.'

'As I remember, I brought the boat.'

'Yes, thanks for bringing my boat.'

Artemis used this exchange to move closer to the rear airlock, a tight space where Butler could not follow.

'Ten minutes, old friend,' he said, his voice robotic through the helmet speaker. 'Then you can reel me back in.'

Butler suddenly thought about how Angeline Fowl would react when she heard about this latest escapade.

'Artemis, wait. There must be another way . . .'

But his objection bounced off a wall of perspex as the airlock dividing wall slid down with a noise like ball bearings rolling around the bottom of a can.

'I don't like that ball-bearing noise,' said Mulch. 'Doesn't sound very watertight.'

No one argued. They knew what he meant.

On the other side of the divider, Artemis was having a few misgivings of his own. He had just noticed the mercenaries' name for the ship, which was painted on the inside of the ocean door in what was supposed to look like blood but could not be or it would have long since washed off.

Probably some rubber-based solution, thought Artemis, but the base of the mercenaries' paint was not what bothered him – it was the name itself, which was *Plunderer*, in Gnommish of course. The verb *plunder* was pronounced *ffurfor* and the *er* suffix that changes the verb to a noun has, in Gnommish, the sound *fer*, which would imply that one is derived from the other. Grammar lesson aside, the pronunciation of the word *plunderer* was more or less *fourfourfour*.

Four four four, thought Artemis, pale inside his helmet. *Death death death*.

At which point the hull door slid up with more ball-bearing noises and the ocean sucked him into its deep dark depths.

Take a moment, thought Artemis as the suit's outer skin vibrated and activated the glow orbs at his temples, fingertips and knees. *Don't count, don't organize, just do as Butler advised and focus.*

He did not feel *underwater* though he knew he was. His body did not experience the expected resistance from the ocean, there was no dulling of the motor skills and he felt as though he could move with the same fluency as he always did, though Butler would argue whether his movements were ever fluid.

Which would have been great, had not the giant squid, whose territory he had just invaded, wrapped this glowing intruder in fat tentacles and whisked him off towards his lair.

Ah, the mythical giant squid. Genus Architeuthis, thought Artemis, strangely calm now that he was faced with a catastrophe worthy of all the worrying he'd been doing. *Not so mythical any more.*

⊗ • ⋊ꟼ • ⊖ • ⊗ • ◻ꞵ → • ⋊ • ⊗ ꞵ ⋊ꜰ • ∪ꖦ⊖ꝯ⊖ꞵ⋊

CHAPTER 9: FORBIDDEN LOVE

TURNBALL Root met Leonor Carsby on the remote Hawaiian island of Lehua in the summer of 1938. Leonor was there because she had crash-landed her Lockheed Electra into the northern slope of the island's volcanic ridge and freewheeled into the oddly shaped natural canal known as The Keyhole that cut through the island. Turnball was there because he maintained a winter residence on the otherwise uninhabited island where he liked to drink wine and listen to jazz recordings while he planned his next heist.

They were an unlikely couple but their first meeting took place in the kind of extreme circumstances which often cause hearts to beat faster and believe themselves in love.

Leonor Carsby was a human Manhattan heiress, but also a founder member of the Ninety-Nines, an organization of women in aviation first presided over by Amelia Earhart. When Earhart was lost in the Pacific, Leonor Carsby vowed that she herself would complete the journey which her friend and hero Amelia had begun.

In April 1938 she took off from California with a navigator and extra-large fuel tanks. Six weeks later Leonor Carsby arrived in The Keyhole with neither, having lost both to Lehua's cruel crescent-shaped ridge. It was a miracle she herself survived, improbably protected only by the Lockheed's bubble cockpit.

On his daily patrol Unix had come across the heiress spread-eagled on a flat rock at the water's edge. She was not in good shape: dehydrated, one leg badly broken, delirious and on the edge of death.

The sprite called it in, expecting to be given the execution order, but something about the human woman's face on his screen interested Turnball. He instructed Unix not to do anything, but to wait for his arrival.

Turnball took the trouble to shave, draw his hair back into a ponytail and put on a fresh ruffled shirt before taking the lift from the subterranean cave to the surface. There he found Unix squatting over the most gorgeous creature he had ever seen. Even twisted unnaturally and covered with blood and bruises, it was clear to Turnball that she was an exquisite beauty.

As he stood over Leonor, with the sun behind him, casting long shadows across his face, the aviatrix opened her eyes, took Turnball in and said two words:

'My God.' And then she was lost to delirium once more.

Turnball was intrigued. He felt a thaw round a heart that

had been frozen for decades. Who was this woman who had fallen from the skies?

'Bring her inside,' he told Unix. 'Use whatever magic we have to make her well.'

Unix did as he was told without comment, as was his way. Many other lieutenants might have questioned the wisdom of using the gang's dwindling supply of magic on a human. There was a newbie in the group who still had half a tank in him. When that was gone, who knew how long it would be before they had power again?

But Unix did not complain, and neither did the others as they were all aware that Turnball Root did not handle moaning well, and moaners tended to find themselves stranded somewhere uncomfortable waiting for something extremely painful to happen to them.

So Leonor Carsby was taken into the subterranean cave and nursed back to health. Turnball did not involve himself too much during the early stages, preferring to show up when Leonor was on the point of waking up so he could pretend he had been there the whole time. Initially Leonor did nothing but heal and sleep, but after some weeks she began to speak, hesitantly at first but then questions tumbled out of her so quickly that Turnball could hardly keep up.

'Who are you?'

'What are you?'

'How did you find me?'

'Is Pierre, my navigator, alive?'

'When will I be fit to travel?'

Generally, Turnball handled questions about as well as he handled moaning, but from Leonor Carsby every question caused him to smile indulgently and answer in detail.

Why is this? he wondered. *Why do I tolerate this human instead of simply tossing her to the sharks in the normal fashion? I am spending time and magic on her in extravagant amounts.*

Turnball began thinking about Leonor's face when he wasn't looking at it. Water chimes reminded him of her laugh. Sometimes he was sure he could hear her call to him, though he was on the far side of the island.

Grow up, you fool, he told himself. *Yours is not the heart of a romantic.*

But the heart cannot lie and Turnball Root found himself in love with Leonor Carsby. He cancelled two raids on federal bullion sites to be by her side and moved his office to her room, so he could work while she slept.

And, for her part, Leonor loved him too. She knew he was not human, but still she loved him. He told her about everything but the violence. Turnball styled himself as a revolutionary on the run from an unjust state, and she believed it. Why wouldn't she? He was the dashing hero who had saved her and Turnball made sure none of his cronies shattered this illusion.

When Leonor was well enough, Turnball took her to Mount Everest in his shuttle and she cried tears of amazement. As they hovered there, shrouded by the cold white mist, Turnball asked the question he had been wanting to ask for two months.

'That first moment, my dear, when your eyes met mine, you said, *My God*. Why did you say that?'

Leonor dried her eyes. 'I was half dead, Turnball. You'll laugh and think me silly.'

Root took her hand. 'I could never think that. Never.'

'Very well. I shall tell you. I said those words, Turnball, because I thought I had died and you were a fierce, handsome angel come to take me to heaven.'

Turnball did not laugh and he did not think it was silly. He knew at that moment that this gorgeous petite woman was the love of his life and he had to have her.

So when Leonor began talking of her return to New York and how Turnball would be the sensation of the city, he pricked the ball of his thumb with a quill, drew a thrall rune with the blood and prepared himself a supper of mandrake and rice wine.

VENICE, İTALY, NOW

The giant amorphobot bore Turnball Root to his beloved who waited for him at the basement dock to their house in Venice. The house stood four storeys high and had been commissioned by Turnball himself in 1798 and built from the finest reconstituted Italian marble mixed with fairy poly-mers, which would absorb the gradual shift of the city without cracking. It took several hours to make the journey, during which time the amorphobot kept Turnball and his men alive by periodically surfacing to replenish its cells with oxygen and spiking their arms with saline drips for nourishment. As they travelled, Turnball logged on to the computer in the amorphobot's belly to ensure that all was ready for the next stage of his plan.

Turnball found that he was very comfortable working in this sheltered environment with the world flashing by. He was insulated yet in control.

Safe.

From the corner of his eye, through the bleary mask of gel, Turnball was aware that Bobb Ragby and Ching Mayle now regarded him with something approaching worship following the spectacular nature of their escape. Worship. He liked that.

As they approached the Italian coast, Turnball felt his calm smugness desert him as a nervous serpent crawled into his stomach.

Leonor. How I have missed you.

Since Turnball had acquired a computer, there had been barely a day when they had not written to each other, but Leonor refused to participate in video-calls, and of course Turnball knew why.

You will always be beautiful to me, my darling.

The amorphobot thrummed the length of Venice's Grand Canal, skirting the mounds of rubbish and corpses of murdered princes until it stopped in front of the only sub-aquatic gate with an omni-sensor. The bot winked at the sensor and the sensor winked back, and, now that everyone was all pally, the gate opened without blasting them with the recessed Neutrino lances on its pillars.

Turnball winked at his crew. 'Thank goodness for that, eh? Sometimes that gate is a little unfriendly.' It was difficult to talk with the slow surge of gel over one's teeth, but Turnball felt the comment was worth it. Leonor would like that one.

Turnball's crew did not answer; their accommodation inside the gel bot was a little more cramped than their captain's. They were squished together like salted slugs in a cone.

The bot elongated itself to flow easily down the narrow channel to Turnball's underground dock. Strip lights glowed in the gloom, drawing them underneath the house. Deeper and deeper they went until at last the bot expelled Turnball gently on to a sloping slipway. He straightened his coat, tightened his ponytail and walked slowly along the ramp towards the slight figure waiting in the shadows.

'Put the others to sleep,' he told the bot. 'I need to talk to my wife.'

A plasma charge crackled through the bot, knocking out the fairies inside. Unix barely had time to roll his eyes before passing out.

Turnball took a halting step, nervous as a teenage elf about to take his first moon flight.

'Leonor? Darling. I have come home to you. Come and kiss me.'

His wife hobbled forward from the blackness, leaning heavily on an ivory-topped cane. Her fingers were gnarled, with glowing rheumatoid knuckles, her body was angular and unnatural, with sharp bones stretching the heavy lace of her skirt. One eye drooped and the other was closed completely and the lines on her face were scored deep by time and black with shadows.

'Turnball. As handsome as ever. It is so wonderful to see you free.' Leonor's voice was a mere rasp, laboured and painful.

'Now that you are home,' she said, taking an age, 'I can allow myself to die.'

Turnball's heart lurched. He had palpitations and a red band of heat tightened about his forehead. Everything he had ever done suddenly seemed all for nothing.

'You cannot die,' he said furiously, rubbing the pad of his thumb, heating the rune. 'I love you, I need you.'

Leonor's eyelids fluttered. 'I cannot die,' she repeated. 'But why not, Turnball? I am too old for life. Only my longing to see you again has kept me alive, but my time has passed. I regret nothing, except that I never flew again. I wanted to, but I didn't . . . Why was that?'

My hold is weakening. The old spell has died.

'You chose a life with me, my darling,' he said, rushing the last steps to her side. 'But now that I have found the secret to eternal youth you can be young again and soon you will fly wherever you want to go.'

Turnball felt the tiniest pressure as her fragile hand squeezed his fingers. 'I would like that, my dear.'

'Of course you would,' said Turnball, steering his wife to

the basement lift. 'And now you should rest. I have a lot to organize before we leave.'

Leonor allowed herself to be led, feeling, as always, powerless to resist her charismatic husband.

'That's my Turnball. Always coming to my rescue. One of these days I will rescue you.'

'You do rescue me,' said Turnball sincerely. '*Every* day.'

A barb of guilt pricked his heart as he knew he could never allow Leonor to fly again. For if she could fly then she might fly away.

Turnball was shocked and frightened by how feeble Leonor had become. Somehow the simple act of marrying a fairy had slowed down her ageing process, but now it seemed that he could delay her decline no longer. Turnball took his fear for his wife, turned it into rage and pointed it at his crew.

'We have a historic opportunity here,' he shouted at the small group, who were assembled in the second-storey library, 'to strike a blow at the heart of our ancient enemy and also secure a supply of magic that will never run dry. If one of you useless jail rats fails in his task that I have spent long lonely months planning, there will be nowhere on this earth you can hide from me. I will hunt you down and peel the skin from your head. Do you understand?'

They understood. Historically, Turnball's threats were usually vague and stylish – when he got down to specifics then the captain was close to the edge.

'Good. Good.' Turnball took a breath. 'Is everything ready, Quartermaster?'

Quartermaster Ark Sool stepped forward. Sool was an unusually tall gnome who had until quite recently been an internal affairs officer for the LEP. Having been demoted to private following an investigation into the ethics of his own methods, Sool cashed in whatever years he had and decided that he would use the accumulated knowledge of decades of criminal investigation to make himself some of the gold that gnomes were almost hypnotically attracted to. He advertised his services at the Sozzled Parrot and had soon been picked up by Turnball, anonymously at first, but now they were meeting face to face.

'Everything is ready, Captain,' he said, tones clipped, back straight. 'The shuttle we acquired from the LEP pound has been fitted out as an Atlantis ambulance. And I managed to trim the budget quite a bit and took the liberty of ordering a few new dress suits for you.'

'Excellent work, Quartermaster,' said Turnball. 'Your share has just gone up three per cent. Initiative pays. Never forget that.'

He rubbed his hands. 'How soon can we leave?'

'As soon as you give the word, Captain. The ambulance is on the jetty and ready for push off.'

'The laser?'

'Modified as requested. Small enough to fit in your pocket.'

'I find myself liking you quite a bit, Sool. Keep it up and soon you will be a full partner.'

ℛᎧᏰ→•⫶◊◯⌘ᏒᏆᏃ•⊕◯◊•⊖ᏒᏃ•ᏰᏜ•ᏃᎧℱ

Sool bowed slightly. 'Thank you, sir.'

'Any casualties while you were doing the shopping?'

'Not on our side, sir,' said Sool.

'And who cares about the other side, eh?'

Turnball liked the idea of blood being spilled. It made the entire exercise seem worthwhile.

'Now, we all know I am a selfish fairy – that's what's kept us alive and prospering apart from our recent stint at the Council's pleasure. If I get what I want, then we all flourish. And what I want is a source of magic strong enough to make my wife young again. And if that source of magic can also make your dreams come true, so much the better. Until recently there was no everlasting source, but now the demons have returned from Limbo bringing a mighty warlock with them. A young demon who has taken the unusual name of Number One.'

'A smarmy little upstart,' said Sool. 'Won't salute or wear a uniform.'

'I'm taking one per cent of your share back for interrupting,' said Turnball gently. 'Do it again and I'll take an arm.'

Sool opened his mouth to apologize but on consideration decided that another little bow would suffice.

'You're new. You'll learn. And if you don't, at least Mister Ragby will have a nice meal. He loves limbs.'

Ragby made the point by gnashing his large teeth.

'So, to continue, uninterrupted, there is now a demon warlock in Haven. If we can take him, then he shields us forever and he brings my Leonor back to me. Questions?'

Bobb Ragby raised a finger.

'Yes, Mister Ragby?'

'Won't this Number One be hard to get to?'

'Ah, excellent question, Mister Ragby. Not quite as stupid as you appear, after all. And you are right. *Generally* a person of this importance would be hidden away like the last stink-worm at a dwarf sludge pool party, but in the event of a disaster at sea, where the medical staff are stretched to their limits, such a powerful warlock will be pressed into service by the medical warlocks. So we will find him in the aquanaut *Nostremius*, the floating hospital.'

A broad smile spread across Ragby's face. 'And we have a fake ambulance.'

'We do indeed, Bobb. You put things together quickly.'

Ching had a question too. 'A person like that, with all this power, surely the LEP are going to come after a person like that?'

This was exactly the question Turnball wanted asked. He was delighted by how this presentation was going. 'Let me answer your question with one of my own, just to get your mind working, because I have faith that you're not just a stupid goblin. Do you know why I had the space probe crash into the prison shuttle?'

Ching's reptilian face wrinkled in concentration and he absently licked his eyeballs as he thought. 'I think you done that so the Leppers would ass-ume we were dead.'

'Correct, Mister Mayle. I orchestrated a huge catastrophe so everyone would believe we had been killed.' Turnball shrugged. 'I don't feel bad about that. We are at war with the Leppers as you call them. If you take sides in a war, then you can expect to be a target. I might feel a little bad about the next catastrophe. I'm a little sentimental about hospitals; I was born in one.'

Bobb raised the same finger again. 'Uh, Captain, was that a joke?'

Root beamed a charming smile. 'Why, yes it was, Mister Ragby.'

Bobb Ragby started to laugh.

The Atlantis Trench, now

Artemis Fowl felt the tentacles of the giant squid tighten round him. Saucer-sized spherical suckers latched on to his pressure suit, slobbering on the surface, searching for purchase. Each cup was lined with rings of razor-sharp chitin teeth, which gnashed viciously on Artemis's protected limbs and torso.

Eight arms, if I remember correctly, thought Artemis. *Which is two fours. Die! Die!*

Artemis almost giggled. Even in the death grip of the biggest squid ever to be seen by a man he was persisting with his compulsive behaviour.

It won't be long now before I am counting my words again.

When the squid's biting suckers could not gain access to the tender meat inside, it held Artemis away from the giant mantle.

The next stage of the squid's assault was to batter Artemis with one of its two longer tentacles, which it swung like a mace. Artemis felt the jarring blow, but his suit did not rupture.

'One two three four five,' shouted Artemis defiantly. 'Wear the suit and stay alive.'

Number poetry. Back to square one.

Three times more the squid struck and then it drew Artemis close in circling bands of fat tentacle and took his entire head inside his gnashing beak. The noise was exactly what Artemis had always imagined it would sound like if a giant squid tried to crack his sea helmet.

If I get out of this, I will start thinking about girls like a normal fifteen-year-old.

After several heart-stopping minutes, the squid apparently gave up and dashed Artemis down in a nest of bones and sea junk that it had assembled on a high shelf at the side of an underwater cliff.

Artemis lay on his back and watched as the creature expanded its mantle cavity, filled it with hundreds of gallons of seawater, then contracted the mantle, shooting itself into the near pitch black of deep water.

Artemis felt that in the circumstances a slang word was justified.

'Wow,' he breathed. 'Of all the things that have almost killed me, that was the most fearsome.'

After several minutes, Artemis's heart rate slowed enough to extinguish the flashing heart readout on his suit and he felt that he could move without throwing up.

'I've moved position,' he said into his helmet, in case Foaly's phone, which was stuck into the helmet over his forehead, was still actually functional. 'I intend to try and take some bearings so you can come and rescue me.'

'Moved position?' said Foaly's voice, which was transmitted faintly by vibration through the helmet's polymer, so that it seemed to come from everywhere. 'That's an understatement. We're going to try to catch up.'

'Look for landmarks,' said another voice, Butler. 'We can use them to triangulate with Foaly's phone to pinpoint your position.'

This was a hopeful plan at best, but Artemis felt that it was better to have something to do other than just wait for his air to run out.

'Actually, how much air do I have?'

Foaly, of course, was the one to answer that technical question. 'The suit has functioning gills that draw oxygen from the ocean, so it will keep breathing long after you're dead, so to speak. Not that you're going to die.'

Artemis turned over and raised himself on to all fours. Any difficulty he experienced was due to his body being in shock from the cephalopod attack and not the pressure suit, which was functioning perfectly and which would later go on to win an industry award for its performance that day.

Take five steps, Artemis urged himself. *Just five. Whatever you do, don't stop at . . . one less than five.*

Artemis took five shuffling steps, feeling his way along the ledge, carefully avoiding shuffling off into the abyss. He could probably survive the drop, but he had no desire to have to climb back up again.

'I'm on a long flat ledge, on the lip of the trench,' he said softly, anxious not to disturb any vibration-sensitive creatures, sharks, for example.

He realized that the squid had dropped him into some kind of nest. Perhaps the creature did not actually sleep here, but it seemed to feed in the spot and collect things that interested it. There were several skeletons, including the gigantic ribbed remains of a sperm whale, which Artemis first mistook for a shipwreck. There were small boats, huge brass propellers, great chunks of gleaming quartz, phosphorescent rocks, various crates and even a mangled orange deep-sea submarine with grinning skeletons inside.

Artemis moved quickly away from the craft even though his intellect assured him that the skeletons could not harm him.

Pardon me if I don't completely trust my intellect these days.

He noticed that in all this rubble there did not appear to be any fairy-made articles, even with Atlantis just over the crest.

Then Artemis saw that he was mistaken. There was, no more than ten metres from him, a small, slick metallic computer cube with unmistakable fairy markings that seemed to float just above the surface of the ledge.

No, wait, not floating. Suspended in gel.

Artemis poked the gel gingerly and when there was no reaction apart from a gentle fizzling spark he plunged his sheathed hand into the gel up to the shoulder, grasping the cube by a corner. With the aid of the suit's servo motors, he easily pulled it free.

Wreckage from the probe, perhaps, he thought, then said aloud, 'I have something. It could be pertinent. Are you seeing this, Foaly?'

There was no reply.

I need to get back to the ship, or into the crash crater. Somewhere away from the giant squid who wants to nibble my flesh and suck my marrow.

Artemis immediately regretted thinking the *suck my marrow* bit, as it was far too graphic and now he felt like throwing up again.

I don't even know which way to go, Artemis realized. *This entire venture was ill advised. What were the chances I would find a clue at the bottom of the ocean?*

An ironic statement, as it would turn out, because he held a vital clue in his hands.

Artemis swung his head this way and that to see if whatever was caught in the beams of his helmet could spark off an idea. Nothing, just an almost transparent fish propelling its bloated body with stubby fins and filtering plankton through its circular nostrils.

I need something to happen, thought Artemis a little desperately. The idea had occurred to him that he was lost alone underneath six miles of crushing ocean with not much of an idea what to do next. Artemis had always performed well under pressure, but that was usually the intellectual pressure a person might experience at the end of a taxing chess match, not the kind of pressure that could splinter a person's bones and squeeze every bubble of air from their lungs. Actual water pressure.

As it turned out, *something* did happen; the squid came back, and he bore in the grip of his larger tentacles what appeared to be the space probe's nose cone.

I wonder what he wants that for? wondered Artemis. *It's almost as if he's actually manipulating a tool.*

But to what end? What nut would a giant squid wish to crack?

'Me,' Artemis blurted. 'I'm the nut.'

Artemis could have sworn the squid winked at him, before bringing the five-tonne chunk of spacecraft swinging down towards the morsel of meat in its blue shell.

'I'm the nut!' Artemis shouted again, a little hysterically it must be said. He backpedalled along the ledge, the suit's motors lending him a little speed. Just enough metres per second to feel the force of the swing but not the metal itself. The probe's prow cut through the rock like a cleaver through soft meat and carved a v-shaped trench that ran between the soles of Artemis's feet.

So much for being a genius, thought Artemis bitterly. *One grand gesture and I'm fish food.*

The squid yanked its weapon free from the rock and raised it high, pumping its mantle cavity full of water for the next effort. Artemis's back was literally against the wall. He had nowhere to go and made an easy target.

'Butler!' called Artemis, purely out of habit. He had no real expectation that his bodyguard could miraculously materialize at his side, and even if he did it would just be to die there.

The squid closed one huge eye, taking careful aim.

These things are smarter than scientists think, thought Artemis. *I do wish I had been able to write a paper.*

The prow came hammering down, compressing water then pushing it aside. Metal filled Artemis's vision and it occurred to him that this was the second time this particular prow had almost crushed him.

Except this time it's not almost.

But it was to be *almost*. An orange circle pulsed in Artemis's helmet readout and he prayed that it was a sign that an electromagnetic connection had been established between his suit and the ship.

It was. Artemis felt a gentle tug, then a fierce one that yanked him off the ledge straight up towards the hovering mercenary craft. In the light of his suit beams he could see a magnetic plate in the ship's belly. Underneath him the squid abandoned its improvised mallet and bunched itself for pursuit.

I'll probably slow down before I hit that plate, Artemis thought hopefully.

He didn't, but the impact hurt a lot less than a blow from an armed giant squid.

Generally the diver would be taken inside immediately, but in this case Holly decided that it would be best to leave Artemis where he was and put a little distance between them and the squid, which Artemis would later agree was the correct decision even though at the time he was screaming.

Artemis craned his head round to see the massive dome of the squid's head jetting after him, tentacles behind rippling like skipping ropes, skipping ropes with razor-lined suckers and enough power to crush an armoured vehicle, not to mention the ability to manipulate tools.

'Holly!' he shouted. 'If you can hear me. Go faster!'

Apparently she could hear him.

Holly took the ship deep into the impact crater and when she was absolutely sure the squid was off their scopes she flipped the magnetic plate and Artemis was dumped into the airlock, still clutching the fairy box to his chest.

'Hey, look,' said Mulch, once the airlock had drained. 'It's the nut.' He ran in small circles around the bay squealing: 'I'm the nut. I'm the nut.' The dwarf stopped for a laugh. 'He cracks me up, really.'

Butler hurried to Artemis's side. 'Cut him some slack, Diggums. He just tangled with a giant squid.'

Mulch was not impressed. 'I once ate one of those things. A big one, not a tiddler like that fellow.'

Butler helped Artemis with the helmet. 'Anything broken? Can you move your fingers and toes? What is the capital of Pakistan?'

Artemis coughed and stretched his neck. 'Nothing broken. Digits all mobile and the capital of Pakistan is Islamabad, which is noteworthy for being purpose built to be the capital.'

'OK, Artemis,' said Butler. 'You're fine. I won't ask you to count to five.'

'I would rather count in fives if you don't mind. Foaly, congratulations on building such a sturdy phone with an excellent tracking program.'

Holly hit the water flaps to slow the ship's forward motion. 'Did you find anything?'

Artemis held out the hardware cube. 'Wreckage from the probe. This was covered in some kind of gel. Interesting texture, loaded with crystals. Something of yours, Foaly?'

The centaur clopped over and took the small metal box. 'It's the heart from an amorphobot,' he said fondly. 'These little guys were the perfect foragers. They could absorb anything including each other.'

'Maybe they absorbed this Turnball guy and his buddies,' said Juliet, half joking.

Artemis was about to explain in patronizingly simple terms exactly why this wasn't possible when it occurred to him that it was indeed possible – not only that, it was probable.

'They weren't programmed to act as rescue vehicles,' said Foaly.

Holly scowled. 'If you tell me one more time that those amorphobots weren't programmed to do something, then I will have to shave your hindquarters while you sleep.'

Artemis crawled to the steel bench. 'Are you saying that you people knew about these amorphobots all the time?'

'Of course we did. They attacked us in Iceland. Remember?'

'No. I was unconscious.'

'That's right. Seems like ages ago.'

'So I endured trial by squid for nothing?'

'Oh no. Not for nothing. It would have taken me minutes to make the connection and even then it would only have been a theory.' Foaly typed a code into his phone, releasing it from the pressure suit's helmet. 'Whereas now we can check the programming.'

Foaly hooked his phone to the bot's brain and was delighted to see its readout light up. He ran a few checks and was easily able to pinpoint the shadow program. 'This is a little puzzling. The bot was sent new mission parameters by the control orb. Charmingly enough, it's actually telling its gel to kill us all right now. That's why we never detected any outside interference – there was none. It's a simple little shadow program, a few lines of code, that's all. Simple to kill.' He did so with a few taps of the keyboard.

'Where is this control orb?' asked Artemis.

'It's in my lab, in Haven.'

'Could it have been tampered with?'

Foaly didn't have to think about this for long. 'Impossible, and I'm not just being typical me and denying my equipment is responsible. I check that thing most days. I ran a systems check yesterday and there was nothing out of the ordinary in the orb's history. Whoever set this up has been feeding the probe instructions for weeks, if not months.'

Artemis closed his eyes to blot out the shining fours that had appeared in his vision, floating around the craft's interior, hissing malignantly.

$$\text{᛭ᛒᚱᚼ᛫ᚿᛊᛁᚢ᛫ᛊᚠᚱᚦᛒ᛬᛭᛫▢᛫ᚿᛁᚢ᛫ᛒ}$$

*I manage to survive a giant squid attack and now I'm worried
by hissing fours. Great.*

'I need everyone to sit in a line, on the opposite bench,
small to tall.'

'That's the Atlantis Complex talking, Mud Boy,' said Holly.
'Fight it.'

Artemis pressed the heels of his hands into his eye sockets.
'Please, Holly. For me.'

Mulch was delighted with this game. 'Should we hold
hands, or chant? How about: *five keeps me alive, four makes my
bottom sore?*'

'Number poetry?' said Artemis sceptically. 'That's ridiculous. Please, sit where I ask.'

They did, reluctantly and grumbling, Foaly and Mulch
arguing for a moment over who was smaller. There was no
argument over who was tallest. Butler sat hunched at the
end, chin almost between his knees. Beside him sat Juliet,
then Foaly, then Mulch and finally Holly who had set the ship
on neutral.

Five, thought Artemis. *Five friends to keep me alive.*

He sat, still clad in the pressure exo-skeleton suit, watching his friends and taking strength, letting his ideas build.

Finally he said, 'Foaly, there must have been a second orb.'

Foaly nodded. 'There was. We always grow a back-up. In
this case we used the clone because the original was damaged.
Only minor damage, true, but you can't take chances with
space travel. The first was sent off to be incinerated.'

'Where?'

'Atlantis. Koboi Labs got the contract. This was obviously before we realized how deranged Opal is.'

'So, if we accept that Turnball Root got hold of the second orb and had it repaired by Vishby, or whoever else worked for him, then would the probe obey commands from that orb?'

'Of course. No questions asked. They could be sent by any computer with a satellite link.'

Butler raised a finger. 'Can I say something?'

'Of course, old friend.'

'Foaly. Your security sucks. When are you guys going to learn? A few years ago the goblins built a shuttle, and now you have convicts running your space program.'

Foaly stamped a hoof. 'Hey, pal, less of the judgemental attitude. We've stayed hidden for thousands of years. That's how good our security is.'

'Five ten fifteen twenty,' shouted Artemis. 'Please. We need to work quickly.'

'Can we tease you about this later?' said Mulch. 'I have some great material.'

'Later,' said Artemis. 'For now, we need to work out where Turnball is going and what his final objective is.'

When there was no argument, he continued. 'If we assume that Turnball used his orb to control the probe and used these amorphobots to carry him away, can we track the amor-phobots?'

Foaly's head movement was somewhere between a nod and a shake. 'Possibly. But not for long.'

Artemis understood. 'The gel dissipates in salt water.'

'That's right. The friction between the water and the bots wears down the gel, but as soon as it separates from the brain it begins to dissolve. No charge, no cohesion. I'd say with a melon-sized bubble, you might get a few hours.'

'It's already been a few hours. How much longer do we have?'

'It may already be too late. If I was allowed out of my school desk, I might be able to tell you.'

'Of course, please.'

Foaly swung his arms forward, lifting himself from his awkward seated position, and clopped into the cockpit where he quickly entered the gel's chemical make-up into the gyro's rudimentary computer and dropped a filter over the portholes.

'Luckily for us the mercenaries decided to leave the scanners intact. Everyone pick a window. I've run a scan for a specific radiation and the gel trail should show up as a luminous green. Shout if you see something.'

They all took a porthole, except Holly, who sat in the pilot's chair ready to take off in whichever direction the trail led.

'I see it!' said Mulch. 'No, wait. It's a really angry squid looking for his little nut. Sorry. I know that was inappropriate, but I'm hungry.'

'There,' called Juliet. 'I see something, portside.'

Artemis switched to her porthole. Winding from the depths of the crater was a wispy stream of shining bubbles that disappeared as they watched it, the lower bubbles separating into smaller blobs then towards the end of the trail some were disappearing altogether.

'Quickly, Holly,' said Artemis urgently. 'Follow those bubbles.'

Holly opened the throttle. 'Now there's an order I never thought I'd hear from you,' she said.

They sped after the bubble trail in the mercenaries' gyro, though Foaly did argue that technically they were not bubbles but globules, for which information he received a punch on the shoulder from Juliet.

'Hey, don't punch me,' protested the centaur.

'Technically that was a rap, not a punch,' corrected Juliet. 'Now this . . . this is a punch.'

The trail grew fainter before their eyes and Holly quickly programmed in a projected course whenever the globules changed direction just in case they disappeared altogether.

Artemis sat in the co-pilot's chair with a hand over one eye and his other hand in front of his face.

'The thumb is generally acknowledged to be a finger,' he told Holly. 'In which case we're safe, because that makes five fingers. But some experts argue that the thumb is completely different and is one of the things that sets us apart from the animals and in that case we only have four fingers on each hand. And that's bad.'

He's getting worse, thought Holly anxiously.

Butler was stumped. If someone were threatening Artemis, the correct protective action was usually pretty obvious: *Clobber the bad guy and confiscate his weapon.* But now the bad guy was Artemis's own mind, and it was turning him against everyone, including Butler.

How can I trust any order Artemis gives me? the bodyguard wondered. *It could simply be a ruse to get me out of the way. Just like Mexico.*

He squatted beside Artemis. 'You do have faith in me now, don't you, Artemis?'

Artemis tried to meet his eyes but couldn't manage it. 'I'm trying, old friend. I want to, but I know that soon I won't have the strength. I need help, and soon.'

They both knew what Artemis wasn't saying: *I need help before I go out of my mind entirely.*

They followed the gel trail eastwards through the Atlantic and round the tip of Gibraltar into the Med. In the early afternoon the trail died suddenly. The last green bubble popped and suddenly they were fifteen metres underwater, two miles outside the Golfo di Venezia with nothing but yachts and gondolas in the gyro's scopes.

'It has to be Venice,' said Holly, bringing the ship to periscope depth, taking the opportunity to fill the air tanks and equalize. 'It's right in front of us.'

'Venice is a big city,' said Butler. 'And not an easy place to search. How are we going to find these guys?'

The amorphobot brain in Foaly's hand suddenly beeped as it established a link with its brethren. 'I don't think that's going to be a problem. They're close. Very close. Very, very close.'

Artemis was not happy with his melodramatic statement. '*Very, very* close? Really, Foaly? You're a scientist. How close, exactly?'

Foaly pointed to the gyro's hatch. 'That close.'

The next minute or two were frantic and seemed to have an entire day's worth of happenings compressed into a few moments. To Artemis and Foaly the whole thing was just flashes of colour and blurred movement. Butler, Holly and Juliet saw a little more, being trained soldiers. Butler even managed to get off the bench, which did him absolutely no good whatsoever.

The gyro's hatch made a sound like a giant plastic bottle being stepped on by a giant foot, then simply disappeared. Rather, it appeared to disappear. It was actually torn backwards with great force then hurled into the sky. The hatch eventually lodged in the shaft of the bell tower of San Marco Piazza, which caused quite a bit of consternation in the city, especially for the painter whose rope was severed by the spinning hatch and who plummeted thirty metres to land on his brother's back. The brothers were already fighting and this didn't make things any better.

Back in the gyro, water immediately began flooding the ship's interior, but most of the available space was filled by the rolling forms of six amorphobots, which flowed into the bay, chittering as they selected their targets. It was all over in less than a second. The bots pounced on their targets, quickly engulfing them in turgid gel, and spirited them into the azure blue of the Mediterranean.

As they were whisked towards the murky form of a fairy ship in the depths, each prisoner had his or her own thoughts about what had happened.

Artemis was stunned by how much this abduction reminded him of his time spent battling through the mind-screen in his own brain.

Holly wondered if her weapon would work inside the gunk, or if it had been disabled yet again.

Foaly couldn't help feeling a little fondness for the amorphobot that held him prisoner; after all he had grown it in a lab beaker.

Juliet tried to keep Butler in sight. So long as she could see her brother, she felt reasonably safe.

Butler thrashed for a moment but quickly realized that his efforts were futile and so drew himself in like a newborn, conserving his energy for one explosive movement.

Mulch was also considering an explosive movement. Maybe he couldn't escape but he could certainly make this blobby thing regret picking him up. The dwarf pulled his knees slowly to his chest and allowed the gas in his tubes to collect into long bubbles. Eventually he would have enough force to blast through or else he would be left floating in what would look like the world's largest lava lamp.

Turnball Root was having a reasonably good time. He would have been having a wonderful time, but for the fact that his darling Leonor was not in the condition he would like her to be, and he was worried that if he was able to restore

Leonor's faculties, she would quickly tumble to the fact that he was not quite the principled revolutionary he had always pretended to be and he would lose her love. Leonor had a strong sense of morality and she would definitely kick up a fuss at the idea of him imprisoning a demon warlock to keep her forever young. Turnball glanced at the thrall rune on his thumb. The intricate set of spirals and characters that had kept Leonor on the hook, but the power of which was weakening all the time. Would she have left him without it? Maybe. Probably.

Turnball was possibly the world's foremost expert on runes. They suited his situation as they only required a tiny spark of magic to kick-start them and thereafter operated on the power of the symbols themselves. Different people reacted differently to rune control. Some could be controlled for decades while others would reject the black magic and go instantly insane. Leonor had been the ideal thrall because a large part of her wanted to believe what Turnball told her.

With his modified laser, Turnball could enslave anyone he wished, for as long as he wished no matter how they felt about him, and without the need for a single spark of magic.

Like these new prisoners for example. A veritable treasure chest of talents at his disposal. One never knew when a teenage mastermind would come in handy, or a technical centaur, especially when it was well known that the little demon trusted them both. With those two and the warlock, he could start his own principality if he chose to.

Yes, I am having a reasonably good time, thought Turnball. *But soon I will be having an excellent time. Just one more set of people to kill. Maybe two.*

The amorphobots had entered the ambulance through the airlock and morphed into one in the ambulance's only cell. Actually the bot holding Mulch Diggums was excluded from the morph as the other bots could not identify the chemical spectrum of the gas bubbles inside the dwarf's body and did not frankly like the look of Mulch anyway and so, though he tried to meld with the others, the bot was repulsed and wobbled lonely in the corner.

Turnball Root descended the spiral staircase from the bridge and literally swaggered into the cell to gloat.

'Look here,' he said to Unix, who stood at his shoulder, grim as ever. 'The finest fairy and human minds all gathered together in one cell.'

They hung before him suspended in smart gel, unable to do much besides take shallow breaths and move like sleepy swimmers.

'Don't even bother making the effort to call for help or shoot your way out,' Turnball continued. 'I am jamming your phones and weapons.' He leaned close to the bot's shimmering surface. 'Here's one of Julius's little pups. Didn't we shoot her already, Unix?'

A leery smile tightened the sprite's jaw, though it did not make him seem a nicer person.

'And the great Foaly. Saviour of the People. Not any more,

my little pony. Soon you will be my thrall and delighted to be so.' Turnball wiggled his hand at the captives and they could see the red runes painted on his finger and thumb.

'And what have we here?' Turnball stopped in front of the Butlers. 'Crazy Bear and the Jade Princess. I missed you once before but it won't happen a second time.'

'What about me?' Mulch managed to say, and the bot translated the vibrations of his larynx into sound.

'What about you?'

'Don't I get a description? I'm dangerous too.'

Turnball laughed, but softly so the noise would not awaken Leonor who slept in the berth upstairs. 'I like you, dwarf. You have spirit, but nonetheless I shall kill you as you are of no use to me, unless you fancy a position as jester. A fat, smelly jester. Obviously I am assuming that you smell bad. You certainly look as though you might.'

Turnball moved on to Artemis. 'And, of course, Artemis Fowl. Ex-criminal mastermind and current psychotic. How is the Complex going, Artemis? I bet you have a *bad* number. What is it, five? Four?' Artemis must have flinched because Turnball knew he had guessed correctly. 'Four, then. And how do I know you suffer from Atlantis? You should ask your *friend* Foaly. He's the one who supplies me with pictures.'

Artemis was not at all surprised to find that some of his paranoia was actually justified.

Turnball paced along the line like a general delivering a pre-battle pep talk. 'I am delighted that you are all here, genuinely delighted. Because you can be useful to me. You see, my wife is very old, and to save her life and bring her youth back I need a very powerful magician.'

Artemis's eyes widened. He got it straight away. All of this to lure N°1 out of Haven.

'Your friend Number One will be helping out with the injured on the *Nostremius* and we were going to go in there, masquerading as patients, and bring him out with my super-duper modified lasers, but there was always going to be the niggly problem of the little fellow perhaps getting a magical bolt off before I enthralled him. But now, Holly Short, one of his best friends in the whole world, is going to fetch him for me.'

Turnball turned to Unix. 'Tell the bot to spit out Captain Short.'

Unix consulted a computer rendering of the bot and its contents on a wall screen. With a flick of his finger, he dragged Holly from the gel. Almost instantaneously the bot did the same. Holly felt as though she were being vomited from the belly of a beast on to the cold metal floor. She lay there gasping as her lungs accustomed themselves to breathing pure air once more. She opened her eyes to see a grinning Turnball looming over her.

'I'm remembering more and more about you as time goes by,' he said, and kicked her hard in the ribs with one black boot. 'And I remember that you put me in prison. But never mind, eh. Now you can make up for it by doing me a good turn.'

Holly spat a blob of gel on to the deck. 'Not likely, Turnball.'

Turnball kicked her again. 'You will address me by my rank.'

◊•8→•⨞⟊ᖴ⍭ᕊ•8⏽•⋃ᕱᕊⱸ⊃⌇⊗⍭ᕊ⊗•⩕ᕊ

Holly spoke through gritted teeth. 'I doubt it.'

'I don't doubt it,' said Turnball, and put his boot on her throat. From his pocket he pulled what looked like a pen light.

'This looks like a pen light, doesn't it?'

Holly could not speak, but she was guessing the slim cylinder was something more sinister than a light.

'Yet it is quite a bit more than that. You may have guessed that black-magic runes are something of a hobby of mine. Illegal, yes, but almost everything I do is illegal, so why start worrying now? What this little laser does is burn the rune directly into the skin of the person I wish to enslave. No magic necessary. So long as I have the corresponding rune on my person, then you are my thrall forever.'

Turnball showed his finger to Holly, the one with Vishby's rune still inscribed on the pad, the magic of which could be transferred to her now that Vishby was dead. 'And guess what, my dear? A free slot just opened up in my organization.'

Root activated the laser and hummed for a moment until the tip turned red, then he jammed it into Holly's neck, branding her with his binding rune.

Holly bucked and screamed in a black-magic fit.

'Not so gentle as the touch,' noted Turnball, stepping out of puke range just in case.

The fit lasted less than a minute, leaving Holly rigid on the floor, breathing abnormally fast, eyelids fluttering.

Turnball licked the blood rune on his own finger.

'Now, Miss Short, what say we go and kidnap a warlock?'

Holly stood, arms stiff by her side, eyes unfocused.

'Yes, Captain,' she said.

Turnball clapped her on the back. 'That's more like it, Short. Isn't it liberating not to have a choice? You just do what I say and nothing is your fault.'

'Yes, Captain. Most liberating.'

Turnball handed her a Neutrino. 'Feel free to kill anyone who gets in your way.'

Holly checked the battery level expertly. 'Anyone who gets in my way, I kill them.'

'I like these lasers,' said Turnball, twiddling the rune pen. 'Let's do someone else. Tell the bot to pop young Fowl out of his bubble, Unix. It will be nice to have a pet genius.'

Unix dragged his finger across the touch-screen and Artemis flopped gasping to the floor like a fish out of water.

THE AQUANAUT *NOSTREMIUS*, ATLANTIS TRENCH

The young demon warlock who chose to call himself Nº1 was feeling extremely sad. He was a sensitive little fellow, though you would not think it to look at his grey armour-plated hide and the squat head that seemed to push its way out of his lumpy shoulders, but he felt others' pain, and this trait, according to his master, was what made him such an excellent warlock.

There was a lot of pain in the fairy world today. The Martian probe disasters in Iceland and the Atlantis Trench were the worst fairy disasters to have occurred in recent times. To the humans, injury on this scale would probably not even make it on to the big news stations, but the fairy folk were small in number and cautious by nature so to have two probe-related disasters in one cycle was horrific. But at least a larger catastrophe had been averted by the efficient evacuation of Atlantis.

N^{O}1 had barely begun to grieve for the loss of his friends in Iceland, when the LEP had informed him that Holly, Foaly and Artemis had actually survived. Commander Trouble Kelp asked him to go to Atlantis on the *Nostremius* hospital ship to help heal those injured by the probe's blast wave. The little demon had immediately agreed, hoping that he could distract himself for a short period at least by using his powers to help others. And now news had filtered through that Holly's escape pod had gone down at sea and all hands were presumed lost. It was too much to process: dead, alive, then dead again. If Holly had had some magic in her system N^{O}1 might have been able to sense her out there somewhere, but he could feel nothing.

So for the past several hours N^{O}1 had worked himself ragged laying hands on the injured. He had knitted bones, sealed gashes, repaired ruptured organs, drawn salt water from lungs, draped veils of calm over hysteria and, in some extreme cases, wiped the entire pile-up from people's memory. For the first time since he had blossomed as a warlock, N^{O}1 was actually feeling a little depleted. But he could not leave right now as word had just come over the aquanaut's speakers that yet another ambulance had docked.

I need to sleep, he thought wearily. *But not to dream. I would only dream of Holly. I cannot believe she's gone.*

And something made him look up at that moment and he saw Holly Short walking down the corridor towards the quarantine door. The sight was so unexpected that N°1 was strangely unsurprised.

It's Holly, but she's moving weirdly. As though she's underwater.

N°1 finished the bone knit he was working on, then left the clean-up to a nurse. He shambled towards the security door, where Holly was having her retina scanned. The computer accepted her LEP credentials and popped open with a pneumatic hiss.

N°1 skipped outside to prevent Holly entering.

'We have to keep that area germ free,' he said, sorry these had to be the first words he uttered to his resurrected friend, 'and you look like you just escaped from toxic garbage.' Then he hugged her tightly. 'You smell like a toxic dump too, but you're alive. Thank goodness. Tell me, did Foaly survive? Please say he did. And Artemis? I couldn't bear it when I heard you were all gone.'

Holly did not meet his eyes. 'Artemis is sick. I need you to come.'

N°1 was immediately desolate, his mood swinging rapidly like a small child's. 'Artemis is sick? Oh no. Bring him in and we can take care of him here.'

Holly turned back the way she had come. 'No. He can't be moved. You need to follow me.'

N°1 jogged after his friend Holly without a moment's

hesitation. 'Is it a broken bone, is that it? Artemis can't be moved? Is Foaly OK? Where did you guys go?'

But there were no answers for the little demon, and all he could do was follow Holly's square shoulders through the throngs of walking wounded, past the cots that had been erected in the hallways. The smell of disinfectant burned his nostrils and the cries of the injured seared his heart.

I'll just fix Artemis quickly. Maybe lie down for a minute, then get back to work.

N°1 was a good soul and it never for a moment occurred to him to probe Holly a little to make sure she was fully herself. It never crossed his mind that one of his closest friends could be leading him into a life of servitude.

Turnball sat by Leonor's bed in the stolen shuttle ambulance, holding her hand while she slept. He felt a little giddy about changing his plan at the last minute. It was quite the cavalier move, and the rush of adrenalin reminded him of his younger days.

'It was all seat-of-the-pants stuff before I went to prison,' he confided to the sleeping Leonor. 'I was a captain in the LEP and running the underworld at the same time. To be honest, there wasn't much of an underworld before I came along. In the morning I would chair a meeting of the task force that was trying to apprehend me, and in the evening I would be doing black-market deals with the goblin gangs.' Turnball smiled and shook his head. 'Good days.'

Leonor did not react, as Turnball had thought it best to

give her just a drop of sedative until the warlock had restored her youth. He knew from her talk of death that he was losing his grip on his wife and she was not strong enough to survive another thrall rune.

So, sleep, my darling. Sleep. Soon, all will be as it was.

As soon as Captain Short returned with the demon. And if she did not? Then he would board the *Nostremius* and take the warlock by force. Perhaps he would lose a crew member or two, but they should be glad to die for their captain's wife.

One level down, in the brig, Bobb Ragby was on guard duty, a duty which he was enjoying immensely as he considered it payback for all the years he himself had been lorded over by guards. It didn't matter to Bobb that his gel-bound prisoners weren't actually the people who'd watched over him; that was just their bad luck. He was taking special pleasure in teasing Mulch Diggums whom he had long considered a competitor in the *top criminal dwarf* competition that he played in his head during the long hours spent on the toilet thanks to a diet of processed food.

Turnball had ordered him to split the amorphobots for safety and now one hung in each corner of the cell like a giant wobbling egg sac.

If any of them act up, then use the shocker feature at your own discretion, Turnball had said. *And if they try to shoot their way out make sure we get that on video so we can have a good laugh later.*

Ragby had decided he would definitely use the shocker at the first provocation, maybe before the first provocation.

'Hey, Diggums, why don't you try to eat some of the gel, so I have an excuse to electrocute you?'

Mulch did not waste his energy talking; he simply bared his enormous teeth.

'Yeah?' said Ragby. 'They ain't so big. The more I look at you, Diggums, the less I believe all that junk your little groupies spew back at the Sozzled Parrot. You don't look like much of a burglar to me, Diggums. I think you're a phoney. A fraud, a tale-spinning liar.'

Mulch brought a hand up to his face. *Yawn*.

Artemis had been returned to the grip of his amorphobot once the branding had been completed, and with nothing to do but think in its clammy folds he could feel whatever was left of his battered personality slipping away. The rune on his neck had taken hold of his willpower in a vice-like grip and, while he could think and speak at the moment, it took a lot of effort and he guessed that he only had those rudimentary functions because Turnball hadn't given him any specific instructions yet. Once he had his orders, then he would be powerless to resist.

Turnball would be able to order me to do anything, he realized.

Through the distorting field of gel, Artemis could see Ragby taunting Mulch and thought that perhaps it would be a good idea if he joined the argument.

Speaking through the gel was a tricky affair that involved forming the words through clenched teeth, which kept the gel out but allowed it to pick up vibration in the throat.

'Hello, Mister Ragby,' he said. The amorphobot sprouted a gel speaker and translated the vibrations into words.

'Hey, look,' said Ragby. 'The thrall speaks. What do you want, Mud Boy? A little shock, is that what you want?'

Artemis decided that highbrow intellectual argument was not the way to go with this person and decided to go straight for the personal insult.

'I want you to have a bath, dwarf. You stink.'

Ragby was delighted to have a little diversion. 'Wow. That's like actual grown-up fighting talk. You do know that your bodyguard is out of action?'

If Butler had been equipped with laser eyeballs, Bobb Ragby would have had holes bored right through his skull.

What are you up to, Artemis? wondered Butler. *This kind of insult is not your style.*

'I don't need a bodyguard to dispose of you, Ragby,' continued Artemis. 'Just a bucket of water and a wire brush.'

'Funny,' said Ragby, though he sounded a little less amused than previously.

'Perhaps some disinfectant, so your germs would not spread.'

'I have a fungus,' said Ragby. 'It's a real medical condition and it's very hurtful of you to bring it up.'

'Awww,' said Artemis. 'Is the big, tough dwarf in pain?'

Ragby had had enough. 'Not as much pain as you,' he said, and instructed the bot to pass a charge through its gel sac.

Artemis was attacked by shards of white lightning. He jittered for a moment like a marionette in the hands of a toddler, then relaxed, floating unconscious in the gel.

•)ᛒᛟ)ᛉ)ᚩᚱᛞ•→•ᚱᛄᛟ⊕ᛁᛟᚱ•⊙ᛒᚻᛞ•ᛟᚱ•

Ragby laughed. 'Not so funny now, are you?'

Butler growled, which would have been menacing had not his bot speakers translated it as a robotic purr, then he began to push. It should have been impossible for him to make any impact without traction, but somehow he actually managed to distend the gel, causing the bot to chitter as though being tickled.

'You guys are hilarious,' said Ragby, and allowed Butler to wear himself out for a few minutes, before he grew bored and shocked the bodyguard. Not enough to knock the big human out, but certainly enough to calm him down a little.

'Two down,' he said cheerily. 'Who's next?'

'Me,' said Mulch. 'I'm next.'

Bobb Ragby turned to find Mulch Diggums rolled into a ball, rear end pointed directly at Bobb himself. The rear end was not covered by material, or, in other words, it was a bare bottom and it meant business.

Ragby, as a dwarf himself and a subscriber to *Where the Wind Blows* monthly, knew exactly what was about to happen.

'No way,' he breathed. He should shock Diggums, he knew, but this was too much entertainment to pass up. If things got out of hand, he could press the button, until then no harm in watching. Just in time he remembered to press record on the security cameras in case the captain wanted a look later.

'Go on, Diggums. If you actually break free, then I'll present my own backside for a good kicking.'

Mulch did not reply; breathing was too difficult inside the

gel to go wasting any precious energy trading insults with Bobb Ragby. Instead he wrapped his forearms round his shins and bore down on his colon, which was inflated like a very long balloon snake.

'Go, Mulch!' whooped Ragby. 'Make your people proud. Just so as you know, this will be up on the Ethernet in about five minutes.'

The first bubble to emerge was cantaloupe sized. These big bubbles were known among dwarf tunnellers as *corkers* from back in the days when corks were used to cap bottles. Often a corker had to be cleared before the main flow could begin.

'Good-sized corker,' Bobb Ragby admitted.

Once the corker was out of his system, Mulch followed it with a flurry of smaller squibs that emerged into the gel with an initial speed that was quickly arrested by the bot's gel.

'Is that it?' called Bobb, a little disappointed, truth be known. 'Is that all you got?'

That was not all Mulch had got. A hundred more assorted squibs quickly followed, some spheres, some ellipsoids and Ragby swore he saw a cube.

'Now you're just showing off!' he said.

The bubbles just kept on coming in various sizes and shapes. Some were transparent, some suspiciously opaque and a few had wisps of gas inside that crackled when they hit the gel.

The bot chittered nervously, the metal hardware heart flashing orange as its built-in spectrometer struggled to analyse the gas's components.

'Now *that* I have never seen,' said Bobb, his finger hovering over the shocker button.

Still the bubbles flowed, inflating the amorphobot to twice its original size. Its chitterings climbed the octaves until eventually they shattered nearby medical beakers and climbed to ultrasonic wavelengths, too high for the humans and fairies to hear.

The shrieking has stopped, thought Bobb. *That must mean the danger is past.*

He couldn't have been more wrong.

Mulch was virtually invisible now behind the bubbles, his image twisted and refracted by their curved surfaces. More and more bubbles were produced. Mulch seemed to be the dwarf equivalent of a clown's car that could hold more passengers than would seem to be allowed by the laws of physics. The amorphobot was stretched to its limits and its surface was dappled by the pressure. It began bouncing on the spot, venting bursts of the mysterious smoky gas.

'Well, Mulch, it's been fun,' said Bobb Ragby, and reluctantly pressed the shocker button, which as it turned out was the wrong thing to do. Even the amorphobot tried to refuse the order, but Ragby insisted, jabbing the button again and again until the familiar crackling sparked from two nodes on its metallic heart.

Any first-day chemistry student could have told Ragby never to put sparks near a mystery gas.

Unfortunately Ragby had never met any first-day chemistry students and so it came as a total surprise to him when the gas passed by Mulch Diggums ignited, bubble after bubble, in a chain reaction of mini-explosions. The bot expanded and ruptured, gel jets erupting from its surface. It bounced from floor to ceiling then pinballed across the cell, running Ragby over like a giant tyre. It was a testament to Foaly's design and standards that the amorphobot held its integrity even under such extreme circumstances. It transferred gel from un-scorched sections and grafted them on to ruined areas.

Ragby lay stunned on the deck while the bot came to rest across the hatch, shuddering and heaving. In cases like this it had a deep-rooted self-preservation order that Turnball had not thought to override. In the event that a sample collected by one of the amorphobots proved dangerous to the bot's systems, then that subject was to be immediately ejected. And this pungent dwarf was definitely dangerous, and so the damaged amorphobot hawked Mulch Diggums on to the blackened deck where he lay, smoking.

'I should never have had all that vole curry,' he mumbled, then passed out.

Bobb Ragby was the first dwarf to recover.

'That was something,' he said, then spat out a lump of charred gel. 'You got out, darn it if you didn't, so I suppose by rights I should present my behind for a kicking.'

Ragby lowered his wide bottom towards Mulch's uncon-scious face, but got no reaction.

'No takers?' he said. 'Well, you can't say I didn't offer.'

'Here,' said a voice behind him. 'Let me kick that for you.'

He twisted his neck round just in time to see an enormous

boot heading for his behind, and behind that boot there was an angry head, which in spite of being a little out of focus because of Bobb's perspective, unmistakably belonged to the human Butler.

Mulch had never believed he would actually get out of the amorphobot's belly, but he had hoped to distract Bobb Ragby for a few moments so that Foaly could come up with one of his genius techy plans.

And that was exactly what had happened. While Ragby had been occupied watching the gastrobatics of his fellow dwarf, Foaly had been busy syncing the bot core Artemis had picked up at the impact site with the core in his own amorphobot. In a laboratory it would have taken him about ten seconds to connect and send a string of code to shut out the instructions from the stolen control orb, but, suspended inside an amorphobot, it took the centaur at least half a minute. As soon as the readout flashed green, Foaly networked with the remaining bots and instructed them to dissolve.

Half a second later, Juliet and Foaly flopped to the floor, tears in their eyes, gel in their windpipes. Artemis lay unmoving, still unconscious from his electrocution.

Butler landed on his feet, spat and attacked.

Poor Bobb Ragby never had a chance, not that Butler did much to him. All it took was one kick, then the dwarf's terror took hold and jetted him straight into the lip of a metal bunk. He collapsed with a surprisingly childlike moan.

Butler turned quickly to Artemis and checked his pulse.

'How's Artemis's heart?' asked Juliet, bending to check on Mulch.

'It's beating,' replied her brother. 'That's about all I can tell you. We need to get him over to that hospital ship. Mulch too.'

The dwarf coughed then muttered something about beer and cheese pies.

'Do you mean beer, and cheese pies? Or beer-and-cheese pies?' Juliet glanced at her brother. 'Mulch may be delirious – it's hard to tell.'

Butler took Bobb Ragby's gun from his belt then tossed him bodily on to Foaly's broad back.

'OK. Here's the strategy. We take Artemis and Mulch across to the *Nostremius*'s sickbay then I retrieve Holly if necessary.'

Juliet's head snapped back. 'But Foaly can do –'

'Get moving,' thundered Butler. 'Go immediately. I do not want to talk about it.'

'OK. But if you're not with us in five minutes I'm coming after you.'

'I would appreciate that,' said Butler, propping Mulch on Foaly's back, then the unconscious Artemis. 'And if you could bring any troops you find along the way that would be great.'

'Troops on a hospital ship?' said Foaly, trying his best not to smell what was on his back. 'You'll be lucky.'

Mulch's tongue lolled out, resting on the centaur's neck. 'Mmm,' he mumbled around his tongue. 'Horse. Tasty.'

'Let's go,' said Foaly nervously. 'Let's go right now.'

The ambulance was a small ship compared to the massive aquanaut which loomed over them. The little craft had two levels: a sickbay and cell downstairs and on top of the spiral staircase a bridge with a small trucker's cabin, and apart from a couple of nooks for storage and recycling, and the room in which they'd been imprisoned, that was it. Luckily for Butler and the others the umbilical across to the *Nostremius* was on the bottom level.

Ching Mayle was peering across through the umbilical, obviously waiting for Holly's return with the demon warlock.

'Please,' whispered Juliet, when they saw the goblin at the hatch, 'allow me.'

Butler was holding both Artemis and Mulch steady on Foaly's back. Bobb Ragby he was not so worried about. 'Knock yourself out,' he said. 'Or, rather, knock the other guy out.'

Being a wrestler, Juliet could not simply run at Ching Mayle and knock him out – she had to add a little drama.

She ran down the corridor crying hysterically. 'Help me, Mister Goblin. Save me.'

Ching removed his fingers from the bite marks on his skull he was forever scratching, which of course meant that they never healed properly.

'Uh . . . Save you from what?'

Juliet sniffled. 'There's a big ugly goblin trying to stop us leaving the ship.'

Mayle reached for his gun. 'There's a what?'

'A big ugly guy, with all these septic dents in his head.'

Ching licked his eyeballs. 'Septic dents? Hey, wait a minute . . .'

'Finally,' said Juliet, and pirouetted like an ice-skater, whacking Ching Mayle with her signature jade ring. He tumbled into the umbilical passage, sliding down to the low point. Juliet caught his weapon before it hit the deck.

'One more down,' she said.

'You couldn't just punch him in the head,' grumbled Butler, leading Foaly past her. 'Boo hoo. Help me I'm a girl. What kind of modern woman are you?'

'A smart one,' said Juliet. 'He never even got a shot off.'

Butler was not impressed. 'He should never have got a hand to his gun. Next time, just hit the goblin. You're lucky he didn't blast you with a fireball.'

'Oh no,' said Foaly, pushing through a rope curtain that seemed to be coated with disinfectant, and into the umbilical passage. 'No flame near the umbilical. This is a pressurized tube with an oxygen-helium mix, heavy on the oxygen because of the pressure. One spark in here and, first, we explode, then the tube ruptures and the ocean squashes us flat.'

One by one they stepped into the umbilical. It was an incredible construction. A double-skinned tube of transparent super-tough plastic, strengthened with a wrap of octagonal wire. Air pumps hummed loudly along its length and light orbs drew deep-sea creatures to it, including Artemis's giant squid, which had wrapped itself around the umbilical's central span and was gnawing the wire frame with its beak. Its chitin-lined suckers scraped the plastic, smearing long welts along the tube.

'Don't worry,' said Foaly confidently. 'That creature can't get through. We've done a thousand stress tests.'

'With actual giant squid?' asked Juliet, understandably concerned.

'No,' admitted Foaly.

'So just computer tests, then?'

'Absolutely not,' said Foaly, offended. 'We used a normal squid and a tiny umbilical model. It worked quite well until one of my dwarf lab assistants fancied some calamari.'

Juliet shuddered. 'It's just that I have a thing about giant squid.'

'Don't we all?' said Foaly, and clopped past her down the umbilical.

The passage was fifty metres long with a slight incline at either end. The walkway beneath their feet was coated with a slightly tacky substance to prevent any accidental sparking and there were fire-extinguishing scatter bombs at regular intervals that would automatically coat the tube with powder in the event of a fire breaking out.

Foaly pointed at one of the fire-extinguishing bombs. 'In all honesty, those are for show. If so much as a spark gets loose in here, not even the squid is going to survive.'

They proceeded across to the aquanaut, feeling the cold of the ocean radiate through the walls, breathing the sharp oxygen-rich air. The *Nostremius* hospital ship loomed above, four storeys high, curved green walls dotted by a thousand glowing portholes, anchored to the seabed by a dozen bus-sized anchors. Umbilicals stretched from several ports and shadowy figures could be seen shuffling across from their ships to the *Nostremius*. It was a sombre, surreal image.

Foaly led, carrying Artemis, Mulch and a snoring Bobb Ragby and complaining every step of the way.

'Passengers. Centaurs don't carry passengers. Just because we have a horse's torso doesn't mean we have a horse's temperament. This is demeaning, that's what it is.'

Neither Juliet nor Butler took any notice. They were in a dangerous stretch right now and any confrontation had to be quickly contained or it could mean a watery grave for them all.

On Foaly's back, Artemis moaned and stirred. Butler patted his shoulder.

'You just stay asleep, young man. No need to wake up now.'

As much respect as Butler had for Artemis's abilities, he couldn't think how they could help in this situation, especially with that angry-looking rune burned into his neck.

They were two thirds of the way across when the hatch on the *Nostremius* end slid open, and Holly stepped through followed by Nº1.

There was no emotion in Holly's eyes, but she calmly assessed the situation and drew the Neutrino from her holster, taking a quick bead on Butler's forehead. From the look on her face, she could have been about to shoot a dart at a fairground target.

'No, Captain Short,' said Turnball's voice from behind Butler. 'No guns in here.'

Turnball stood at the entrance to the ambulance with Unix, as ever, at one shoulder and Ark Sool hovering at the other.

Juliet was on rear-guard duty. 'It's the jolly pirate,' she called to her brother. 'And his merry idiots. I think without guns that we're in pretty good shape. Should I go over there and beat some respect for life into them?'

Butler held up two fingers. *Wait.*

This was a nightmare scenario for any bodyguard: stuck in the middle of a transparent tube, several miles underwater with a murdering band of fugitives at one end and an enthralled but still highly skilled police officer at the other.

Poor N°1 had no idea what kind of drama he had stepped into.

'Holly, what's going on? Are we in the middle of one of your big adventures? Should I zap someone?'

Holly stood impassively waiting for instructions, but Butler heard what N°1 had said. 'No magic, Number One. One spark could blow up this entire platform.'

N°1 sighed. 'Can't you people ever just go on a picnic or something? Do there always have to be explosions?'

Artemis moaned again, then slid from behind Mulch off Foaly's back on to the walkway.

Standing in the doorway of the stolen shuttle ambulance, gazing down the umbilical towards Butler, Turnball realized he had a few marked cards in the deck. 'Ah,' he said. 'My little genius awakes. This should make our game interesting.'

Butler turned sideways to make himself a smaller target. There were to be no guns in this showdown, but there could be blades. 'Go back inside,' he called to N°1. 'Go in and shut the hatch.'

The demon warlock tapped Holly's shoulder. 'Should I go in, Holly? Would that be the best thing to do?'

Holly did not answer, but with that touch N°1 felt the rune spell that squatted like a parasite on her mind. It seemed purple to him and malignant and somehow aware. In his imagination, the reptilian rune crouching on Holly's brain snarled at him and nipped with venomous teeth.

'Oh,' said N°1, withdrawing his finger sharply.

I could undo the spell, he thought. *But it would be delicate work to avoid brain damage and there would definitely be sparks.*

He took a slow step backwards, but Holly quickly walked round him and smashed the heel of her hand into the door mechanism, sealing it for as long as it took for maintenance to get a fairy down there. Which would be way too long.

'No running away, young Master Demon,' called Turnball. 'I have need of your magic.'

My magic, thought N°1. *There must be something I can do. The* mesmer *doesn't require any sparks.*

'Listen to me, Holly,' said the demon warlock, his voice multilayered with magic. 'Look into my eyes.'

Which was as far as he got before Holly brought the edge of her hand down in a chopping motion that hit N°1 accurately in the gap between the armour plates on his chest and neck. Right in the windpipe. The demon collapsed to the ground gasping. It would be minutes before he could do as much as squeak.

Turnball laughed cruelly. 'Rune trumps *mesmer*, I would say.'

Butler tried to ignore the more extreme circumstances, such as the explosive gas they were breathing and the giant squid giving him the evil eye from outside the umbilical tube, and treat the situation as a common alley brawl.

I have been in this situation a dozen times. Admittedly we are flanked, but Juliet and I could take these and a dozen more. Holly can fight, but she is mesmerized and that will slow her down. Why is Turnball so confident with only a gnome and a sprite by his side?

'Ready, sister?' he said.

'Say the word.'

'I'll take Turnball and his friends. You contain Holly without doing any damage if you can manage it.'

'OK, brother.'

'What should I do?' asked Foaly, trying to keep the whinny out of his voice.

'Stand over Artemis and Mulch. Keep them safe.'

'Very well, Butler,' said the centaur, feeling utterly helpless as he always did in violent situations. 'You can count on me.'

Butler and Juliet switched sides, touching hands briefly on the way past.

'Be careful. Holly is quick.'

'You too. I don't trust that Turnball guy.'

$$\text{⊗⠃•◌◔♈•✦◌⟩⚱•⚘•⚖⠃⚚•◉⚏◊•◠⊗⠃}$$

Both of these statements would shortly prove themselves true. Unfortunately Butler had formulated their plan of action without two vital pieces of information. First of all Holly was not mesmerized, she was enthralled by a rune, and where the *mesmer* slowed the enchanted person down, runes certainly did not. In fact, they gave the victim access to more life force than they would normally have, which is why long-term thralls must not be allowed to get too excited for too long or they will literally burn themselves out. The second piece of information Butler did not have was the fact that Turnball had anticipated he might have to fight his way through an umbilical and so was armed accordingly.

The Butlers went down within seconds of each other. Juliet ran full tilt for Holly, no chatter or exaggerated wrestling moves – Holly was a serious opponent. The serious opponent stood listlessly, arms dangling until the last possible moment, then she ducked low, so quickly that it seemed a ghost image hung in the space where she had been, and swept Juliet's legs from under her. Juliet banged her head hard on the walkway and by the time her vision cleared Holly was on her chest with her Neutrino levelled at Juliet's head.

'No sparks,' panted Juliet. 'No sparks.'

'No sparks,' repeated Holly dully, then stuffed the gun barrel down the front of Juliet's Jade Princess leotard and pulled the trigger. Juliet spasmed once then collapsed. There were no sparks.

At the other end of the conduit, Butler had not rushed forward with quite so much gusto. If things were as they seemed, he could easily defeat Turnball and his little hench-fairies. Perhaps a menacing approach would be enough to scare them into running away.

Turnball seemed a little irritated and not at all scared. 'Mister Butler, as a manservant to a great strategist, didn't it occur to you that another great strategist such as myself might have anticipated this moment, or one like it?'

Butler's stomach sank. *Turnball is armed.*

Butler's only option was to cover the remaining distance before Turnball managed to aim his weapon. He almost made it, but then *almost* in a fight is about as useful as rubber needles in a knitting contest.

Turnball unclipped the stumpy weapon on a lanyard behind his back and shot Butler eight times in the chest and head. The bodyguard's eyes rolled back in his head but his momentum drove him forward, and Turnball had to skip smartly to one side to avoid being crushed. Ark Sool and Unix were not so lucky. Butler landed on them like a meteor, driving every last gasp of air from their bodies and breaking several ribs.

'*Olé!*' said Turnball, who had made a point of attending the bullfights whenever he was in Spain, not seeming too upset by the loss of his crew.

The vibrations set off one of the fire-extinguisher powder packs, which must have been on a hair trigger, and filled the umbilical with floating white powder.

'*Oh, the weather outside is frightful,*' sang Turnball, pointing his gun at Foaly, who was trying to at least look brave. 'Do you like my weapon? It was developed for crowd control during the first goblin riots. Purely chemical. Shoots zolpidem tartrate knock-out pellets. Gas powered, with dissolvable shells. No sparks. Sometimes low-tech is the way to go.'

Artemis suddenly drew a lungful of air, as though he had just breached the ocean's surface.

'Ah, my genius surfaces. Stand up, Artemis. I command you.'

Artemis lurched to his feet, his head and clothes matted with white powder.

'Choke that centaur for me, would you?'

There followed an uncomfortable minute while Artemis tried to find some purchase on Foaly's broad neck, then squeezed with all the power in his fingers, which was not very much. Foaly was more embarrassed than hurt.

Turnball wiped a tear from his eye. 'Oh, this is too much. But I indulge myself – Leonor is waiting. Come here, Artemis, and you too, Captain Short. Bring the demon. We must be gone from here before the ambulance generator blows.'

Artemis and Holly did as they were told with the emotion of automatons. Holly yanked poor, gasping Nº1 along by the collar of his tunic and Artemis stepped past Foaly without a glance. Outside the conduit, the fish and squid paid close attention to this fascinating diversion from the dreariness of everyday sub-aquatic life.

Suddenly, Turnball was impatient to be off.

'Come now, my thralls. Where is the speed you are famous for?'

Artemis did speed up, showing a nimbleness that anyone who knew the boy would not associate with him.

'That's more like it,' said Turnball. 'I may keep you, Artemis.'

'That's nice,' said the human boy. 'I'll tell him when I see him.'

'Ehm,' said Turnball, puzzled, then the boy who looked like Artemis Fowl jabbed Turnball in the gut with stiffened fingers.

'Butler showed Artemis that one a thousand times,' said the boy. 'He didn't listen, but I did.'

Turnball wanted to say something, but he was winded, and even if he hadn't been he had no idea what he would have said.

'For I am not Artemis Fowl, villainous elf,' said Orion, twisting the gun from Turnball's fingers. 'I am the young romantic who always knew his day would come, so I listened to Butler and I am ready.'

Turnball got enough breath back for one word. 'How?'

'Artemis knew he had to escape the power of the rune, which controlled his mind but not mine, so he goaded your cretinous minion into shocking him, which released me.'

Turnball clasped his stomach. *Of course. Atlantis stage two.* He rested both elbows on his knees and rasped at Holly. 'Kill him. Kill the boy.'

Orion pivoted and aimed the gun at Holly. 'Please, sweet maiden. Do not force my hand for I will strike for the good of all.'

Holly threw Nº1 aside and ran full tilt, side to side.

'Artemis could never shoot,' she snarled.

Orion squared his shoulders, and extended his hands, supporting his right hand with his left. Both Artemis and Orion were ambidextrous but, unlike Artemis, Orion favoured his right hand. He remembered what Butler had said time and time again.

Sight along your arm. Breathe out and squeeze.

The first pellet caught Holly on the cheek, the second on the forehead and the third on the shoulder, which took a second to penetrate. Holly's speed took her halfway up the curved wall before her body gave out and she slid back down on her face.

Orion turned to Turnball who was sneaking up on him. 'Be still, foul demon.'

'Hey,' said No1, who was getting his breath back.

'Apologies, gentle mage,' said Orion. 'I was referring to my piratical foe.'

'Four,' said Turnball, with some desperation. 'Four four four.'

Orion laughed a haughty hero's laugh. 'No such luck, Turnball Root. Your evil plans have been thwarted. Accept your fate.'

Turnball's face turned slowly purple, a family trait.

'I need the demon,' he bellowed, spittle spraying from his lips. 'Turn him over or we all die.'

'Too late for hollow threats, my friend. You have been outfoxed. Now sit still while my compadre, the noble steed, binds your hands.'

Turnball took a whooping breath and stood erect. 'No. I have one card left to play. The ambulance is rigged to explode. The autopilot is smashed and the generator has been exposed – there is no turning back. Give me the demon and I will pilot the shuttle deep into the trench then escape in the belly of an amorphobot. There is room for one more besides Leonor. I can take you instead of Number One.'

Foaly sucked his lips. 'Ah. OK. Little problem with that plan. I dissolved the bots.'

'So that was your plot,' said Orion fiercely, brandishing the gun like a cutlass. 'You would take what you wanted and then bury the evidence in the explosion.'

Turnball shrugged, suddenly calm. He had always known a day like this would come. 'It has worked for me before.' He consulted a timer on his wrist computer. 'In five minutes the shuttle explodes and we all die. If you will excuse me, I must go to my wife's bedside.'

He turned to find his wife a little closer than expected. Leonor stood framed by the umbilical's curtain, leaning heavily on her walking stick, face pale in the glow from the light orbs.

'Turnball, what's happening?' she said, her breath laboured, but both eyes were open and they were clear. Clearer than they had been since they'd first met.

Turnball rushed to her side, supporting her with one arm.

'Yes, my dear. You should lie down. Things will be better soon.'

Leonor snapped as she had not for a long time. 'You just said the ship will explode.'

Turnball's eyes were wide with surprise – his beloved wife

had never snapped at him before – but he kept a gentle smile on his lips. 'What does it matter, so long as we are together? Even death will not separate us.'

From somewhere, Leonor found the strength to stand straight. 'I am ready for my long sleep, Turnball. But you are young, these people are young, and is that not a hospital ship we are moored to?'

'Yes, yes it is. But these people are my enemies. They have persecuted me.' Turnball licked the rune on his thumb, but Leonor was beyond his power now.

'I think that perhaps you were far from blameless, my dear, but I was blinded by love. I have always loved you, Turnball. I always will.'

Orion was getting anxious. The seconds were ticking away and he had no wish to see his beloved Holly at the heart of an explosion.

'Step aside, madam,' he said to Leonor. 'I must pilot this ship deep into the trench.'

Leonor raised her stick shakily. 'No. I will take this journey alone. I have outstayed my welcome on this earth and shut my eyes to what was happening around me. Now at last I will fly where I never thought possible.' She stroked Turnball's wet cheek and kissed him. 'At last I can finally fly again, Turnball.'

Turnball clasped his wife's shoulders tenderly. 'You can fly, you will. But not now. This flight is death and I cannot be without you. Don't you want what we had?'

'Those times are gone,' said Leonor simply. 'Perhaps they

should never have been. Now, you must let me go, or else you must try to stop me.'

This was an ultimatum that Turnball had been dreading since first applying the rune to Leonor's neck. He was about to lose his wife and there was nothing he could do about it. His emotions played across his face, and a network of lines appeared around his eyes as though drawn by an invisible pen.

'I must go, Turnball,' said Leonor softly.

'Fly, my love,' said Turnball, and he seemed in that moment as old as his wife.

'Let me do this for you, my love. Let me save you, as you saved me all those years ago?' Leonor kissed him again and withdrew through the curtain.

Turnball stood for a moment, shoulders shuddering, chin down, then he pulled himself together.

He faced Orion and jerked a thumb towards the ambulance. 'I should go. Leonor will never make it back up the steps on her own.'

And with such an ordinary statement he was gone, the hatch sealing behind him.

'Understated but graceful,' said Orion. 'A nice exit.'

The Butlers were both unconscious, which would be a source of some ribbing and embarrassment later, so they did not see the stolen ambulance shuttle detach itself from the umbilical conduit and peel away from the *Nostremius*, Leonor and Turnball clearly visible at the cockpit controls. And they completely missed the shuttle diving deep into the Atlantis Trench in a long graceful arc.

⊕✲•⬡⅄⟩⟨⚡•⟲⟍•⊕✲⬠•◉⊕•⊖⊕•⊕⊗•⊷→•⚓

'That woman is quite a pilot,' said Orion. 'I imagine they are holding hands now and smiling bravely.'

Moments later a hellfire blossom grew from the depths of the trench, but the explosion was quickly extinguished by the millions of tonnes of water bearing down on it. The shock currents, however, raced along the raised ridge, dislodging centuries-old coral and rippling the untethered end of the umbilical conduit like a child would a skipping rope, sending the squid scurrying for safety.

The tube's occupants were jumbled together, heroes and villains alike, and swept to the *Nostremius*'s door, which moments later was opened from the inside by a confused technical officer, a hardened sea gnome who, to his eternal shame, squealed like a baby sprite when he came face to face with a gigantic human covered in white dust.

'Zombie,' he shrieked, and, unfortunately for him, two of his shift buddies were in the airlock behind him and it cost him three weeks' pudding rations to buy their silence.

EPILOGUE

ARTEMIS woke to find Holly and Foaly leaning over him. Holly seemed concerned whereas Foaly was scrutinizing him, as one would a lab experiment.

I am not in pain, thought Artemis. *They must have given me something.*

And then: *I should lighten the mood.*

'Ah, my princess. Noble steed. How does the morning find you both?'

'D'Arvit,' said Holly. 'It's the knight in shining armour.'

'Hmm,' said Foaly. 'That's how Atlantis goes. As it progresses, you can never predict what will set it off. I thought the cocktail of drugs would bring back Artemis but at least Orion will tell us what Artemis is up to.' He leaned in closer. 'Orion, you noble youth. Do you happen to know the password for Artemis's firewall?'

'Of course I do,' said Artemis. 'It's D-O-N-K-E-Y space B-O-Y.'

Foaly was halfway through writing this down when the penny dropped.

'Oh, ha ha, Artemis. Most hilarious. I knew it was you all the time.'

Holly did not laugh. 'That wasn't funny, Artemis. Atlantis Complex is no joke.'

At the mere mention of the disease, Artemis felt the nest of malignant fours stir at the back of his head.

Not again, he thought.

'It would really help if you two swapped places,' he said, trying to sound calm and in control. 'Also, could you close those two porthole blinds all the way? Or open all the way, but not in the middle like that. That makes no sense.'

Holly wanted to shake Artemis until he snapped out of it, but she had talked to Dr Argon of the Psych Brotherhood and he had told them to humour the human until they could get him checked into the clinic.

Opal Koboi's old room is still free, the doctor had said brightly, and Holly suspected he was already thinking of titles for the inevitable book.

So she said, 'OK, Artemis. I'll get the blinds.'

As Holly tapped the little sun icon beside the blind, lightening the glass, she noticed the shoals of exotic fish basking in the pod light from the *Nostremius*'s stern fins.

We are all swimming towards the light, she realized, and then wondered when she'd become so philosophical. *Too much thinking is one of the things that put Artemis where he is now. We need to deal with this problem.*

'Artemis,' she said, forcing a note of positivity into her voice, 'Doctor Argon wondered if you had any kind of record of . . .'

'My descent into madness?' completed Artemis.

'Well, he actually said, the Complex's progression. He said keeping a journal of some kind is common among sufferers. They feel a great need to be understood after . . .'

Again Artemis completed the sentence. 'After we die. I know. I feel that compulsion still.' He tugged off the ring from his middle finger. 'It's my fairy communicator, remember? I kept a video diary. Should make terrifying viewing.'

Foaly took the ring. 'Let me zap that down to Argon. It will give him a little insight before he gets you strapped into the crazy chair.' The centaur realized what he had said. 'Sorry. Caballine is always saying how insensitive I am. There's no crazy chair, it's more like a couch or a futon.'

'We get it, Foaly,' said Holly. 'Thanks so much.'

The centaur clopped to the hospital room's automatic door. 'OK. I'll send this off. See you later and watch out for those evil fours.'

Artemis winced. Holly was right; the Atlantis Complex was not funny.

Holly sat on the chair beside his bed. It was a very high-tech bed with stabilizers and impact cushions, but unfortunately a little short.

'You're growing, Artemis,' she said.

⇥ • ⚔ • 𓅱 𓈗 𓆓 𓍢 𓎡 𓅱 𓅓 𓏏 ⇥ • 𓂓 𓏏 𓐍 𓂋 𓅱 𓎡 𓅱 • 𓎡 ⚔

Artemis smiled weakly. 'I know. Not fast enough in some ways.'

Holly took his hand. 'You can try to upset yourself if you want but you won't be able to. Foaly pumped enough sedative into you to put a horse to sleep.'

They both smiled at that for a moment, but Artemis was in a melancholy mood.

'This adventure was different, Holly. Usually someone wins and we are better off at the end. But this time so many people died, innocents, and no one has benefited. And all for love. I can't even think of Turnball as a villain – all he wanted was his wife back.'

Holly squeezed Artemis's fingers. 'Things would have been a lot worse without us around. Number One is alive, thanks to you, not to mention everyone on this hospital ship. And as soon as we have you back to your old self, we can get working on saving the world with your Ice Cube.'

'Good. That's still my priority, though I might want to renegotiate my terms a little.'

'Hmm. I thought you might.'

Artemis took a sip of water from a cup on his locker. 'I don't want to go back to being me completely. My old self is what brought on Atlantis Complex in the first place.'

'You did some bad things, Artemis. But you wouldn't do them again. Let them go.'

'Really? You can just let things go?'

'It's not that easy, but you can do it with our help, if it's what you really want.'

Artemis rolled his eyes. 'Potions and therapy, heaven help me.'

'Doctor Argon is a bit of a fame hound but he's good. The best. Also, I'm sure Number One can give you a magical detox, get the last of those sparks out of your system.'

'That sounds painful.'

'Maybe. But you'll have friends around you. Good friends.'

Artemis sat up on the pillows. 'I know. Where's Mulch?'

'Where do you think?'

'I think he's in the galley. Possibly inside one of the refrigerators.'

'I think you're probably right.'

'How about Juliet?'

Holly's sigh was both affectionate and frustrated. 'She's organized a wrestling match between herself and a jumbo pixie who passed a comment about her ponytail. I am currently pretending I don't know anything about it. I should go and break it up soon.'

'I pity the pixie,' said Artemis. 'And how about Butler? Do you think he can ever trust me again?'

'I think he already does.'

'I need to speak to him.'

Holly glanced towards the corridor. 'You'd better give it a minute. He's making a delicate phone call.'

Artemis could guess who he was calling. He would have to make a similar call himself soon.

'So,' he said, trying to sound more light-hearted than he

actually felt with the Atlantis Complex bubbling at the base of his temporal lobe.

Arrange this, it said.

Count that.

Beware four. Four is death.

'I hear that you were on a date with Trouble Kelp. Are you two planning on building a bivouac any time soon?'

Butler thought he might be developing claustrophobia. It definitely seemed as though the walls were closing in. It didn't help that the corridor he was crouched in was built for people half his size. The only place he could stand up properly was the gymnasium, and that wasn't really the place to make a private call as his baby sister was probably beating the stuffing out of a jumbo pixie in there at the moment, playing it up for the assembled crowd of patients and medics who would soon adore the Jade Princess.

Butler slid down the wall into a sitting position and held out Artemis's phone.

Maybe there's no network, he thought hopefully.

But there was. Four bars. Artemis had built his phone to access all available networks, including military and fairy. A person would have to be on the moon before Artemis's phone would fail.

OK. Stop putting it off. Make the call.

Butler scrolled through the contacts and selected Angeline Fowl's mobile phone. It took a few seconds to connect as the call had to go through Haven up to a satellite and back to

Ireland, and when it did ring the tone was the fairy triple beep.

Maybe she's asleep.

But Angeline picked up on the second ring.

'Artemis? Where are you? Why haven't you called?'

'No, Mrs Fowl. It's me, Butler.'

Angeline realized that Butler was calling her on Artemis's phone and naturally jumped to the worst possible conclusion. 'Oh my God! He's dead, isn't he? I should never have let him go.'

'No, no. Artemis is fine,' said Butler hurriedly. 'Not a mark on him.'

Angeline was crying into the phone. 'Thank goodness. I would blame myself. A fifteen-year-old, off to save the world, with *fairies*. What was I thinking? That's it now. Finished. A normal life from now on.'

I can't even remember normal, thought Butler.

'Can I speak to him?'

Here we go.

'Not at the moment. He's . . . eh . . . sedated.'

'Sedated! You said he wasn't hurt, Butler. You just said there wasn't a mark on him.'

Butler winced. 'There isn't a mark on him. Not on the outside.'

Butler swore he could hear Angeline Fowl fuming. 'What is that supposed to mean? Are you turning metaphorical in your dotage, man? Is Artemis hurt or not?'

Butler would have much preferred to be facing down a SWAT team than delivering this news, so he chose his words carefully. 'Artemis has developed a condition, a mental condition. It's a little like OCD.'

'Oh no,' said Angeline, and for a moment Butler thought she had dropped the phone, then he heard her breathing, fast and shallow.

'It can be controlled,' he said. 'We're taking him to a clinic right now. The best clinic the fairies have. He is in absolutely no danger.'

'I want to see him.'

'You will. They're sending someone for you.' This wasn't actually the case, but Butler vowed that it would be, seconds after he hung up the phone. 'What about the twins?'

'The nanny can sleep over. Artemis's father is in São Paulo at a summit. I'll have to tell him everything.'

'No,' said Butler quickly. 'Don't take that decision now. Talk to Artemis first.'

'W-will he know me?'

'Of course he will,' Butler replied.

'Very well, Butler. I'm going to pack a bag now. Tell the fairies to call when they're ten minutes away.'

'I will do.'

'And, Butler?'

'Yes, Mrs Fowl?'

'Look after my boy until I get there. Family is everything, you know that.'

'I do, Mrs Fowl. I will.'

The connection was severed and Angeline Fowl's picture disappeared from the little screen.

Family is everything, thought Butler. *If you're lucky.*

Mulch stuck his head round the door, beard dripping with some congealing liquid that seemed to have whole turnips trapped in it. His forehead was covered in bright blue burn gel.

'Hey, bodyguard. You better get down to the gymnasium. This jumbo pixie guy is killing your sister.'

'Really?' said Butler, unconvinced.

'Really. Juliet just does not seem to be herself. She can't put two moves together. It's pathetic really. Everyone is betting against her.'

'I see,' said Butler, straightening as much as he could in the cramped surroundings.

Mulch held the door. 'It's going to make things really interesting when you show up to help.'

Butler grinned. 'I'm not coming to help. I just want to be there when she stops faking.'

'Ah,' said Mulch, comprehension dawning on his face. 'So I should switch my bet to Juliet?'

'You certainly should,' said Butler and lumbered down the corridor, stepping around a pool of turnip soup.

•ᘮᐯᏇᏏᎯᏰ•⧆◻◖ᕼ⦿→•ᏕᎲᎯ•ᘮᏍᏰ•⩩•⧆

Your story starts here . . .

Do you **love books** and
discovering new stories?
Then **www.puffin.co.uk**
is the place for you . . .

• Thrilling adventures, fantastic fiction
and laugh-out-loud fun

• Brilliant videos featuring your favourite authors
and characters

• Exciting competitions, news, activities,
the Puffin blog and SO MUCH more . . .

www.puffin.co.uk

ARTEMIS FOWL

THE GRAPHIC NOVEL

Of course, it had started with the Internet.
But then it always does.

Alien abductions. UFO sightings.
Leylines. Ancient stone circles.

And the People.
It always came back to the People.

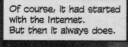

Trawling through gigs of data, he had compiled a database from the thousands of references to fairies he'd found from countries all over the world.

Each human civilization had its own term for the People. But there was no doubt that the reports referred to the same hidden race.

Many stories whispered of a special book carried by each fairy.

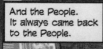

It was their bible containing the history of their race. It also contained their laws, their rules... and their weaknesses.

RELIVE THE ADVENTURE, THE MAGIC,
THE MIND-BLOWING TECHNOLOGY,
THE BEGINNING.
AS YOU'VE NEVER SEEN IT BEFORE.

THE
GRAPHIC
NOVEL